# RESCUING HER KNIGHT

## THE DE WILTONS ~ BOOK ONE

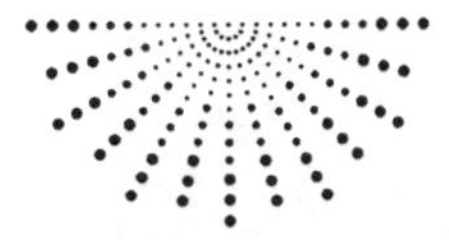

## ROSIE CHAPEL

# Rescuing Her Knight

Rosie Chapel

First printing: 2021
ISBN: 978-0-6450738-4-3 (Paperback)
ISBN: 978-0-6450738-5-0 (E-book)

Ulfire Pty. Ltd.
P.O. Box 1481
South Perth
WA 6951
Australia

www.rosiechapel.com

Cover Designed by Tina Adams

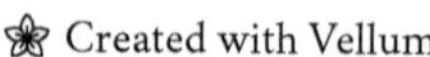 Created with Vellum

*For Aunty Edna, with all my love.*

# ACKNOWLEDGMENTS

To Melanie, Jackie, Maria and Amy – my incredibly patient sounding boards. Thank you for putting up with my nonsensical questions – you ladies keep me sane.

Heartfelt gratitude to Janet for her canny eye.

Special thanks to Melanie and Jackie for generously offering to proofread the final manuscript.

Profound appreciation to Tina Adams for this stunningly beautiful cover – the inspiration for Kitty and Adam's romance.

To my many author friends – thank you for your awesome support.

Thanks to Graham from Fading Street Publishing Services for wielding his editing magic.

Last, but definitely not least, to my amazing husband – thank
you for your patience, support and technical wizardry!

Contrary to popular expectations, the majority of fairy tales
are not pleasant.
Many are littered with all manner of villainy.
The overarching theme in almost every story, however, is
that good defeats evil,
and the hero *always* rescues the heroine...

...occasionally the roles are reversed!

# PROLOGUE

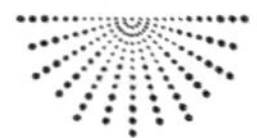

## EASBY HALL - AUGUST 1798

It was an idyllic summer's afternoon. The smattering of white fluffy clouds appeared deliberately designed to emphasise the dazzling blue of the sky.

The subtle fragrance of honeysuckle drifted on the balmy air, along with the warble of birdsong and the buzz of lazy insects. From beyond the gardens rang the sound of children playing.

Several adults sat in a loose circle on the stone flagged terrace, relaxing in the shade thrown by the house. The women sipped cool lemonade; the men opting for wine or perhaps a brandy.

Something about the poses of the four couples suggested an abiding friendship; a notion confirmed by their topics of conversation — had anyone been listening.

Unusually, in this era, although their marriages had been arranged, each man was devoted to his wife. An affection reciprocated. Taking every opportunity to get together, even if only briefly, their easy camaraderie had led to their offspring being similarly disposed to each other. Not all bound by blood, and despite a fourteen-year age gap between oldest and youngest, the children were closer than many siblings.

The tranquil scene was shattered by a piercing screech and, as one, the adults rose from their chairs to hurry in the direction of the racket. The screams continued unabated and when the first parent rounded the hedge delineating the formal gardens and the orchards, he was met by a sight which made him question whether a massacre was in progress.

A little girl, covered in blood, was being tended to by an older boy also liberally spattered. The other children were hovering, their mouths agape.

"Please stop wriggling, Kitty. I know it hurts but I need to stop the bleeding." Using his kerchief, the boy was trying, desperately, to staunch the blood welling from the child's leg.

"Mama, I want Mama." Kitty sobbed, her tears smearing two tracks down grubby cheeks.

"Mama is coming," the adult spoke from above them.

The boy swung his gaze upward, relief painting his features and his voice. "*Papa*. Please help. We were running, and Kitty tripped, and…" he faltered. It was clear what had happened. "There is so much blood." For all his pluck, his face had taken on a slightly green tinge.

"Good lad. Here, I'll carry her. Come on, poppet. Let's get you indoors and see to your knee." Carefully, the gentleman scooped Kitty into his arms,

"*Adam*," hiccuping, Kitty reached out a chubby hand to the boy.

He grasped it, squeezing her fingers gently. "Papa will look after you," Adam said with a child's unwavering faith in their parents' abilities to fix everything.

By this time, the remaining adults had arrived, gathering

their respective children, and giving them a quick once over to ensure no one else was hurt.

"We are all fine," Adam volunteered. "Just Kitty."

Over the heads of the youngsters, the adults shared a grin. It was always 'just Kitty'. The child seemed to attract mishaps. If it wasn't falling flat on her face — and she could trip over air — it was cutting herself on a sheet of paper, or stabbing herself with a quill, or dropping something — usually breakable and usually onto her toes.

A month shy of seven, Katherine de Wilton or, as everyone called her, Kitty, was a walking disaster. It never bothered her. She picked herself up or righted whatever she had knocked over and carried on. She was unfailingly sunny, even in the face of adversity, which made this accident all the more serious.

Kitty rarely cried. When she broke her arm the previous winter after taking an awkward tumble while learning to ice skate, she didn't cry. When she was given the news about her grandfather's death, she was more upset about her mama being sad. The only other time any of them present could recall seeing her weep was when one of the dogs died.

"Mama," her shrieks had dwindled to a forlorn wail as her mother, Frederica de Wilton, Lady Grafton, came forward.

"I'm here, precious, no need for such a rumpus. Uncle Reginald will take you inside." Frederica stroked damp curls out of her daughter's face. "You *do* get into some scrapes."

Kitty sighed dramatically. "Mama, I am six. Things are *bound* to happen when you're six." Her long-suffering tone indicating to her listeners this ought to be blindingly obvious.

"Where's Adam?" She twisted around to find her rescuer.

"I'm here, Kitty." The youth's face materialised in her line of vision.

"Thank you. You are my knight in shining armour." She bestowed on him a watery smile.

Barely fourteen, Adam blushed to the roots of his dark brown hair. "No, I'm not," he mumbled.

The other children cheered when they heard this. "Yes, you are. Our knight. Adam Marchmain, Knight of the Garden." They began to march in front of the adults, repeating their declaration as a nonsensical ditty. Then before anyone could stop them, ran off. Adventures awaited.

Adam lingered, keeping step with his father, unsure whether it was appropriate to play when one of their number was wounded. *Knights were supposed to attend to a damsel in distress, weren't they?* When they reached the terrace, his father, taking pity on him, bent his head and told his son to scoot.

"Go on, Adam. Kitty will be much better after a bath."

"Are you sure?"

"I am certain. If you are worried, come back in half an hour. You'll see, she will have all but forgotten she took a tumble."

"It is a nasty cut, Papa."

"I can see that, but I do not think she will lose her leg." Reginald Marchmain's tone was jovial. A heartening sign to Adam, who knew when his father spoke like this, the situation was not dire.

"All right. Half an hour?"

Reginald nodded and Adam fled in search of the others.

Kitty was duly bathed, the water turning a lovely shade of brown as the mud and a prodigious assortment of detritus was washed off. Clean, and in a fresh dress, she was conveyed to the library.

One of their number, David Wells — the Marquis of Clarence and Adam's uncle — who possessed a little medical knowledge, inspected the injury. Adam was correct, it was nasty. A relatively long and jagged laceration under Kitty's knee.

"I think you ought to call for the doctor," he said, placidly. "It might need suturing.

"What does that mean, Uncle David?" Kitty was staring at her knee with gruesome avidity.

Frederica crouched by her daughter who was lying on the couch. "It means the doctor uses a needle and cotton to tie the edges of the cut together. Similar to how I sew."

Kitty's eyes widened, then she giggled. "Mama, you are silly. You cannot sew people. I am not a tapestry, or a doll."

"I am very much afraid, you can. Doctors do it all the time."

Kitty's courage drained away like the last of the bathwater. She shook her head. "No, no, no, no, no. That is not a good idea. Putting holes in a person's skin. I don't want to be sut… stut… sewn up. I will look like Betsy."

Betsy was a very old and very well-loved doll; one Frederica had played with as a child. Betsy had been repaired numerous times and she was now more stitch than doll. Kitty took Betsy everywhere, even to bed.

"You will not look like Betsy…"

Kitty pinned her mother with a penetrating and uncannily adult stare.

"…well, perhaps a teeny tiny bit, but sweetheart, if the doctor thinks your leg needs stitching, you will need to be my brave girl and let him."

By now, Kitty was all for running away, but any movement made her leg bleed. Truth be told, she was feeling queasy and, reluctantly, submitted to her mother's tender care.

~

The doctor arrived and decreed the wound did indeed require suturing. "It will keep bleeding if we do not," he explained to Kitty, who by now was decidedly averse to the whole idea.

"Come now, Kitty. It will only take a minute. If you let Doctor Arthurs treat your leg, I will ask Uncle Reginald whether you might have an ice." Frederica was past caring whether bribing her daughter was appropriate. Kitty was scared and rightly so. Suturing wounds was not for the faint hearted. If an ice persuaded her, it was worth it.

"I shall go and check," Reginald disappeared to speak to one of the maids out of Kitty's hearing.

Adam poked his head around the door. "How is Kitty?" he asked.

"Adam."

Kitty's whimper had him scuttling over the carpet to her side.

"Does it hurt?"

"Yes, and the doctor wants to sew it." Panic laced her tones.

Adam sank to his knees next to the sofa. "Only the most valiant of soldiers dare be sutured," he remarked, contemplatively. "They usually get a medal."

"I am only six. I doubt there is a medal for being a brave six-year-old."

"I'll wager there is." Hoping he was not about to be proved wrong, Adam lifted his head to scan the faces of the adults surrounding him — his mother, Kitty's parents, and the doctor. Ernest de Wilton, Kitty's father, in immediate understanding, nodded and left the room. Adam kept up a stream of chatter distracting Kitty, while the doctor readied his instruments.

Reginald returned to inform Kitty a large bowl of chocolate ice was being prepared at this very moment

Dr Arthurs rinsed the needle in vinegar, then threaded it. He shot a glance at Frederica who inclined her head and settled behind Kitty, wrapping the small girl in her arms.

"Kitty, this will be painful, but I will be as quick as possible. You need to be a..." he looked at Adam, "...valiant soldier."

Kitty's bottom lip wobbled.

Adam inched closer and took her hand.

"Please will you tell me a story, Adam?" Her face was sheet white and, even though Adam was just a lad, he could tell she was terrified.

"I don't know any stories," he hedged.

"Once upon a time..."

Adam stared at her, slightly confused. *Wasn't he supposed to be the one doing the telling?*

"...that's how they start." Her hot little hand seized his.

Grinning, Adam scoured his brain for a story, any story. It was a long time since he cared to listen to stories, they were for babies.

Dr Arthurs began.

The instant the needle punctured Kitty's skin, she squealed. Two fat tears spilled over. "B-b-b-b..."

"Once upon a time, in a land faraway there was a beautiful princess, whose name was Caterina." Adam rushed to interject.

Kitty pressed her lips together, gripping his fingers tightly, her other hand clutching her mother's arm.

"She had curly blonde hair, and green eyes."

"Ohhhh, 'tis me," Kitty exclaimed.

"One day, she was out riding her horse—"

"What was the horse's name?" Kitty croaked as the doctor pulled the needle.

"Mmmm… Bluebell."

"I love bluebells." The little girl beamed at Adam

"I know. Do you want to hear the story or not?"

"Continue," she intoned imperiously, causing Frederica to smother a grin.

There was a loud hiss when the thread was drawn through.

Noticing Kitty's expression, Adam hurried on.

"The princess was riding Bluebell through the woods and through the meadows. They rode for a long time until they came to the river which marked the border of her father's lands. The princess had never travelled beyond the boundary and wanted to explore. The river was deep and fast flowing. Bluebell hesitated at the water's edge, but the princess failed to recognise the danger and urged the mare forward."

"Ohhhh, what happened?" Engrossed by the story Kitty was becoming less aware of the needle's sting.

"Bluebell struggled to keep her footing. Realising they might be swept away, the princess panicked and called for help. Bluebell joined in, neighing loudly, and between them, they created a fair din. Suddenly, on the opposite bank, another horse appeared. A huge black stallion, ridden by a tall stranger.

"Before Caterina could repeat her plea, the stranger and his horse were in the river splashing towards her. The man grabbed Bluebell's reins and led them out of the torrent. As soon as they reached the safety of the bank, the stranger dipped his head, and turned to ride away.

'Wait, kind sir. You saved my life, or at the very least preserved me from a drenching. Such a brave act deserves a reward.' The princess cried.

'No reward is necessary. It is my pleasure and honour to rescue so beautiful a maiden.'

The princess blushed. "Thank you. I am in your debt.'

'Fair lady, there is no debt.' The rider bowed his head, and with a wave of his hand was gone. The end." Adam, who had no idea what to say next, finished abruptly.

"Is *that* it?" A disgruntled Kitty chimed in.

The doctor snipped the last suture.

"Knights rescue damsels in distress but always leave without giving their name. 'Tis in all the books. Anyway, Dr Arthurs has finished."

"What happens?" Kitty folded her arms and glowered.

"Don't be rude, Kitty. Adam has told a charming story and here is Uncle Reginald with your ice," Frederica reproved.

"I will finish it another time," Adam vowed, rashly.

"Promise?"

"I promise."

Kitty's father came in bearing a cushion, on which lay a medal. In actuality it was an old but impressive-looking coin, which Reginald had procured from somewhere.

With a flourish, he presented it to his small daughter, effectively diverting her.

For a while, the story was forgotten.

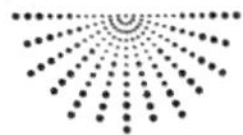

# CHAPTER ONE

GRAFTON MANOR ~ AUGUST 1805

Stretched out on a wooden bench, Kitty de Wilton was lost in another world. It was a glorious day, and she was reading in her favourite nook — the arbour beyond the water gardens. Here it was secluded and peaceful.

Three of her cousins were staying and, much as Kitty loved them, they were exhausting, prompting her to vanish whenever the occasion presented itself. She could hear their high-pitched voices mingling with those of her siblings, bellowing to one another. Their unrestrained exuberance making Kitty chuckle.

Almost fourteen, Kitty was the oldest of the de Wilton children. Her brothers, identical twins, Ernest — named after their father — and Emory, had recently celebrated their twelfth birthday, while the youngest of their clan, Georgina was a puckish eight-year-old.

Of late, Kitty had become quite introspective, in stark contrast with her usual ebullience. The hijinks she used to embrace with fervour no longer held the same appeal.

She fidgeted on the seat, and for no particular reason thought of Adam Marchmain. She hadn't seen him since he went up to Oxford. *He must be twenty-one now. How the years had flown.* Hitching her skirts, she inspected her left knee, running light fingers over the scar.

Unbidden, memories surfaced.

*After Papa had bestowed the coin — currently secreted away in her treasure box in her bedroom — Kitty devoured the scrumptious chocolate ice, so quickly she gave herself a headache.*

*Despite feeling wretched, she had no mind to miss any more of the fun, refusing, point blank, to go to bed. A compromise was reached and she, with bad grace, agreed to remain on the terrace.*

*Initially, the other children played nearby, but soon their natural enthusiasm took them further and further from the house. Before long they were out of sight.*

*Her knee throbbing, and disposed to sulk, Kitty was surprised when Adam reappeared hauling a small cart. He came to a halt at the bottom of the short flight of steps leading from the terrace to the lawns.*

*"Aunt Frederica, may I wheel Kitty in this?" he beseeched her mother. "I will be very careful not to tip her out."*

*His earnest request elicited a series of benevolent smiles.*

*"Oh, Mama, pleeeeeeeeease." Kitty adopted her most winsome expression, while batting her eyelashes at her parent.*

*Frederica swallowed a bark of laughter. "Of course, you may. Thank you, Adam, you are very considerate."*

*"We didn't want Kitty to feel left out." Embarrassed at being the centre of attention, he squirmed under the adults' scrutiny.*

*Lord Grafton carried his daughter to the cart, in which someone had placed a rug and a cushion. Kitty settled in, and Adam pulled her around to where the others had congregated. Her shouts of merriment were reward enough to the young lad.*

*"Oh, what fun." Kitty clasped her hands together. "I have a*

*grand carriage and my very own knight in shining armour. You will always be my Knight of the Garden, Adam Marchmain."*

*Adam bowed and, flushing bright red... again... replied, "As you will always be my princess."*


Kitty sighed. She missed Adam. He could always be relied upon to come up with the best games, the best capers. For the remainder of that summer, he took it upon himself to become a kind of guardian, encouraging her high spirits while reining in her wilder exploits.

In turn, as she grew older, Kitty introduced Adam to the wonder of books. Whenever their families gathered, especially if the weather proved too inclement to play outside, the pair read stories to the other children.

Sometimes they acted them out, everyone given a part. The results were raucous and often hilarious, but they were not harming anyone, and it kept them busy for hours.

Oddly, the one thing Adam never did was finish his story.


She heard Adam had enlisted in the Royal Navy. Britain was at war with France. A war her father blamed on a lunatic called Napoleon. Rumours abounded in the broadsheets that this Napoleon person was going to invade Britain.

"The unmitigated gall of the man," Ernest de Wilton had groused, when he thought his children were out of hearing range.

Kitty, who wanted to know everything about everything, had developed a knack of making herself invisible, garnering all kinds of information. Most was not for the ears of thirteen-year-olds and *definitely* not suitable for young ladies.

It did not take her long to conclude, irrespective of whether it was on land or sea, any battle would result in the loss of lives. Since then, whenever she could sneak into her father's study, Kitty scoured the broadsheets for information.

The news was rarely positive, although so far England had repelled any threat. Adam was about to enter the fray, and there was a reasonable possibility he could be killed.

To Kitty, a world without Adam Marchmain was inconceivable.

The drum of approaching feet jerked her from her melancholy reverie.

"Kitty, Kitty, tell us a story," Araminta, Kitty's ten-year-old cousin, implored.

Kitty grinned at the eager faces in front of her. "What kind of story?"

"The one about the Knight of the Garden."

"Not again. You always choose that one."

"We love it," they chorused.

"Fair enough, but you must pick another story next time. Make yourselves comfortable."

After a bit of shoving and a lot of giggling, six expectant faces tilted upwards to Kitty.

"Once upon a time, in a land faraway…" she paused.

"…there was a princess named…" they chanted in unison. Every time she told the story, Kitty picked a different name.

"Hmmmm… now what was her name? Daffodil?"

"No," came the answer.

"Apple Blossom?"

"Nooooooooo," they chortled.

"Elderberry?"

"Kitty…"

Taking pity on them, she said, "Nessa."

"Ohhhhhhh, 'tis my turn," a little voice piped up. Vanessa was Araminta's younger sister. The same age as Georgina, the pair could be relied upon to get into all kinds of naughtiness.

"Now hush and listen." Kitty wove her tale, which expanded with every telling. From a simple story of a knight rescuing a princess, it had evolved to include dragons and witches, fairies and goblins, kings and queens. In deference to the boys, she had incorporated tournaments and quests.

The story unfolded to a silent audience. It was about the only time the children were peaceful unless asleep. Kitty was reaching the climax of the yarn when a loud crack shattered the stillness. They all jumped, and the three younger girls squealed.

Kitty turned to see Adam striding towards them, resplendent in his naval uniform. Over his shoulder she spied Juno, his mare, tethered to a tree. *How had she missed the thunder of hooves crossing the dry ground?*

"Adam," everyone crowed.

"Nice to see how entertained you are by my story."

"*Your* story?" Nessa's nose crinkled in puzzlement.

"Adam was the one who began this story when you were naught but a babe," Kitty explained.

"Why?"

"Kitty had tripped over and hurt her knee. It was so bad the doctor had to suture the cut and I made up the story to distract her," Adam said.

"I 'member," Emory joined in. "There was lots of blood. Derek said your leg was going to fall off."

In the ensuing banter, Derek — older brother of Araminta and Vanessa — blushed scarlet, while all of them peered at Kitty's skirts to see whether she had two legs.

"My legs are fine. I can still chase you rascals." Kitty

chuckled, to a gale of laughter from the other children and cries of 'you will never catch us.'

"Mind, I do not recall dragons and wizards in my tale," Adam mused, folding his arms, and trying to look stern.

The children 'oooohed.'

"As *I* recall," Kitty countered, loftily, "*you* did not finish the story, even though you promised you would." Her mouth tilted in a cheeky smirk.

"Another time, perhaps." The tall young man grinned. "I cannot tarry, I came to say goodbye."

"Goodbye? Where are you going?" everyone, except Kitty, clamoured.

"To London, then Portsmouth, then I do not know. The High Seas I daresay."

Ernest begged Adam for all the details, as did Emory and Derek; the lads being enamoured of the British Navy. Sensitive to the fact there were four girls, Adam talked about his training and the places where he might be posted, without going into gory details.

After describing the *HMS Nimbus*, the ship he had been assigned to, he explained his likely duties, shrewdly skirting mention of battles and naval engagements, to the boys' badly concealed disappointment

Kitty listened in silence.

Adam caught her eye and sent a reassuring smile.

She reciprocated, but it was half-hearted. To the undiscerning ear, it sounded as though he was off on a great crusade, but she was not fooled by his cheerful descriptions. She had seen the numbers of dead and wounded, who were listed with harrowing frequency in the newspapers. Her heart ached.

. . .

For reasons she could not fathom, Kitty wanted a private moment with her knight. She threw out casually, "I do believe I overheard Cook say she was baking ginger biscuits this morning."

She tapped her chin in apparent thought. "I am certain she could be persuaded to—" Whatever else she was going to say was lost as Georgina and Vanessa squealed their excitement and bolted across the grass, Araminta on their heels.

The three boys were torn. *Ships or biscuits.*

"Go," Kitty urged. "I think you have squeezed every last scrap of information from Adam."

Ernest eyed Adam, quizzically.

Adam lifted his hands, palms up. "Your sister is correct, fresh biscuits ought not be missed. If you are not quick about it, the girls will eat every last one."

Emory looked at Derek, then tugged on his twin's sleeve. "Come on, if we go the other way, we shall beat them." With a whoop, they bolted.


"So, my Knight of the Garden, you are about to set out on a crusade? 'Tis more than a ride across an estate." Kitty studied Adam, committing his features to memory… just in case.

He was tall, taller than her Papa, she surmised. His straight, chestnut-brown hair was tied in a cue and lay neatly on the stiff collar of his uniform. His rich, mahogany-coloured eyes, currently twinkling down on her, were framed by dark lashes. A straight nose over firm lips.

She canted her head. His was an angular face. Not handsome as such but arresting. A face not easily forgotten.

"Do I pass muster?" he asked, after at least a minute when neither of them spoke, amusement playing around his mouth.

"My apologies, I have a need to memorise you. I am under

no illusion as to the dangers you are about to face and…" To remind Adam he might die was unconscionable. "Forgive me, that was thoughtless."

"There is naught to forgive. I am cognisant of the hazards of life at sea. I shall endeavour to stay alive but can only place my trust in the Good Lord and those whom I serve with and under, that we return unscathed. I…" He hesitated and shuffled from foot to foot awkwardly.

"What is it, Adam?" Kitty coaxed. "'Tis unlike you to be diffident."

"I wondered, if… whether… perhaps…" a red stain flushed up his cheeks, and Adam ignored the voice of reason which insisted this was a gross breach of etiquette. "Might I beg a kiss from my princess?" This last came out in a rush, but in spite of his embarrassment, he held her astonished gaze.

At any other time, Kitty would have burst out laughing at so unusual request. To ask a thirteen-year-old girl, even one soon to be fourteen, for a kiss was not something expected from a man of twenty and one, and a naval officer to boot. Today, something in Adam's stance stifled her mirth.

She stood up from her bench and executed a neat curtsy, her soft lilac gown billowing out like a wave of her favourite bluebells.

"Adam Marchmain, Marquis of Teasdale, Knight of the Garden, Officer of His Majesty's Navy, it would be my honour to bestow upon you a kiss."

She was about to stretch up onto her tiptoes when Adam dropped to one knee. Without thinking, she grasped his hand, so as not to over-balance and, bending ever-so slightly, brushed her lips to his hot cheek.

"Stay safe, my knight," she murmured.

"I give you my word," he replied just as quietly. Rising to

his feet, he bowed with a flourish and pressed a kiss to her knuckles.

Kitty stared into his dark eyes, an emotion she would not recognise for a decade, teasing at the edge of her consciousness.

"I do not think I can say goodbye," she muttered, treacherous tears threatening.

"Perhaps we ought simply to say until we meet again."

She considered that and nodded. "Far preferable. So, my Lord Teasdale, until we meet again."

"Until we meet again, my Lady Katherine de Wilton."

Grabbing her book and her wrap, Kitty all but ran along the path towards the house.

She stopped once to glance over her shoulder.

Adam waved and, after remounting Juno, headed in the direction of Easby Hall — his father's estate, which bordered that of the Grafton's.

Unbeknownst to either Kitty or Adam, the next time they met, their lives had changed beyond all recognition.

# CHAPTER TWO

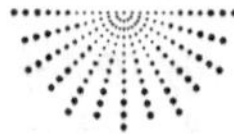

GRAFTON MANOR ~ APRIL 1815

*T*wo elegantly clad ladies were sitting in the library, savouring a cup of tea and a plate of cakes so tiny they were barely a mouthful, but utterly divine. It was mild for the time of year, and the French doors stood open. The gentle breeze wafting into the room carried with it a sweet fragrance.

Lady Frederica Grafton and her bosom friend Prudence Marchmain who bore the lofty title Duchess of Easby, were watching a younger woman attempting to teach a tiny child to walk.

"How long has it been?" Prudence asked.

"Coming up two years." Frederica sighed. "She has still to revert to the Kitty we used to know. She is much too reserved. Even her voice remains unrecognisable. If I had only known…"

"Frederica, my dear, you *cannot* hold yourself responsible. None of us had the faintest idea. Kitty did a sterling job of feigning happiness. One should not speak ill of the dead, but that man was a monster."

"I wish there was a way we could lift her spirits. She only smiles when she is with Evie. I praise the Good Lord *he* never had the opportunity to subject that angel to his abominable behaviour." Her antipathy for the dead man was unequivocal.

Prudence nodded her agreement. "Small mercies, small mercies."

During the lull in their conversation, childish giggles could be heard. The two ladies regarded the little girl who plonked onto her bottom for the umpteenth time that afternoon, fondly. The young woman sank onto the grass and swung the child into her arms, showering her face with kisses.

"She needs a diversion, Prudence," Frederica brooded. "She needs to be distracted long enough that her soul starts to shine once more. My depth of grief is as though my daughter has passed away, but there she is, although a mere shell of who she once was. I am at a loss as to how to bring her back to life."

Prudence listened to her friend, the inkling of a plan nudging at the periphery of her mind. If they could make it happen, it might save two lives, perhaps even four. "I may just have the answer," she mused.

Something in Prudence's voice snagged Frederica's attention. "I know that tone." She grinned. "Come on, spill." Her use of the slang their children had insisted on employing making them chuckle.

"Adam."

The single word was enough for Frederica to understand where her friend might be going with this.

"Adam," she echoed. "Of course."

"I am at my wit's end with him, He is a surly grouch most of the time. I understand why, but his dour behaviour is affecting Oscar. He has run off every nursemaid. The last one stayed scarcely a week." Prudence threw up her hands. "I despair."

"What makes you think Kitty could succeed where others have failed?"

"Because we tell her precisely what has been going on. Kitty and Adam have been friends since before she learnt to walk. There is little about him she does not know, bar latterly. We can lay it all out for her and let her decide.

"I daresay the challenge will be enough to persuade her, but the clincher will be the possible damage he is doing to Oscar. Adam does not care to interview prospective staff in whatever capacity and has delegated the task to me." Her gurgle of wicked laughter, at odds with her obvious gentility.

"You are shameless, Prudence Marchmain." Mirth twitched at Frederica's lips. "Surely he will recognise Kitty when they meet again."

"I doubt it. You said yourself, Kitty no longer sounds like she used to, and Adam's injuries prevent him from seeing with any clarity. Moreover, he assumes her to be happily wed and living with her husband miles from here. The last person he would expect to be engaged as a nursemaid and eventual governess, is Kitty."

Frederica rolled the idea around her head. It could backfire, badly. Hopefully if that day ever came to pass, it would be too late. "It has merit, but will Adam accept a nursemaid who has a child of her own?"

"I shall couch it in terms with which he cannot argue. I can be very persuasive when necessary."

"That you can, my dear." Frederica grinned.

With indecorous gusto, they applied their considerable intelligence to the scheme. It *had* to work, neither Prudence nor Frederica could countenance it failing. Their children had borne enough. It was time to banish the darkness and bring some felicity back into their lives.

∽

Katherine Lovell, Viscountess Asquith, widow and mother, was blessedly ignorant of the plot being hatched in the library.

Her sole focus these days was Evie, no one else mattered. Evie was the reason Kitty dragged herself out of bed every morning and, so far, the only person who could bring a smile to her face, despite the strenuous efforts of her family.


Kitty had returned to Grafton Manor not quite two years ago. Frederica was pleasantly surprised, if marginally nonplussed when the butler announced Lady Asquith. Kitty had not sent word of her impending arrival.

Surprise became shock when her daughter entered the parlour.

Although visibly pregnant, Kitty had faded to a shadow of her former self. Her once curvaceous figure was gaunt, and her features pinched. Dark circles marred the delicate skin under her eyes and her hair, unravelling from its bun, hung limply around her shoulders.

Kitty had met her mother's disbelieving gaze and collapsed in tears.

Frederica assumed control. Enveloping Kitty in her arms, she had ushered the distraught woman to a chaise. Rocking her daughter until the storm subsided, Frederica listened with growing horror as Kitty's sorry tale unfolded.

Frederica had hardly seen her daughter since the latter's marriage. Godfrey, Kitty's husband had whisked his new wife away to his sprawling estate near Yarmouth and the two families were rarely in London at the same time.

Following Godfrey's sudden death, Kitty had written to her mother suggesting she not attend Godfrey's funeral.

Given the circumstances of his demise, it was a low-key affair, a short ceremony with a handful of mourners.

Frederica, who had bowed to her daughter's request, wished she had not.

Until Kitty's return, her family had assumed she was content and settled in her new life, little knowing the fetters by which Godfrey had governed his wife.

He had been the impeccable suitor and, to all appearances, head over heels in love with Kitty. He had courted her, romanced her and was, ostensibly, devoted to her. A state of affairs which stopped almost the minute they had spoken their vows.

His callous mistreatment began in the carriage on the way to Asquith Place, his family's country seat in Norfolk. He never raised a hand to his wife, but his words cut as deeply as any blow.

Systematically, he cowed Kitty's youthful effervescence, and her joie de vivre, eventually crushing her spirit. She lowered the register of her voice so as not to precipitate the volley of insults her bright chatter engendered. One minute he could charm the birds out of the trees, the next flay them with vitriol.

Neither was Kitty the only person to bear the brunt of his boorish attitude. His staff both in London and Norfolk were treated with similar disdain. Many left without so much as a goodbye, let alone references, electing to risk life on the streets rather than work for so unstable a master.

Kitty learnt when it was acceptable to speak and when it was judicious to remain silent. She discovered, after many, *many* mistakes, which gowns would please him, and which could trigger a tantrum.

He alleged that she was involved in numerous dalliances. Accused her of making eyes at every man within a twenty-mile radius. Refused to believe her when she tried to account for her whereabouts at any given time.

Slowly, Kitty's world contracted to her suite of rooms. Even a constitutional around the scrupulously tended lawns could incite a tirade.

Initially, and one of the reasons Kitty kept her trepidation about his erratic mood swings to herself, was that he came to her bed with unexpected sensitivity. He took her innocence with gentleness. His kisses were both ardent and tender. Briefly, Kitty felt adored, cherished.

Regrettably, as with his temper, this too deteriorated until she dreaded the nights. He was not cruel, and he did not force her, but he made it plain she was his property to do with as he saw fit. Moreover, it was easier to succumb than deny.

Godfrey's death had caused a minor sensation. He was murdered in a back alley, deep in London's Rookeries, allegedly following a bitter and protracted dispute relating to a failed and unnamed business deal.

The night he was killed was one of the happiest in Kitty's recollection, which also induced pangs of guilt. Godfrey's death was not quick, neither was it painless.

Although perhaps it was Fate meting out her own form of justice, Kitty endured a crisis of conscience, because, in the privacy of her bedchamber, she had wished him dead.

Had Kitty but known it, her reaction was typical of someone who had been subject to prolonged abuse, whether physical or verbal. With no one to talk to, she bottled it up, allowing it to fester.

That was until the day her doctor informed her, she was increasing.

Kitty, brought low by a spell of inexplicable sickness while in London, allowed her maid to convince her an appointment with the de Wilton's doctor was essential.

The affable gentleman, who had known Kitty's family for years, confirmed the maid's intuition. His diagnosis prompted Kitty to gape at him in slack-jawed incredulity.

"H-how... b-but... I d-do not..." she had clamped her mouth shut to steady herself. "My apologies, Doctor Bertram, my mouth refuses to follow instruction. How is this possible?"

The doctor had studied her, speculatively. "Because your husband bedded you, Lady Asquith."

She had blushed. "Yes, I know *how* it happens, but he... he is dead," she replied, baldly.

"Lady Asquith, you are at least four months gone, did you not notice the changes to your body?"

*Four months. Her husband had been killed about four months previously.* A grim smile tugged at the corners of her mouth at the irony. Had Godfrey been alive it was conceivable he would denounce the child, claiming she had seduced one of the grooms, or a gardener.

She could not understand why he had married her, except that to him the whole thing was some macabre game. To exert complete control over another person and bask in their misery. The man had been a venomous blackguard. The crude profanity the only suitable appellation.

"Forgive me, doctor. If you knew anything of my life you would understand why I questioned your pronouncement. Yes, my husband bedded me, but since it has been two years without issue, I had begun to hope children were not in my future."

Something in Kitty's voice had stayed the doctor's instinctive response. He ran an experienced and fatherly eye over the young woman, taking in her bruised features, pallid complexion, and fatigued demeanour. Barely twenty and two years old, Kitty was already a widow. Mind, there were a lot of widows resulting from the war which continued to rage.

"That is one of the saddest things I have ever heard, Lady Asquith, and I am sorry."

She straightened her shoulders. "It was what it was. By the grace of God, I am no longer burdened, but now I have another life for which I am about to become responsible."

"What of your family?"

"I have not told them."

"Oh, my dear. It is unhealthy to suppress such distress, for it may manifest in melancholy. Your Mama would be deeply perturbed if she thought you felt unable to apprise her of what you have…" he considered his words carefully, "…suffered."

"I doubt any of them will believe my tale of woe, Dr Bertram. Asquith was careful to present himself as an exemplary husband on the few occasions he could not avoid a brush with my family."

"Lady Asquith—"

"Please call me Kitty, Doctor. You have just examined me. You have known me since I was born. All this lady-ing becomes tiresome after a while. Moreover, I abhor my title as you might imagine." One corner of her mouth lifted slightly, warming her face momentarily.

"As you wish, Lad… Kitty," the doctor acceded. "As I was saying, if your mother could see you now, she would be most upset. You cannot disguise that you look unwell, haggard even. It is imperative you take care of yourself if you hope to carry your child to term. There are dangers enough without the added concern of ill-health."

"What do you suggest?" She had guessed his answer before he spoke.

"Go home. You husband is dead, you are increasing. It would not be unexpected given your situation. I guarantee, the moment Lady Grafton claps eyes on you, she will be both saddened and relieved. The former because you have kept this from her, and the latter because you have mustered the courage to tell her," he elaborated at Kitty's quizzical expression.

Kitty let his words roll around her head. "The Asquith estates…"

"You have stewards? A man of business?"

She nodded.

"Let them earn their keep. Nothing, I repeat, nothing is more vital than your well-being for the next few months. Please do not let him win."

Kitty's head shot up and she pinned the doctor with stunned green eyes. "Let him *win?*"

"Yes, if you permit him to rule your life even after his death, he has won. You have been afforded the chance to step out from his oppression, to become the spirited girl… young woman… you used to be. Do not waste the opportunity."


That was the first day in a long and difficult climb back to some semblance of normality. Kitty handed over the entire administration of the Asquith and Lovell estates to five eminently dependable stewards and one trusted solicitor, a decision she did not regret. She had contemplated selling some of the properties but her solicitor, a Mr Trimbell, had convinced her not to be precipitous.

After apprising her staff in London and Norfolk of her

intentions, Kitty thanked them for their care under arduous conditions. Reiterating their positions were not in jeopardy, she promised, should any wish to leave, they would take with them glowing references.

Her belongings packed, she departed without a backwards glance.

~

# CHAPTER THREE

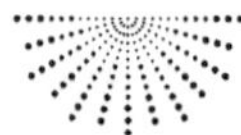

## EASBY HALL ~ APRIL 1815

"Adam," an optimistic voice called along the airy corridors of Easby Hall. An answering hail directed Prudence Marchmain to the study, where she found her son sitting in one of the aged leather chairs, staring into space.

"Adam, there is someone I should be pleased for you to meet."

"Not another do-gooding nursemaid," Adam Marchmain, Marquis of Teasdale, griped. "Can you not leave me in peace?"

"Come now, you know Oscar needs someone. He is five years old and requires more than childish games to keep him occupied. 'Tis time he began basic lessons. Are *you* equipped to teach him?"

"Do you delight in mocking me?" The man gave a humourless guffaw. "How on God's good earth could I possibly teach him?"

"You could stop being a grump, that would be a start," Prudence muttered under her breath.

"Beg pardon?"

"Nothing, my dear." She smiled sweetly. "Now, to business. I have interviewed a most suitable candidate. She is a widow, with a daughter, who…"

"A daughter? Oh, Mother…"

"Please, hold your complaints until I have explained, tsk,"

His mother's exasperation pulled the hint of a grin from Adam. "I apologise, Mama, do continue." He opened his hands in a gesture of compliance.

"She has a young daughter who, I have assured her, will be welcome, and I believe will be good for Oscar. Something to divert him, make him feel important. He worries about you, Adam, and it is not healthy for a child of his tender years to be so encumbered."

Adam swallowed the retort on the tip of his tongue. There was little point in arguing, his mother would get her own way and, he acknowledged, she was correct in her assertion.

Oscar was altogether too formal and polite for a child his age. He should be scampering around the grounds getting into mischief, not helping his crippled father avoid misplaced chairs or prevent him from tripping over a step.

"Fine," he relented grudgingly. "Do I have any say in the matter?" He quirked a brow.

"Not a single one." She beamed at her son. "I think she might be exactly what this house needs." With that cryptic comment, Prudence Marchmain swept out of the room.


Adam allowed himself a smirk. His mother was irrepressible. To say she was a duchess with all the weight the title bore, she often acted like a giddy girl. When she got together with Frederica de Wilton… the grin became a chuckle. He let that thought dangle as another pricked at his consciousness.

Kitty de Wilton, no… she was married to some viscount. Adam racked his brain, but the name eluded him. *Where was she these days?* His mother had told him. She kept him abreast of the lives of all those with whom he grew up, but he was unable to recall. Images flooded his mind of halcyon days when none of them had a care in the world.

How quickly life changed. The older ones were either married or at university or serving in one arm or other of the military. The younger ones at school or being tutored in how to become the ideal wife.

He frowned and levered himself out of the chair. With practised ease he walked over to the open French doors, without banging into any of the neatly positioned furniture, and narrowed his eyes. Blurry shapes and splashes of colour were all he could discern. Frustrated he slammed his palm on the door jamb.

"Bloody useless," he ground out. Closing his eyes, Adam leant his head against the cool wood and breathed in the fresh spring air.

He tried to cling to those happy childhood memories, but as ever, the minute he let down his guard, they were banished, superimposed by his waking torment.

He could not recall the last time he had slept without nightmares. Without hearing the screams of his fellow crew, not quite muffled by the incessant artillery fire. Without the stench of burning flesh. Without the all-pervading, metallic odour of blood and death. Without feeling the excruciating agony.

Four years ago.

The day his life was shattered.

In his mind's eye, Adam could see the moment before all hell broke loose, as though it was yesterday.

~

His ship, *HMS Nimbus* was involved in the battle for the key island of Vis in the Adriatic. Napoleon's domination over this stretch of water off the Mediterranean allowed him to transport troops and supplies to the Balkans.

Aware of this, the British navy seized Vis, from where they conducted lightning raids on enemy shipping. While successful, their tactics galvanised the French into action.

Inevitably, the persistent sparring precipitated an outright battle. The British squadron, led by Captain William Hoste was outnumbered three to one, which may have lulled the French into a false sense of security.

Hoste's brilliant strategy proved superior to that of the French, but it was a gruelling twelve hours before he could claim victory. Both sides sustained heavy casualties — personnel and vessels.

Adam was wounded when the *Nimbus* took cannon fire towards the end of the engagement. The French formation began to disperse, allowing the British squadron to pull ahead.

Bringing up the rear, the *Nimbus* was raked by one of the French frigates. The distance between the ships meant the damage was not as devastating as it might have been, but still resulted in twenty casualties. Three killed and seventeen wounded, eight of those, grievously.

Adam was thrown across the gun deck during the salvo, his body riddled with shards of exploding wood, leaving him scarred and virtually blind. The ship's surgeon said he should count himself lucky. The gunner who had been standing not three feet from him was blown to smithereens, his remains splattering those nearby.

*Lucky!* Nothing about it was lucky. By battle's end, Adam had lost a number of good friends, and not just from his ship. *HMS Nimbus* had since been dismantled, her crew reassigned, and he had been discharged. Yes, it was with honour, but his life, his career had been unceremoniously yanked out from under him.

He had relished being a sailor. Life on the open sea, while not easy, had been exhilarating, in spite of the ever-present dangers. It made men out of boys, taught them deference, comradeship, and dignity. Your shipmates became your family, and you relied on them, loved them even — warts and all. Privations and limitations aside, he had felt at home on the waves. Everything was less… complicated than on land.

Back on English soil, Adam spent several months in hospital, until the doctor was confident his physical wounds were healing satisfactorily. His body was criss-crossed by scars, and the blast had ruined his eyesight.

He could distinguish between light and shadow, changes in colour and, when in proximity to a person, was able to make out their features. Beyond a few feet, solid shapes had been reduced to blurry blobs and often merged into one another.

His doctor had tried to reassure him, there was a possibility the impairment was temporary; his tone implying the complete opposite.


There was more bad news to come.
It transpired Adam's young wife had died giving birth to
their son.


In 1809, Adam's ship went into dry dock for what would be a protracted period, while undergoing necessary repairs. On extended leave, he had visited with his friends, who persuaded him into the heady whirl of the elite. It was a relief, for a time, to pretend the world was at peace. To forget the hardships of life at sea. To revel in the extravagant lifestyle so beloved of Society.

Gwendolyn was a friend of one of his cousins, whom Adam had met, quite by chance, at a ball. There was a spark, and a gentle courtship began.

In the midst of a war, while not fought on English shores, to those directly affected or involved, life seemed fleeting. The fear their country may yet be conquered, inspired many a swain to ask for his lady's hand. Perhaps impetuously.

Adam, who found Gwendolyn enchanting, was one such suitor. Their families approved the match, and they were wed a month later. They moved into The Laurels, Adam's London residence and settled into married life.

Barely eight months after their nuptials, Adam was recalled to the *Nimbus*. Repairs complete, she was to join the fleet in the Mediterranean. During the fortnight before his departure, Adam and Gwendolyn had spent every available moment together.

He promised to take care. He whispered words of love as they clung to each other the night before he left. He swore he would return to her. She kissed him into insensibility and told him her heart was his forever.

She waved him goodbye from the steps of their home.

It was the last time they saw each other.

For a while, Adam wallowed in a grief which threatened to overcome him. What was the point of living? He had lost his wife, his career, his sight. His body ached from the battering it had received.

The mere thought of getting out of bed, of putting one foot in front of the other was enough to burrow under layers of blankets and hibernate like a wild animal.

. . .

His mother was the one who pulled him out of the doldrums. Prudence visited Adam as often as possible while he was in St Bart's — the London hospital specialising in battle injuries and trauma. So appalled was she by the devastation men could inflict on each other, she undertook to chat with as many of the wounded as she was able, inspiring her friends to do likewise.

Some patients had no family, and even the briefest of visits brightened their day. Although unheard of for a member of the nobility to spend time in the oft grim wards of St Bart's, voluntarily, Prudence was not to be swayed. If their measures had a positive effect on even one patient, the minimal discomfort they might experience was worth it.

One day, fearing Adam was on the brink of something disastrous, Prudence perched on the edge of his bed and took him to task in brisk no-nonsense tones.

"Oscar is a helpless babe who needs his father. You have a duty to your son. I thought you a courageous man. Those of your comrades who visit, never fail to cite the esteem with which you treated those of lesser rank, while respecting your superiors. I listen to them laud your bravery under fire, your steadfast loyalty to your crew, and your conscientious approach to any dispute. You are an officer, Adam, 'tis time you behaved like one."

"The boy does not know me, and what do *I* know about being a father? I have never met the child. I did not even know Gwen was increasing. I missed it all, Mama. She died, and I was not there to comfort her or tell her I loved her. I missed it all."

Before he could prevent it, a tear rolled down Adam's cheek, then another. He blinked fiercely to stem the tide. Too late.

Without drawing attention to her son's distress, his mother shifted on the bed to take Adam in her arms. She rocked him as she had when he was a child. The storm was short, but intense, and when it abated, Adam felt somewhat lighter of heart, although the weight pressing down on him had not lifted entirely.

Two weeks later, Adam went home to Easby Hall.

With some trepidation, it must be admitted, Adam met his baby son. It was a moment which remained etched in his soul. Oscar was almost a year old, gabbling gibberish interspersed with the odd recognisable word.

Saddened that Adam could not distinguish Oscar's features clearly, Prudence described the child. He had dark blond hair, and currently his eyes were blue, but were beginning to show a hint of grey. This last reminded Adam of Gwendolyn, who had striking grey eyes.

When Oscar saw Adam, his little face illuminated in a smile wide enough that Adam was able to perceive it, leaving him bewildered. His child could not possibly know him, but with so small a gesture, Oscar stole his heart.

Adam's learning curve was steep. It was rare for fathers of his class... of any class... to assume responsibility for a child as that was typically the domain of the mother.

Prudence was a Godsend. Mother of four children, and in defiance of her exalted status, she had eschewed wet nurses and nannies, electing to nurture her children herself.

Her advice and support were a boon to the young man who was trying to come to terms with the loss of his wife, not to mention his disability.

# CHAPTER FOUR

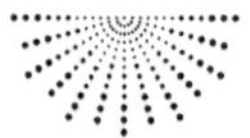

Oscar was the one shining beacon in Adam's life. Accepting some things required a woman's touch, Adam became father and mother to the tiny scrap of humanity.

With Prudence's guidance, he navigated the complexities of being a sole parent. Acknowledging he was fortunate to have plenty of staff to support him, he did as much as possible by himself.

Adam's diminished eyesight, while improved, was the biggest stumbling block... figuratively and literally. He worried he would trip over something and drop his son or, worse fall and land on the boy, crushing him. Prudence, with the help of her staff, re-arranged the furniture so as to leave wide swathes of uncluttered floor, which became trusted pathways.

With tedious regularity, Adam was led around Easby Hall, listening to his guide describe everything around them, down to the last detail. These hours created pictures in Adam's mind, allowing him to visualise the whole of the house as distinctly as if his eyes had never been damaged.

The day Adam walked around his home unaided, was a personal triumph.

Adam, while perhaps not happy with his life was almost content.

That was until Oscar needed a nursemaid.

Adam wrested his mind back to the present. Dwelling on what might have been was futile. No amount of 'what if's' could change the past. *Another nursemaid?* His head was already aching, and he had yet to meet this paragon. Adam knew his behaviour with the succession of women his mother had appointed, to be truculent, but he could not marshal the will to curb it.

With their shrill, twittery voices, slightly patronising attitudes, and well-intentioned platitudes, they only served to frustrate and irk. Two of them had decided he might be quite the catch and flirted outrageously. One even going so far as to move furniture, deliberately, so she could 'happen upon the scene' at the opportune moment to swoop in and rescue him. It was maddening.

Oscar's tuition was crucial. He would be duke one day, and Adam had no mind to deprive his son of the best education, but he preferred it not to happen too soon. This interlude with his son was to be prized. It would be gone soon enough. The two of them were close, much closer than many fathers and sons of the nobility.

As soon as Oscar was old enough to comprehend his father's limitations, he had taken it upon himself to become his escort. Adam had no clue how the boy managed to work out his routine, but he had.

Oscar bounced into Adam's bedchamber, punctually, at nine every morning. He took his father's hand and steered him along the many corridors and down the stairs to the dining room. They ate breakfast together, after which Oscar shepherded Adam to the study, or the estate office or wherever he had to go that particular day.

Adam, capable of making his way to any and all parts of his home or the grounds, used these precious snatches of time to cement the bond with his son. He talked about anything and nothing, the majority of which Oscar could not understand, but that did not bother the child unduly.

As the months ticked by, and Oscar's comprehension increased, their conversations became more intelligible. Oscar was always full of his day, nattering nineteen to the dozen about what he had been up to. Joyous moments.

Then came the string of nannies and their interfering ways. Their presence had created an animosity, Adam found difficult to repress. He became tetchy and, with little provocation, his temper frayed.

Adam's tolerance disintegrated spurring him, as his mother had so eloquently put it to Frederica, to run off every last nursemaid, some before they had been shown their assigned bedchamber.

Looking back, he recognised this was when Oscar's reserve had manifested, perhaps an unconscious attempt to soothe his father's agitation.

The realisation brought Adam up short. When *he* was five, he had been tearing around the grounds with his cousins and friends. Playing hide come seek in the woods, climbing trees in the orchards, tumbling into the house as the sun set. Grubby but happy.

*Oh, what he would give to feel happy.*

. . .

Adam bowed to the inevitable. For Oscar's sake he would do his best to behave in a manner of which his mother would approve.

He pushed himself off the jamb and oriented himself in the room. "Mama," he called, walking slowly towards the library door. "*Mama.*"

"Yes, dear?" Her reply floated to him from the floor above.

He angled his head in its general direction. "When does she arrive?"

Adam had no idea of the radiant smile which wreathed his mother's face. Nor did he hear Mrs Wilderby, the house-keeper, with whom Prudence had been talking, clap softly in satisfaction.

Instilling a bland note into her reply, Prudence leant over the balustrade. "I have arranged for her to arrive on Sunday afternoon. That will give her a little time to become familiar with the Hall before she starts her duties proper on Monday morning. Is that suitable?"

"Thank you, Mama, that is quite suitable."

"Excellent. I shall be down for tea shortly."

He heard her voice fade as she crossed the landing towards the east wing. Spinning on his heel, Adam went in search of Oscar.

"Stage one accomplished." Prudence grinned in a most un-duchess-like fashion as the pair walked briskly across the vast landing towards the guest chambers.

"Mrs Wilderby, while typically a governess is not entitled

to a maid, these are unusual circumstances. I am considering assigning Mabel in the guise of mother's help. What do you think?"

"I think Mabel is a good choice, your Grace. She's a sensible girl, dependable and trustworthy." Not needing to add that if any of these qualities was absent, the girl would be dispatched with alacrity. "How much do you want her to know?" the housekeeper asked.

"I think we ought to tell her the truth. Even though Kitty is hardly recognisable as the child who used to charge head-long around this estate, like you, many of the staff here will remember her. I have no doubt Lord Teasdale will eventually fathom out my ruse, but I hope we can keep it in play long enough for them both to recall that life can be fun, not a chore." Prudence had apprised her housekeeper something of Kitty's circumstances, the latter genuinely sympathetic.

"Easby Hall has always been a place where happiness thrives, your Grace," Mrs Wilderby said comfortingly. "I am sure it will cast its spell again."

Prudence patted her housekeeper's arm. "Why June, that is one of the nicest things you have ever said. I am so glad you feel it too."

"Aye, well, you and his Grace are a pleasure to work for and no mistake. There's them as not so fortunate." Her cheeks colouring a faint pink, Mrs Wilderby bustled along to the suite of rooms allocated to Kitty and her daughter, leaving Prudence in her wake.

Prudence chuckled. *Oh no, Mrs Wilderby, we are the ones who are fortunate.*

The remainder of the afternoon was devoted to ensuring everything was prepared for the new arrivals.

~

Five miles away, as the crow flew, Kitty Lovell was pacing back and forth across the terrace of Grafton Manor. *This was a bad idea. No... this was positively the worst idea.* Adam would recognise her immediately, how could he not? They had known each other for two decades. Surely, she had not changed *that* much.

It was going to be a farce of epic proportions. *What did she know about being a nursemaid, or a governess anyway?* Evie was too young to require lessons of any kind and, although Kitty believed herself a loving mother, she often made mistakes.

Reaching the low wall marking the end of the flag stones, she turned to march in the opposite direction. Her internal debate nowhere near its conclusion.

Aunt Prudence's scheme had sounded so benign when first proposed. To help Adam with his son. Where was the harm? Kitty's mind wandered back two days, to the moment his mother broached the possibility.

"He is in desperate need of someone who won't be upset by his... errr... crotchety temperament." Prudence had encouraged

"Why do you think I will be any different from the others?" Kitty had countered.

"Because you and Adam share an affinity. Even when you were a little girl, Adam never flustered you. The few instances when he was upset or irate, it was you who was able to fix whatever perturbed him without making it a big drama. You always could. You refused to take umbrage if he growled at you, and you never backed down. He admired your spirit and your lack of pretension. You secured his respect the day you split your knee, and it has only increased through the years."

"That is all well and good, but he is supposed to think I am a qualified governess, engaged by you, who has come to care for Oscar. I cannot be his friend *and* a stranger."

"Just be you, my dear. Kitty de Wilton." Prudence purposely used her maiden name, mindful of the enmity the younger woman bore for anything connected to her husband.

"You know Adam's eyes are impaired?" She raised a brow and Kitty nodded. "While he has regained some of his sight, I doubt it will ever be restored fully. This works in our favour. You might not be quite the Kitty of our recollection, but I concur, your features are distinctive. Under normal circumstances it would not take him long to figure it out. Our advantage is your voice. You have been home nigh on two years, but your voice is unrecognisable."


Kitty had shuffled under her aunt's sympathetic gaze. Uncomfortably aware of the damage Godfrey had wrought, she remained incapable of invoking the energy required to reverse it. She continued to speak as though fearful of the response. She was too thin, rarely did anything with her hair other than plait it, and tended to wear her old, faded gowns; the ones she left behind when she got married.

It was such a relief not to worry about what colour or material or design of attire she chose. Not to require her hair styling. To be free to walk the floors barefoot. To read whatever and whenever she wanted; another treasured pastime he had prohibited eventually, simply because he knew how much she loved to bury herself in a book.

Women did not need to be well-read, that might upstage their husband… *goodness me, no.* To look good on the arm of their spouse and discuss nothing more interesting than the weather, had been Godfrey's philosophy and woe betide Kitty if she disagreed.

"I am not sure this is a good idea, Aunt Prudence. Adam is a clever man."

"I accept we cannot fool him indefinitely. If we can maintain the artifice long enough that Oscar reverts to being a typical rascally five-year-old and stops worrying about his father, I will class our subterfuge as a success. Everything after that is a bonus."

She studied Kitty who was biting her lip in indecision.

"Please, Kitty." Regardless of how close the two families were, it was unheard of for a duchess to plead. "I need my son back."

That she and Frederica hoped the plan would also revitalise Kitty, was neither here nor there, and something neither mother deemed prudent to enunciate.

Kitty asked several more questions, but Prudence had been confident she would consent, if only because it was Adam.

Kitty sank onto one of chairs facing the gardens. The sun was beginning its slow descent, bathing the scene in front of her in a golden haze. Lethargic insects levitated on the breeze. Their hum, hypnotic. Bird song wrapped around her, their avian harmony transcending any man-made music.

She leant back in the chair, breathed in the fragrant air, and waited until the tumult in her mind cleared.

This was for Adam. She would do anything for him, something of which Aunt Prudence was acutely conscious and, if she was honest, her assent was never in any doubt.

"On your own head be it, Kitty Lovell," she muttered. "This could prove to be a great, big, enormous gaffe, or the making of me. Let us hope 'tis the latter."

# CHAPTER FIVE

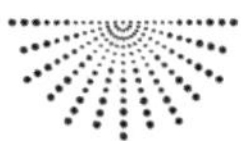

The next few days were a confusion of packing. With the help of her maid, Kitty selected the plainest of dresses, although a mischievous imp coerced her to include some of a brighter hue.

Prudence — of the opinion the less rigid an atmosphere the quicker Oscar would adjust to his new regimen — had said not to worry about a uniform, sober garments would suffice. Since Godfrey had mandated that Kitty be attired in drab gowns, unless they were hosting guests, she had plenty from which to choose.

When she unlatched the trunks, Kitty was swamped by a wave of conflicting emotions. None had been opened since she came home to Grafton Manor. Initially, she could not bear the reminders of her marriage and then it was easier to leave them strapped and stored out of sight in the attics.

As she lifted the lid of the first one, a faint odour drifted towards her. Dried lavender and something else. Something reminiscent of the oft airless atmosphere at Asquith Place.

Whimsically, Kitty labelled it sadness.

. . .

Evie's fascination with the large boxes, interrupted Kitty's musings. The little girl, who could only just see over the rim of the boxes, chattered in unintelligible glee, while chubby fingers tried to grab anything they could reach.

Her antics made Kitty chuckle and on impulse, she lowered her daughter into the nearest trunk. The pair had a grand old time tossing dresses about. Soon, the bedchamber resembled an explosion in a modiste's boutique, but the two at the centre remained unrepentant, giggling with mirth.

In the blink of an eye, Sunday afternoon came around. Frederica suggested Kitty use the open topped carriage. It was a mild, late-spring day and the drive to Easby Hall would take less than an hour. Luggage packed; the only thing left was to say their adieus.

"Please come home when you are able." Frederica would miss her daughter and granddaughter, their parting causing unanticipated sorrow.

"I promise, Mama," Kitty vowed, "but it will depend on my duties. I cannot simply run home when the mood takes me. I shall have a schedule to maintain and am now at someone else's beck and call. Moreover, I am supposed to be from some distance away and, thus, unlikely to know anyone in the vicinity. Perhaps you might find time to visit with Aunt Prudence every once in a while."

"That I shall." Frederica hugged Kitty tightly. "I love you my daughter…" about to add to her sentiment, she decided against it.

"I love you too, Mama. Come, Evie." Kitty hoisted the little girl into the carriage. "Sit there, poppet." She pointed to the corner where a pile of rugs had been arranged to create a bolster seat, which allowed Evie to see over the side of the carriage.

Sam, one of the grooms, clicked the reins. Frederica, Kitty, and Evie waved madly at each other as the coach rattled down the drive.

Once the Manor was out of sight, Kitty sat back, one arm around Evie to ensure she would not fall off her perch and tried to ignore the fluttering in her stomach.

The sound of a carriage trundling up the long drive to Easby Hall, set Adam's teeth on edge. *Hell, and damnation, why had he acquiesced to this lunacy? Another bloody busybody in his home, his parents' home,* he corrected himself.

Unbidden, his thoughts strayed momentarily to Teasdale Mallow, his estate in Wiltshire.

It was years since Adam had visited. He took Gwendolyn shortly after their marriage. He valued the isolation but, it became apparent his new wife favoured the hustle and bustle of London. They had returned to the city scant weeks later.

*Perhaps when Oscar was a little older, they might travel there.* His father had ensured the property's upkeep, but it had been sorely neglected.

Adam focused on his current problem. For his mother's sake, he would make the effort to be civil, but the thought of enduring this rigmarole again, made his chest tighten.

"Papa, Papa, are we going to meet the lady at the door?" His son's question broke into his reverie.

"No, no. Mr Wilderby will escort her here." They were in the library. "It is not proper for a lord to greet a member of staff. They are brought to us." Adam knew he sounded pompous and, to be fair, he did not adhere to such conventions, but he had no desire to loiter on the doorstep while someone as insignificant as a nursemaid arrived.

"Papa, pleeeeeease come," Oscar wheedled, tugging on his father's hand.

Inadvertently aiding Oscar's cause, Frederica poked her head around the door. "Come along, you two. It would be a kindness to greet Mrs Lovell and her daughter as they arrive. Do you not agree?"

"Yes," Oscar squeaked.

"No, in fact I do not," Adam dissented. "'Tis not approp—"

"Oh, do stop being so stuffy," Prudence interrupted his denial and adjured him to smile. She tucked his arm through hers, and with Oscar jigging about at his other side, the three made their way across the hall to the main entrance.

Mr Wilderby masked his surprise at this informality, but when Prudence gave him a sly wink, he grinned. He knew who was about to blow into this house and, along with those of the staff who had been informed, prayed Kitty's presence would work a miracle.

~

When Easby Hall came into sight, Kitty gripped the side of the carriage, the cool of the metal seeping through her gloves. Sucking in one… two… three… four deep breaths, she strove for calm.

A handful of people had congregated on the top step of the flight leading up to the front door. Her forehead creased. *Unusual. Why would so many people meet a nursemaid?*

As they approached, Kitty spotted her Aunt Prudence. *You must remember to call her, your Grace,* she admonished internally. A small boy, jumping up and down, hopefully in excitement, held the hand of a tall man.

Kitty's heart did a funny hiccup. *The tall man could*

*only be Adam.* Glad she could study him, covertly, she was taken aback by the changes the last decade had inflicted. He was broader than she recalled, but his stance was rigid. More than the military bearing she would have expected; it was as though he dared not relax.

While she watched, he bent and spoke to the boy who immediately stilled. *Oh no, that would not do.* A memory flickered. Her eyes narrowed and she itched to rap the man's knuckles. In her opinion, to curtail a child's exuberance, especially one so young was unnecessary.

A smartly uniformed footman crunched across the gravel as the carriage came to a halt. He opened the door, dropped the step, and offered Kitty his hand.

Recognition dawned and Kitty, climbing down, greeted him in undertones. "Elias, thank you. 'Tis glad I am to see you."

Elias, who had been with the Marchmain family, since he was a boy, gave her a warm smile and bowed. "Not half as glad as we are to have you, Lady Asquith."

"Please, I am Mrs Lovell from now on, and this is Evie." She stretched into the carriage to lift out her daughter.

"Permit me, my L... Mrs Lovell," Elias appealed.

"That would be very kind." Kitty nodded.

Elias hopped up the steps and gathered Evie in his arms. "I am honoured to meet you, Miss Evie," the footman greeted in dignified tones.

Evie planted a kiss on his cheek. "Hullo," she chirped distracted by his neatly trimmed sideburns. "Tickles." She giggled.

Elias bit his lip to keep a straight face. Holding Evie in one arm he held his other out for Kitty.

"I shall manage, you have enough to contend with. Evie is a wriggler," Kitty warned. "Shall I bring my valise?"

"Leave all your luggage, my lady. It will be taken to your chambers."

"Thank you again." She dipped her head. They had reached the bottom of the steps.

"Mrs Lovell, how lovely. I hope your journey was untroubled." Prudence sailed down to greet her.

Kitty curtsied. "Thank you, yes, the coaching inn you recommended proved most congenial, and you were correct, their game pie was indeed delicious." Kitty met her aunt's gaze, silent communication passing between them.

"Do come up and meet your new charge." Prudence, a frequent visitor to Grafton Manor was worried Evie might give the game away. Thankfully, that young personage was fixated on Oscar.

Kitty followed the duchess up the sweeping flight of steps coming face to face with Adam Marchmain, her Knight of the Garden. His countenance, once so cheerful was severe, not helped by the spiderweb of scars covering the right side of his face.

"Adam, Oscar, this is Mrs Lovell and her daughter Evie. Mrs Lovell may I present Oscar Marchmain and his father the Marquis of Teasdale."

"Lord Teasdale." Kitty executed a flawless curtsy, bringing her eye to eye with Oscar who marched forward.

"Hullo," he boomed and flung his arms around Kitty's neck almost knocking her over.

"Oscar." Adam's censure was sharp.

Oscar's face fell and he made to return to his father's side.

Kitty reached for the boy's hand. She clasped it gently, and he offered a relieved smile. "I beg your pardon, my lord," she intervened, politely. "'Tis naught but a child's exhilaration. I think it marvellous to be met with such enthusiasm. It sets a most congenial tone."

Adam glowered at the indistinct shape speaking to him. He had the impression she had chastised him, but so shrewdly it felt like a compliment.

"No matter. Welcome to Easby Hall, I hope your sojourn here is pleasant, I do not expect it to be a long one." He spun on his heel.

"We shall see." Kitty conceded to his swiftly retreating back. "May I say what magnificent surroundings. Far more beneficial than London."

She turned to admire the familiar vista.

Breathing in a lungful of balmy air, with its faint fragrance of honeysuckle, it felt like she had come home.

As far as Adam was concerned, he had done his duty. He stalked back to the library, where he poured himself a large whisky. He heard the lilt of voices as his mother along with Mrs Wilderby and Oscar escorted the new arrivals up to their chambers.

Why on earth his mother felt it necessary to provide a suite of rooms in the guest wing was lost on him. By rights, the woman ought to be assigned a small bedchamber adjacent to the nursery.

When he had taken Prudence to task about it, her answer was less than satisfactory. She claimed, due to Mrs Lovell's circumstances, more generous quarters could be afforded, and it wasn't as though they didn't have the space. The justification had sounded contrived to Adam, but he could not for the life of him figure out why.

He sipped the amber spirit, savouring the smoky flavour as it slid over his tongue and down his throat. He might have endorsed this charade, but he intended to avoid the new nursemaid or governess or whatever she was supposed to be, unless absolutely necessary.

~

Upstairs, Kitty and Prudence were chatting about Oscar's requirements.

"I was thinking tomorrow, it being the first day, I would like to assess how much Oscar can cope with. He is not yet six, and I do not wish to overwhelm him. I prefer he look forward to his lessons not find them a chore. A day getting to know each other, with no tuition. I have drawn up a tentative schedule, which I can adjust once I have settled in."

Prudence nodded. "That sounds admirable. I imagine Oscar would thrive on a varied set of tasks. Lots of short lessons separated by some play or reading or a walk."

"That is precisely my thinking. Will Adam consider it impertinent if I include Evie in some parts of our day? We have not been apart since she was born, and the last thing I want is for her to think I have abandoned her. I accept she is too young to understand what I shall be teaching Oscar, but I cannot expect your staff to undertake her care, that is unfair on them."

"Might I suggest Mabel looks after Evie while you are conducting lessons, then she can join you during less structured activities."

"Splendid notion, Aunt Prudence. Thank you." Aware the marquis was downstairs, Kitty gave her aunt a hug. "I admit to being nervous. Adam appears very forbidding. Not at all like the person I recall."

"Now you understand what I meant when I said I need him to embrace life again, and why 'tis imperative you do not let him run you off."

An arch grin curved Kitty's lips. "I am not so easily scared, Aunt. I survived everything Godfrey threw at me and refuse to let another person intimidate me. I might be cracked and bruised, but I am not broken."

"Good girl." Empathy warming her reply, Prudence returned the hug. "Come, I think Mabel has things in hand here. Would you like a stroll around the gardens?"

"I should like that very much. Thank you, Mabel." Kitty sent the maid a grateful smile.

"Oscar, how about we show Mrs Lovell the rose garden?" Prudence suggested.

A bright beam split the boy's face. "Yes!"

"Let me take Evie," Kitty interposed when Oscar pulled the little girl to her feet. "She cannot walk at our pace. When we reach the gardens, you may help her if you wish."

"Goodie." Oscar clapped.

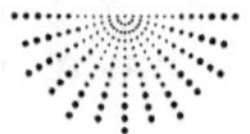

# CHAPTER SIX

*E*asby Hall basked in the mellow splendour of the late afternoon sunshine. Exiting the main house through a door disguised as a window along one of the corridors, Kitty paused, held captive by the vista and the memories chasing through her head.

She could envision a herd of small children running amok across the gardens or dodging around the trees in the orchards. Happy, carefree days, none having any premonition about what life would throw at them. Stopping the rush of images before they turned bleak, Kitty followed Prudence and Oscar.

Upon reaching the rose garden, Kitty placed Evie carefully on her feet and asked Oscar to hold her hand.

"Please do not try to run with her, she will trip over. Evie has only just learnt to walk," Kitty explained.

Oscar nodded and, exhibiting an extraordinary level of patience for so young a child, guided Evie around the flowerbeds. The pair chattered in that peculiar nonsense only small children comprehend, their voices carrying on the balmy air.

. . .

Adam stood by the French doors overlooking the terrace, frustrated at not being able to see the four people whose merry chatter sounded so inviting. *You could join them,* his internal voice chided, *it was your choice to hide in the library.* He dithered, but before he could make a decision, he perceived movement on his right.

"Adam, my dear, do come and sit with us." Prudence ignored Kitty's rapidly shaking head. "You have to talk to him eventually, better now than later," she muttered in undertones.

Raising her voice to its normal level, she continued, "I shall ring for drinks and you can get to know Mrs Lovell."

About to decline, Adam heard himself assent as his feet trod, without vacillation, towards the seats arranged in a loose half-circle on the broad terrace. He grumbled under his breath but coerced his features into what he trusted to be a welcoming aspect.

"Papa, Papa, this is Evie," Oscar's treble tones turned Adam's feigned smile into a genuine grin. Locating a chair, he settled himself and turned in the direction of his son's voice. Slowly, Oscar led Evie to his father; the little girl reeling slightly from the exertion of climbing the unfamiliar steps.

A low voice to his right spoke. "Evie, this is Oscar's father. He is a lord."

Evie canted her head to study Adam. Before Kitty could stop her, she was trying to scramble onto Adam's knee.

"Evie, no..."

Adam's hand went up. "Fret not." He hoisted Evie onto his lap. She squirmed around until she was kneeling, bringing her face to face with Adam. A chubby hand stroked his cheek, inquisitive fingers tracing the scars.

Kitty held her breath, not daring to interfere.

"Pwetty," Evie lisped and planted a kiss right on Adam's lips. Twisting around, she nestled against him. Her head on his shoulder, Evie stuck her thumb in her mouth and fell fast asleep.

Kitty swallowed, trying not to laugh at Adam's stupefaction. "My apologies, my lord. Evie usually has a nap in the afternoon, but today it was not possible. With your permission, I shall take her to bed."

"No need to disturb her, it is no problem." Adam was as surprised as the other two adults when the words tripped over his lips. *The deuce, but what was **wrong** with him?* In truth, Evie's immediate acceptance of him was reminiscent of when Oscar was the same age. There was something inexplicably wonderful about having an infant trust you enough to doze in your arms.

"Oscar, you were very good with Evie." Kitty changed the focus of their conversation. "Thank you for your patience."

Oscar shrugged. "Helping Evie is like helping Papa, if you are not careful, they will trip over or walk into something."

There was a split-second when Kitty thought Adam was going to reprimand Oscar, for what might be considered cheek. The moment passed and Prudence diverted their conversation to other topics.

Mindful of her role, Kitty was more silent spectator than participant in the conversation over dinner, and she excused herself immediately afterward, as would be expected. Later, tucked up in bed, she pondered the events of the day.

Adam's face swam across her vision and her heart ached for the boy she had known. Her knight, full of vitality, whose zest for life had been contagious. She recalled the last time she had seen him, eager to embrace the adventure in which he was about to participate.

Whatever happened, she was determined to peel back the layers until she found that light-hearted boy again.

~

Imperceptibly, Kitty began to work the magic, Prudence and Frederica knew she possessed.

The morning after her arrival, Kitty took Oscar for a brisk walk around the gardens before breakfast. This became a habit unless the weather was too inclement. Kitty never thought to include anyone else, neither did she take Evie. This was for Oscar and her; a time to be outdoors purely for the fun of it, nattering like magpies about anything and nothing.

Breakfast over, the pair disappeared into the schoolroom. Situated down a long corridor off the main hall, this was where all the Marchmain children had begun their education, tucked in a quiet corner of the house.

Two large windows offered a view of the internal courtyard; interesting, but not enough to distract. Four desks, a cupboard — in which was stored books, paper, quills, ink, chalk — and a blackboard on an easel.

Fortuitously, Kitty's own governess had been an avid collector of a monthly publication called *The Lady's Magazine*, currently stored in the schoolroom at Grafton Manor. They had proved to be a mine of information for Kitty because, in amongst the diverse range of topics, were articles on the development of children.

As Kitty had said to Prudence, all she wanted to do on her first day was assess Oscar's abilities. At five years old, the little boy's dexterity, or lack thereof, would preclude him from manipulating a quill with ease, *but* he might be able to form his letters and numbers.

He could learn to count, to read, perhaps even master very basic sums. There was also a way to learn through play. Catching and throwing a ball with accuracy, playing hoops, walking along the top of a low wall, hopping, and skipping, even stacking or lining up pebbles or sticks all contributed to increased coordination, balance, and flexibility.

With no mind to overwhelm Oscar, Kitty divided their day up into equal increments, ensuring she interspersed those tasks requiring concentration with more fun-based pursuits.

She included a quiet time, when she either read out loud from a book of Oscar's choice, or invented a tale. Oscar usually napped; he was still a little boy, his abounding energy notwithstanding.

~

The days slid into weeks; spring became summer. News about the progress of the war filtered through. In June, the Battle of Waterloo was fought. A resounding victory for England and her allies, and the last gasp for Napoleon, who surrendered and was exiled.

It had been a protracted conflict with many lives forfeit. The country seemed to be holding its breath in anticipation of peace, praying husbands, sons, fathers, and brothers might come home safely.

~

Kitty and Oscar settled into a routine, and Prudence was quietly exultant at how seamlessly Kitty slotted into the household. Even though it was a somewhat artificial situation, Kitty had to adapt to a drastic change in status, and the transition from viscountess to governess was not without its challenges.

Being neither servant nor family, the role of governess was oft solitary, and generally undertaken by ladies of noble birth fallen on hard times. Kitty's situation was made slightly more complex because everyone in the household, except Adam, knew the real reason for her presence. Most of them had loved her for years but had to behave as though she was a stranger.

Breakfast and luncheon, she ate with Oscar; dinner was with the family. Kitty spoke when directly addressed and, as a woman of her supposed station ought, kept her opinions to herself. After dinner, unless specifically invited to join the family, Kitty retired to her rooms.

In accordance with the traditional terms of employment for women in her position, she was granted half a day off each week. To go home, if only briefly, was not a viable option. Her cover was of someone who had travelled some distance to take up her post, and she would not know anyone hereabouts. Thus, to remain at the Hall was not unexpected. Kitty didn't mind, there was always plenty to keep her occupied.

Oscar and Evie became fast friends, and the little boy asked Kitty to permit Evie to sleep in the nursery. As Mabel had the adjoining chamber, Kitty was amenable, hiding the tinge of sadness the arrangement engendered.

Her daughter had taken the next step in her development without a backwards glance. Kitty found it harder to adjust. She had no mind to mollycoddle the child, but Evie was not two years old and they had never been apart for a single night.

. . .

Lady Grafton visited periodically which, given her friendship with Prudence, was not unusual. The latter, in the guise of demanding a report on Oscar, invariably orchestrated a few moments for mother and daughter to be together.

If occasionally lonely, for the most part, Kitty was content. She remained reserved, but the shadows lurking in her eyes had diminished, and her features were less wan.

Kitty saw Adam only at dinner, which was both a relief and a regret. He was aloof and rarely contributed to meal-time conversations. Their limited and, admittedly, stilted, interactions only increased her desire to break through the shield he had erected. To see his smile and hear his laughter.

To rescue the knight of her childhood.

Adam maintained his distance and, although politeness itself, laboured to summon up any enthusiasm when he could not avoid speaking to the governess. Despite this, and to his irritation, he was intrigued by the newcomer and her daughter.

Oddly, Evie was the one to put a chink in his armour.

Too young to be inhibited by status, or to comprehend the subtle nuances ebbing and flowing among the adults, Evie treated everyone with the same blithe insouciance. A trait she had inherited from her Mama.

To the amusement of the household, from the day she arrived, whenever Evie saw Adam, she bowed at the waist, her mop of hair sweeping the ground, and addressed him with a stentorian, "Hullo, Sir Pwetty."

The first time it happened, Adam — who had no intention of becoming *friends* with the help or her daughter, especially help he had neither asked for nor wanted — ignored her. The sound of Evie's sad little huff when he refused to acknowledge her, had torn at his soul.

*Had he become so heartless he could not be kind to an innocent child?*

Waving aside Mrs Lovell's apology for her daughter's impudence, Adam had unbent enough to respond. The delight in the little girl's voice, a just reward, and her greeting had become a part of his day to which he looked forward immensely.

This also meant he came into relatively frequent contact with Evie's mother. The woman was a conundrum. He could not fault her behaviour; she was *exactly* what he expected of a nurserymaid-come-governess. Courteous, retiring, and modest. Diametrically opposed, in fact, to those who had held this position previously.

The odd times he questioned her on anything pertaining to Oscar, she answered concisely. Without the simpering titters and what he had supposed to be vacuous smiles which accompanied similar accounts provided by her predecessors.

Once or twice, he had spoken thoughtlessly or with rancour. While others might have taken offence, she brushed it aside or pretended he hadn't spoken at all.

Adam might not be able to see with clarity, but his other senses had heightened and there was something which drew him to Mrs Lovell — something tantalisingly elusive. As though her reticence masked an inner vivacity, deliberately suppressed, yet begging to be revealed.

He puzzled it over until, more than a month later, realisation dawned. He *wanted* to get to know her, to partake of a proper conversation, to find out what lay beneath her unflappable façade.

More than this, he yearned to confide in her, to share his woes. He had the strangest inkling she had the capacity to assuage them.

He found himself listening for her voice, imagining what she looked like. She had even taken root in his dreams, soothing his nightmares. It was infuriating.

Refusing to pander to such whimsy, Adam shoved it aside but, once in a while, her measured tones badgered at the edge of his mind, demanding attention.

*What was it about Mrs Lovell?*

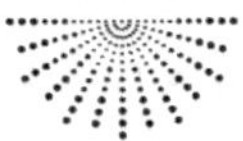

# CHAPTER SEVEN

*I*nitial apprehension aside, Kitty revelled in her work. Oscar, an intelligent child who soaked up his lessons like the proverbial sponge was a pleasure to teach. While some tuition required a desk, the long hot days fostered outdoor pursuits.

Aware they would be confined to the house during the winter, Kitty used the gorgeous weather to their advantage, and conducted the majority of their lessons in the gardens. Often, Mabel and Evie joined them, and the four had a riotous time.

Every afternoon, a book under one arm and a rug under the other, Kitty chivvied her charges across the lawns to one of the sprawling beech trees scattered across the Great Park. Once they were all comfortable, she read a story or three.

Oscar and Evie tended to snooze, especially on the warmer days, allowing Kitty and Mabel to engage in a good old gossip. Mabel, only a couple of years younger than Kitty, had been one of the tweeny maids a decade ago, and recalled the numerous times Kitty and her siblings visited.

Although they grew up on opposite sides of the baize

door, the two women discovered they genuinely valued each other's company, an unlikely friendship blossoming.

"I could get used to this life," Kitty confided one balmy afternoon. She was sitting amongst the massive roots of the tree, propped against the trunk, with little regard for her gown.

"I am sure her Grace would be pleased to have you teach Oscar 'til he goes to school," Mabel replied, her nimble fingers making a daisy chain.

"While the idea is attractive, 'tis unfair on Lord Teasdale for me to continue this ruse indefinitely. Moreover, 'tis obvious his lordship dislikes the notion of a governess. Her Grace informed me he ran off the previous nursemaids."

"That he did, Lad… Mrs Lovell." Mabel caught herself. "Mind they was flibbertigibbets the lot on 'em. Scarce anything but air in their heads, and gracious sakes if they didn't think his lordship would fall in love as soon as look at 'em." She shook her head. "They were a sorry bunch, if you don't mind me saying."

"I don't mind at all. Poor Ad… Lord Teasdale. A grieving widower with a baby boy. He must have looked like an easy mark to women desperate for a wealthy husband, especially if they have come from a noble family.

"Being cast into the role of underling would be an ordeal none expected to face. To have everything you know ripped out from under you, to rely on the generosity of others of your class to take pity on you, cannot be easy to swallow. I am fortunate my husband's death did not leave me destitute."

"How do *you* find it, my lady?" Mabel dared quiz. "A member of the *ton* while temporarily serving them?"

Kitty mused on Mabel's question. "'Tis interesting. I was nervous and perhaps a trifle scared. Being widowed, I have been answerable to no one and confess it is liberating. That said, I fear this scheme will backfire. I have no mind to cause Lord Teasdale any more anguish."

"May I speak candidly, my lady?"

"Of course, and Mabel how many times must I ask you to call me Kitty?" Kitty grinned as Mabel blushed. "You attend to my precious Evie as though she was your own child, not to mention currently we are equals."

"No, my lady, as governess, your status is higher. 'Tis disrespectful to address you by your given name."

"Only if not invited to do so. Please, Mabel." Kitty placed her hand over Mabel's and held the woman's gaze until the latter acquiesced with a tolerant huff. Mabel along with the majority of the household had come to realise, Kitty the adult was no less persuasive than Kitty the child.

"As you wish, Kitty." The absurdity of their conversation struck Mabel, and her lips twitched.

Kitty spotted it and, for no reason either woman could think of, they started laughing

"Now, we have cleared the air, you were about to speak candidly." Kitty cajoled.

"His lordship came back from the war a broken man. His injuries were only the half of it. Her ladyship's death cut him deeply, but I'm of the opinion, as are most here, it were more guilt than the loss of someone he loved dearly."

"How do you mean?" Kitty had been given to understand Adam adored Gwendolyn.

"Don't get me wrong," Mabel sought to clarify. "His lordship cared for his wife, but it was more… hmmm… affection, than an abiding love."

"What was it led to that opinion?" Kitty could not help but pry, amazed Mabel could distinguish between affection and love among the elite. Most hid their feelings remarkably well.

"I was assigned to his lordship's household upon his wedding and did not come back here until he went to sea. Her ladyship removed to her parents' home," she added by way of explanation. Kitty nodded her understanding.

"Part of being staff, is that we are seen and not heard. We are invisible to most, and as such often privy to scenes which perhaps those involved might prefer we did not witness. O'course, we'd never say a word, lawks no, but you become adept at reading faces and behaviour. I reckon as Mr Wilderby knows what his Grace wants, before his Grace does." Mabel chuckled.

"Anyways, while there was no doubt Lord Teasdale was devoted to her ladyship, and her to him, neither minded being apart. They had barely been married five minutes, but they only saw each other at dinner time, and kept separate bedchambers.

"The newlyweds I know want to be together as often as possible and usually share a chamber until the children start coming along. They did spend time together, but..."

"I imagine there are a large number of married couples who do not share a bedchamber." Kitty knew this to be true, especially among the *ton*. "Why, I personally know of several who choose not to."

Mabel's nose crinkled as she tried to articulate what had bothered her about the relationship.

"Yes, but even accepting that, I do not think he loved her. Not like Mr Wilderby loves Mrs Wilderby, or how our Stan loves his Peggy." Referring to her older brother and his wife. "Oh, I'm sorry, my lady," Mabel wrung her hands together, "I'm not explaining this proper like..."

"People of nobility rarely demonstrate their emotions overtly," Kitty interjected. "It is deemed rather vulgar."

"All's I'll say is that it is an awareness. Nothing you can see or even describe adequately, but it's there and you know 'tis enduring. They did not have that." Mabel shrugged, somewhat fatalistically.

It was a long and surprisingly astute speech. Kitty was astonished, never supposing those behind the baize door possessed, or cared to have, such a depth of perception. "Thank you for trusting me enough to speak your mind, Mabel. I have been remiss in my consideration—"

"Do not take on, so. We all have our place," Mabel interrupted.

"I know but…" Kitty opened her palms in a gesture of remorse.

"No buts. 'Tis life, pure and simple. We are fortunate to work for this family who are kindness itself. If spending a little time among us gives you some insight into our world, 'tis a bonus."

Mabel was not being judgemental, and under normal circumstances their conversation would never have happened, but Kitty felt the mild censure all the same. *Perhaps this role reversal was no bad thing*. If nothing else, she was becoming sensitive to those whose lives were not as blessed as hers.

Their conversation moved onto other topics, but Kitty didn't forget.

After a busy day, dealing with estate matters, Adam closed the door to the chief steward's office with a sigh of relief. He rolled his shoulders and stretched his back, aching a little from being hunched over the desk, peering at assorted accounts.

The afternoon was waning, but the air was balmy so, adjusting his bearings, Adam skirted the edge of the building, heading for the terrace.

Finding his favourite chair, he lowered himself into it, and leant back, the sun's rays playing over his face. He had been there scant moments when children's voices floated towards him on the gentle breeze. Straightening up, he listened then swung his head in the direction of the joyful sound. They were coming his way.

He stood, his brain exhorting him to retreat to the house — he did not want Mrs Lovell to think he was *at all* interested in what she was doing — but his legs refused to do his bidding. *You have every right to check on your son's progress,* his heart argued.

He wavered for too long, the thud of footsteps heralding the imminent arrival of at least three people.

"Good afternoon, Lord Teasdale," the voice which had entrenched itself in his dreams hailed him. The low register of her tone was melodious, and Adam had developed a habit of straining to hear it whenever he thought she might be in proximity.

Knowing the new governess often conducted lessons in the garden, Adam had taken to sitting on the terrace. Ostensibly, to relax in the sunshine. In reality it was because, from his vantage point, he could hear any approach. She never failed to speak to him, even though she could easily pass unobserved.

"Good afternoon, Mrs Lovell." His lips quirked. "I hope you have had a productive day."

"We have, thank you." Kitty curtsied. "Oscar is a delight to teach."

"I am glad to hear it." His tone mildly mocking.

"Sir Pwetty." Evie toddled over to Adam. "Cuddle, pwease."

"Evie." Kitty stepped forward to intervene. Before she could, Adam bent and, lifting Evie, swung her in a circle.

"Wheeeeeeeee," the little girl shrieked in glee.

"My Lor—"

"Papa gives the best swings," Oscar confided. "My turn, my turn," he demanded, running to his father who, after standing Evie down, repeated his actions with his son.

Kitty watched with interest. Adam's expression had morphed from grim to jovial, reverting to the young man of her recollection.

Unexpectedly, her spirit soared.

In that moment Kitty recognised what her heart had known for a decade.

The moment a thirteen-year-old girl's *tendre* became love.

*Well, dammit...*

Glad Adam could not see her starry eyes and flushed cheeks, Kitty hid her discovery behind a mask of politeness. "Come children, Lord Teasdale has had a long day, and does not need to be pestered by two rapscallions."

She tempered her instructions with a smile as she picked up Evie. Oscar chortled, kissed his father, and scampered to her side, sliding his hand into hers.

"Thank you for your patience, my lord."

"No matter. 'Tis lovely to see such happy children." He seemed about to say something else but instead, nodded and resumed his seat.

Her recent revelation meant all Kitty wanted to do was stroke his scarred cheek, and kiss those firm lips, to run her fingers through his dark hair. She gulped and, mortified that he might pick up on her musings, croaked something unintelligible and hurried away.

.  .  .

Adam, cursing the sailor who had fired the blasted cannon, twisted in his chair. Squinting at the disappearing group, he discerned a blur of turquoise alongside the more sombre hue of Mabel's uniform. Evidently, Mrs Lovell had eschewed the trademark greys ordinarily worn by women of her station.

He could hear Oscar throwing out questions about skipping and jumping, the two adults answering him as though his prattle was of utmost importance.

*He wanted to be included.* The realisation came as a shock and he tried to push it away, but it harassed him, until he permitted it to roll around his head.

For the first time since his return to Easby Hall, he *wanted* to be part of the daily goings on. Not the official administering of an estate goings on… which to date was all he had paid heed to… the rest of it.

To be part of the conversations he had thus far avoided where possible. To take a ride through the Great Park with his father. To wander aimlessly though the gardens and the orchards with *anyone*. To help Oscar with his lessons. Most of all, he wanted to listen to Mrs Lovell read aloud, to hear her voice wrap around the stories of his childhood.

In the warmth of a lazy afternoon, Adam Marchmain began to live again.

# CHAPTER EIGHT

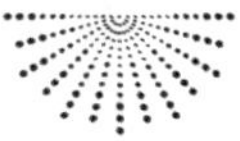

Three days later, an occasion presented itself, and before his head talked him out of it, Adam jumped in with both feet.

Kitty had invented a game. Oscar chose a letter from the alphabet and he had to find things around the house and the gardens beginning with that letter. It often took all day, especially if the letter was one less commonly used.

Adam knew all about this game because of how much Oscar loved it. It had become his favourite lesson, and he was learning to recognise a wide range of objects without realising it.

Breakfast eaten, Evie in the capable hands of Mabel, Kitty and Oscar headed across the hall towards the domestic quarters. They usually left through the backdoor because Kitty thought it improper to use the main entrance.

"Mrs Lovell…" Adam's voice halted them in their tracks.

Kitty turned to see him standing on the threshold of the study. She curtsied. "Lord Teasdale. Good morning, is there something with which I can help you? Something you require?"

"I should like to beg a favour."

Nonplussed, Kitty stammered. "O-of course, my l-lord, if it is w-within my power, I would be glad to help." She stared at him, her jaw slightly open.

"Permit me to join in the game."

There was dead silence.

Kitty was completely at a loss for words. Adam's demeanour had become marginally less severe of late, but this was something she could not have foreseen in a month, nay a year, of Sundays.

"Mrs Lovell…"

Pulling herself together, Kitty assured him he would be most welcome, not quite able to quell the uncertainty in her voice.

"Which letter did you choose today, Oscar?" Adam asked his son who was jiggling about with excitement.

"S." Oscar beamed. "You really want to play, Papa?" His eager question chimed around the spacious hall.

"I really want to play," Adam affirmed.

"Oh goodie." Oscar took his father's hand and led him along the short passage to the green door. "We go this way because it is quicker," he explained.

If any of the staff was surprised to see his lordship walking along the passage adjacent to the kitchens, they kept it to themselves. Mr Wilderby winked at Kitty as she followed Adam and Oscar outside. Kitty shrugged and opened her palms in an 'I have no idea what's happening' gesture, which made the butler chuckle.

. . .

It was another glorious day. A cloudless blue sky, with enough of a breeze to take the edge off the heat. September was on the horizon, and with it would come the harvest, preparations already underway across the estate.

Once beyond the confines of the outbuildings enclosing the courtyard, the trio skirted the walled kitchen garden and the vegetable patch. They were aiming for the wild wood, which was to their right. In the opposite direction, rolling out into the distance, a sea of gold undulated in the breeze; punctuated here and there by a line of trees or a hedgerow. Estate workers could be seen attending to various duties.

"It looks like a fruitful harvest, my lord," Kitty observed, by way of breaking the quiet.

"I am inclined to agree, as long as the weather holds. My stewards concur with your projection. Unusual to find a governess interested in the workings of an estate." There was a note of cynicism in Adam's remark.

"The world is a vast place, everything about it fascinates me," she replied. "From the smallest bird's nest to the great ships which ply the oceans. Moreover, I would be sadly lacking in my duties if I was not cognisant of how an estate is administered. This is Oscar's birthright, and he will need to be educated on every aspect. Becoming duke is more than assuming a title. It is a profession which bears huge responsibility."

Kitty stopped abruptly. She sounded as though she was lecturing Adam.

Changing the subject and before Adam could comment, she urged Oscar to start the game. The little boy hesitated, He was holding Adam's hand, making sure his father did not trip on the uneven ground or walk into a low hanging branch.

Spotting his indecision, Kitty offered tactfully, "Lord Teasdale, Oscar is concerned that while he is dashing around on the hunt for anything beginning with S, you might stumble. Might I be so bold as to suggest you take my arm?" She studied Adam. Given his expression, she could imagine the debate going on in his head.

"I acknowledge we are alone, but we are both widowed, and, with the greatest respect, I have no designs on you or your title." She allowed a tinge of amusement to colour her voice.

"You know about…"

"The previous nursery maids? Yes, her Grace was particularly transparent in that regard." An imp goaded her to add, "Your mother was convinced they had turned you into a testy recluse."

Adam's head snapped around and he pinned her with a keen gaze. Her statement was, perhaps, a confidence too far.

Relieved he could not see her, Kitty gave a merry laugh. "'Tis pleased I am you have not retired to a hermitage. Oscar would miss you." They had reached the edge of the woods. "Are you amenable to entering the trees, I promise to alert you of any hazards."

"You are too kind," Adam muttered. Out of the blue, the woman's laugh tugged at him. A distant memory flittered across his consciousness, gone before he could grasp it. His forehead furrowed as he racked his brain, to no avail. Setting it aside, he rallied his thoughts.

"Where are we exactly." He squinted in an attempt to pinpoint their position.

"We are on the main path into the wood. Ahead there is a fork. The left-hand trail leads to the back of Home Farm, the right will eventually bring you out near the folly on the lake."

Kitty knew these woods like the back of her hand. The mob of children who had spent their holidays at Easby Hall often played hide come seek among the trees, or raced through, seeing who could reach the folly first. It was difficult not blurting it out. She believed Adam would benefit from sharing these memories.

"Did you ever explore these woods as a boy?" she ventured, praying her question would not cause offence.

Adam did not reply immediately. They walked on, coming to the divide.

"Which way would you like to go, my lord."

"To the folly."

Kitty smiled and, unknowingly, squeezed his arm.

Adam felt the increased pressure, a curious frisson snaking out from under her fingers. *Get a grip man, she is the help.*

Kitty repeated her question.

"Yes, yes, I did, along with my siblings, cousins, and friends. These woods were a favourite playground." His lips curved in fond reminiscence. "They were good days. None of us had a care in the world. I never imagined it would come to this."

"It sounds as though you had a lot of fun. Might I beg you to tell me of your friends?" Kitty risked a rebuff but, of late, she had sensed a softening in Adam's intractable attitude.

"Another day, perhaps," he allowed. "Where is Oscar?"

"Not ten yards from us. He is collecting an assortment of things, some of which may even begin with the letter S." Kitty chuckled.

Once again, the memory teased Adam.

"Come let us join him, and he can tell us what he has found." She led him to where Oscar was foraging much like a boar in search of mushrooms.

Kitty guided Adam to a suitable tree stump. Once he was sitting, relatively comfortably, she switched her attention to Oscar's hoard.

"Would you be so good as to put out your hand, palm up?" she asked Adam.

"As long as you promise not to put a large hairy spider on it."

"I promise." She grinned. "Oscar, please tell Papa what you have found and put each item in his hand."

Oscar did as she bade.

"A stone." He balanced the small pebble carefully on his father's palm.

"A stick. Don't drop it." The child warned.

"I will do my best," Adam responded with due gravity, masking a smile.

"You are sitting on a stump, Papa." Oscar leant against his father's knee. "Are you sure you do not want a spider?" he appealed, wistfully.

"Quite sure, you scamp." Adam waggled his eyebrows in mock threat, making Oscar giggle.

"Scamp, another 'S' word," he crowed, then pointed to himself. "I am wearing shoes and a shirt. I can take them off and give them to Papa." He looked at Kitty expectantly.

Kitty chuckled. "And run through the woods in your stockinged feet? My, my, Oscar Marchmain, you are most definitely a scamp."

Oscar bent double with mirth.

"Any more things beginning with S?" Kitty coaxed.

Oscar thought about that for a moment, staring round him, his face scrunched up in concentration. Clapping, he said, "I cannot reach the sun, but I can see it." Then looked at Adam. "I am your son, but I cannot fit in your hand."

The boy's pride in his knowledge, earned him a pat on the head from Adam.

"Clever lad."

"Well done, Oscar," Kitty praised. "Anything else? Do you

remember the name of the birds that fly south for the winter?"

Oscar frowned.

"They zip about catching insects and their name is the same as something we do when we have a drink," Kitty hinted.

"*Swallow,*" Oscar screeched.

"Not so loud, you will disturb the bears," Kitty chided, with feigned severity.

"Mrs Lovell, you know there are no bears in this wood." Oscar gurgled with laughter. "Are we going to the folly?"

"That depends on your Papa. We do not wish to monopolise his day."

"Papa, pleeeeease come with us." Oscar pressed his little hands to his father's cheeks. "Pleeeeeeeease," he entreated.

It was a rare day when Adam denied a request from his son, but he put on a show of thinking about it, inventing appointments he might be missing. He rubbed his chin, thoughtfully.

"Hmmm. I am not sure. What if I am supposed to be meeting Mr Unwin?" The head steward. "Am I due to have morning tea with Grandpapa? Perhaps I have arranged to see Reverend Stainton." The latter being the vicar in the neighbouring village.

"Papa..." Oscar, who was familiar with this game, drew out the word.

"Wait, I have just remembered. They are tomorrow's duties. Thus, I am free. Lead on, Lord Oscar." Adam bowed.

Oscar gave a whoop and shot off through the wood, squealing like a delinquent, rather than the son of a marquis.

The two adults followed more sedately and, to the well-concealed surprise of both, became quite loquacious. By the time they reached the lake — at the centre of which, sitting in splendid isolation on a miniature island, stood the folly — Kitty was almost persuaded she had gone back in time.

She was eight, Adam fifteen and, along with the usual crowd, they were chasing each other over the stepping stones. A light laugh slipped over her lips when she recalled missing her footing and ending up in the water.

"Something amuses you, Mrs Lovell?"

The deep voice by her ear, jolted Kitty back to the present.

"Are you coming over?" Oscar's shout from the little island, allowed her to evade Adam's question.

"Not today," she called. She did not think it necessary to vocalise the reason.

"I am quite capable of crossing the stones," said Adam, mildly.

Kitty bit her lip, trying to come up with an excuse which sounded plausible.

"Trust me, I know how wide the gap is."

"Lord Teasd—"

"I dare you," he taunted with a crooked smile, a roguish glint in his compelling eyes.

Kitty's mouth fell open. "You *dare* me?" she retorted, momentarily forgetting to whom she was speaking.

"I do."

"What her Grace will say I cannot fathom," Kitty fretted. "How do I keep getting embroiled in such lunacy?" she muttered under her breath, unaware Adam heard every word.

"How many other dares have you faced?" he quipped.

Kitty flushed. "Enough," was all she said. Taking his arm, she led him to where the fifteen broad flat stones formed a path to the island. "If you take one step, you will be on the first stone."

Adam followed her directions. Kitty dithered. Did she walk alongside him, risking both of them plunging into the lake or follow him knowing there was no possibility of preventing a tumble if he miscalculated?

Before she could suggest either, Adam was striding across the stones, without a single error, to Kitty's abject relief. When he set foot on the island, he caught Oscar in a hug making his son squeal with jubilation.

"Come along, Mrs Lovell, your turn," Adam called, his cheerful tones ringing over the glistening lake.

Although her skirts were not quite ankle length, Kitty lifted them to be on the safe side — her lack of coordination well-known — and followed with far more caution than was warranted.

Reaching the last stone, she hesitated. The gap between it and the island was wider than she recalled. Maybe it had always been thus, but as child it had not hindered her.

"Mrs Lovell..."

She looked up. Adam had stretched out his hand. It was not done for a servant to take the hand of a lord.

"I can—"

"Take my hand, Mrs Lovell."

Capitulating, Kitty did as he asked and found herself face to chest with him. She tilted her head. Adam was looking down at her. *Dash it all, he was incredibly handsome. His scars detracted not one jot.*

Kitty froze. *They were very close. Would he recognise her?* She strove to remain unaffected, ignoring the tingles trickling along her arm and the thud of her heart.

# CHAPTER NINE

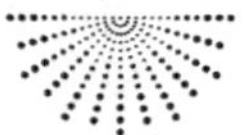

All at once, she wanted to confess to the artifice. Adam did not deserve to be deceived. Kitty bit back the words on the tip of her tongue. She was stuck between a rock and hard place.

While Adam merited the truth, the decision of when to apprise him of it, lay with Aunt Prudence. She would be upset even angry, and rightly so, if pre-empted by a guilt-ridden governess.

Kitty wasn't the only one affected by their clasped hands, Adam too had felt the most peculiar prickle skim over his skin. Standing so close, Mrs Lovell's grimace was unmistake-able. He released her fingers. *Was his touch so abhorrent?* The idea left him disconsolate.

"Is something amiss?"

His solicitous question pierced the fog in Kitty's brain. *He could see her expression?*

"I beg your pardon?"

"You look fierce enough to scare a gang of pirates into relinquishing their booty."

"S-sorry, no, I am fine. Merely a disquieting notion." Kitty schooled her features and turned to check on Oscar. The moment passed and her heart slowed its hammering.

~

The trio returned to the Hall without incident, meaning Kitty did not fall off the stepping stones when she crossed back from the island.

Her reaction playing on his mind, Adam was relieved when Mrs Lovell offered her arm as they walked back. *Perhaps it was not his touch after all.* In his, admittedly limited, exchanges with the governess he had garnered the impression she was an empathetic person, not someone who judged others by outward appearances.

His intuition rarely led him astray, and he hoped he hadn't misread her — blithely ignoring the fact her opinion should not matter to him in the slightest.

As soon as they entered the house, Oscar dashed off to find Evie, eager to tell her about his morning.

"Thank you, Mrs Lovell," Adam said when they parted at the bottom of the stairs. "I thoroughly enjoyed myself. Would you be averse to me accompanying you again?"

"I am sure Oscar would be elated," Kitty replied.

"It will not disrupt your lessons?"

"Not at all. If you will excuse me. I must attend to Evie." She bobbed a curtsy.

Adam, registering the gesture, acknowledged her request. "Of course. Doubtless I shall see you at dinner."

Adam heard the swish of her skirts as she ascended to her chambers. An alluring fragrance tickled his nostrils causing him to twist, his eyes fixed on the ascending shimmer of colour.

*Oh, for the gift of sight.*

❧

The day was the prelude to a new habit and, when they looked back, a catalyst.

As often as his duties allowed, Adam joined Kitty and Oscar. Internally, he reasoned it was because he wanted to spend more time with his son, but he could not deny how much pleasure he gained from being in Mrs Lovell's company.

Aware most governesses were gentle-born woman, forced into the role by circumstance, Adam was also of the understanding the majority were capable of teaching little more than the absolute basics, and not necessarily well.

If their charge was a girl, it was conceivable the governess would be proficient in etiquette, and deportment; schooling the child to be the model wife when the time came. In Adam's opinion, boys benefitted from a tutor, usually the local vicar.

This had been another argument against engaging a governess. One he believed justified, given the debacle resulting from those who had held the position previously.

In her inimitable way, his mother had played on his conscience. She contended that since Oscar had missed out on the nurturing he would normally receive from a mother, hiring a nurserymaid who could also be Oscar's governess until he was eight years old was the sensible alternative.

Mrs Lovell appeared to be the exception. She was well-read, kept abreast of current and political affairs, and possessed a breadth of knowledge, of which a lecturer at Eton or Harrow might be envious.

Altogether courteous and reserved when dining with the family, she was never anything other than relaxed and friendly around Oscar.

In truth, he could not fault her, which both irked and impressed him.

He looked forward to their conversations, which never *ever* circled the weather or any other mundanity. Most importantly, she was an amusing companion.

Witty, bright, jovial, and knew how to make him laugh. She could be coaxed into telling *the* most ribald stories — from where she learnt them, Adam had no clue, and was not game to pry — in a manner which, had Oscar overheard, would have sounded no more interesting than a list of books.

In her turn Kitty was gratified by the frequency with which Adam sought them out. She was not gullible enough to presume it was anything other than interest in his son, but the more time he spent with them, the less grim became his countenance.

She had even managed to make him laugh on more than one occasion. The deep timbre of his mirth echoing around them and reverberating through her. Her satisfaction at this ostensibly impossible achievement, immeasurable.

During their constitutionals, Kitty took it upon herself to describe whatever they came upon, conjuring up the scenes as they strolled by.

Begun when she was explaining to Oscar why there were pigs in the orchards, it had developed into a pleasant practice. She chose a different walk each day, exploring the Great Park, or over to Home Farm, or around the formal gardens.

Without either adult enunciating it, the folly became their favourite haunt. It was a congenial place to conclude a morning's learning. There was a quietude to be found in the middle of the lake, surrounded by gently lapping water and muted calls of the waterfowl.

~

Believing they had reached a cordiality hitherto unexpected, Kitty dared broach the subject of Adam's sight.

It was an unusually cool afternoon, given it was late August, and followed a week of inclement weather which had restricted outdoor activities. Kitty judged it essential for her charge to expend some of his pent-up energy *outside* as opposed to rampaging through the Hall.

After settling Evie for her nap, Kitty suggested a brisk walk, to Oscar's undeniable excitement. Either side of the long drive, stretching around to the Great Park in one direction and the lake in the other, was a sweeping expanse of lush lawn. Oscar could tear about to his heart's content without the slightest chance of him spoiling the carefully manicured garden beds.

Appropriately attired for an afternoon which might conceivably end in grubby knees and scuffed boots, Kitty was ushering Oscar towards the back door, when she heard her name.

"Mrs Lovell, may I accompany you?" Adam's voice arrested their progress.

"Papa, Papa." Oscar jumped up and down in glee.

"If you are prepared to be deafened and pounced upon, you would be most welcome, Lord Teasdale," Kitty replied good humouredly. "Oscar's patience has been sorely tested these last couple of days and 'tis probable he will become riotous."

"I imagine I shall survive the onslaught." Adam's lips twitched. "Lead on."

Oscar grabbed his father's hand and they continued across the hall, through the baize door, and along the cool passageway leading to the domestic entrance.

As soon as they reached the grass, Oscar took off, flying over the lawns like an autumn gale. Giving vent to a series of yells, he tumbled over air, picked himself up and dashed off again. As the adults followed, at a far more decorous pace, Kitty described the child's capers to Adam, whose stern features softened at the image Kitty evoked.

"I am glad he is having fun," he remarked.

"One thing at which Oscar excels, is having fun," Kitty replied, dryly.

Adam's answering chuckle was an attractive sound, the more so because of its rarity.

Kitty studied him surreptitiously. Forgoing both cravat and coat, his attire was casual. Under a simple brown waistcoat, he wore a cream shirt tucked into beige buckskins, completed by a pair of aged, dark brown Hessians. His unruly chestnut hair not confined to its habitual cue, settled against his nape; one dark forelock covering the scars on his right temple.

Even though she knew it was not possible, for a second Kitty had the strangest feeling Adam's twinkling eyes could see far more than the idyllic scene in front of them. Pushing aside such fancy, she asked an innocuous question about the estate, and they fell into the easy conversation which was becoming natural to them.

. . .

By tacit consent, they ended up beside the lake. Oscar was endlessly entertained by the profusion of birds which called it home, and Kitty had spent many hours teaching him about the different breeds and their habitats. Whether they stayed year-round or flew away for some portion of it.

His favourite were the swans. Easby Hall played host to a reasonably sized flock, who remained on or near the lake throughout the year. Today, the majestic birds were at the far side, foraging among the reeds with the ducks.

Oscar ran over the stone slabs to the folly, found himself a convenient rock and hunkered down to watch them. In the still air, the lake was like a millpond. Not a single ripple distorted the surface.

"This is so picturesque," Kitty sighed. "There is nothing quite as inviting as an old folly, floating on a lake."

"Describe it," Adam could not disguise the longing in his voice. The air was redolent with perfume, but he couldn't tell whether the source was late flowering blossoms, or the fragrance of the woman alongside him.

"The lake resembles a mirror. The reflections are so sharp 'tis difficult to distinguish the line between water and land. There is a suggestion of autumn in the slight yellowing of the leaves.

"The waterfowl are having a splendid time rummaging through the reeds. Birds are zipping about catching any insects not quick enough to get out of their way. There is a laziness to the scene, a tranquillity. As though on the edge of slumber."

"That was surprisingly poetic, Mrs Lovell."

Kitty blushed; glad it was unlikely he could see her bright cheeks. "'Tis like a painting. A timeless English scene. Serene, immutable. An unspoken proclamation that whatever goes on beyond our shores, this will endure."

She shrugged and continued shyly, "Heavens, but I sound naive. I know this is a fallacy, my lord, but 'tis one to which I cling. Like the memory of a happy childhood."

Adam patted her hand, currently hooked around his arm. "Never lose your dreams, Mrs Lovell, for oft 'tis all we have."


To Kitty, his remark justified her next topic of conversation... well it would have done, had she been able to articulate it...

"I have a question... if you... would you... not disrespectful... b-but..." she dried up.

"Lost for words, Mrs Lovell?" Adam's tone and the slant of his brow indicating his incredulity.

She blushed and corralled her recalcitrant brain.

"Would you deem me impertinent if I was to ask how hard it is to lose the ability to see? As an adult I mean." Diffidently, she sought to clarify. "I understand for those born without sight, while life is not without its challenges, to them 'tis normal. They do not need to adapt or rethink because they know no difference. How do you cope?"

Adam's countenance grew solemn. He unhooked his arm and stepped away.

She cringed, *dash it all, she was a discourteous chit.*

"Forgive me, Lord Teasdale. Please forget I asked. My query was abominably rude, and I had no mind to make you recall what must have been an egregious experience. 'Tis only that unless an outsider was cognisant of your limitations, they would not know. You move through the house and grounds as though your vision is undimmed."

Kitty was mortified by her audacity. *Aunt Prudence would doubtless give her a well-deserved verbal clip around the ear.*

A strained silence hung between them. It lengthened and

Kitty, who was starting to feel like an overwound clock, could not think of a way to regain their camaraderie.

"Do not take on so. I deem your question just impertinent enough and is one I revisit with regularity." Adam heaved a resigned sigh.

"If I am honest, I may never adjust. I presume you know I am not completely blind. Some days I think my vision is improving, but it is four years, and I have to accept this may be as good as it is going to get. Invariably, there are things I crave to see. Oscar's antics, his smile, or the view from the terrace, to go for a walk unaccompanied."

He shrugged. "Sometimes I am unable to conquer my anger at the hand I was dealt, and curse the *crapaud* who fired the cannon, but we were at war and, to be fair, we were no less guilty."

Adam stared straight ahead; his gaze turned inward. "Then I try to count my blessings, not always with grace, I confess. I have Oscar. I am fortunate to be born into a class whereby I can afford the best medical help and employ staff of the highest calibre who are sensitive to my limitations and needs, and not prone to gossip.

"I hope, in the not too distant future to remove to Teasdale Mallow. I have a hankering to be on my own. I appreciate the support of my family, but I left home when I joined the navy and, as much as I love my parents, I need my own space."

Kitty had to bite her lip to hold back her irreverent bark of laughter. The immense proportions of Easby Hall meant someone could occupy one of the wings and never come into contact with another soul.

As though he had read her thoughts, Adam mused, "I acknowledge the Hall is huge and one could easily get lost within its walls, but 'tis not my home anymore. I came back here when I was released from the hospital because there was no alternative. My parents are kindness itself, and I will remain forever grateful for their support, but 'tis time I stood on my own two feet."

# CHAPTER TEN

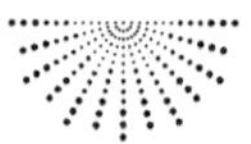

Remembering to whom he was speaking, Adam stopped abruptly. This was too personal. He turned the question onto Kitty.

"And you, Mrs Lovell, what brought you to Easby Hall?"

Kitty did not reply immediately. Preferring not to fabricate her explanation, she opted for minimal but truthful.

"My husband died and four months later, I discovered I was increasing. Life overwhelmed me for a time, and I think I forgot how to function. Your injuries aside, your plight is not dissimilar to mine, and I too returned to live with my parents. It appears, her Grace knew something of my circumstances and believed I could be of use."

She walked to where Adam was standing, his expression remote and, greatly daring, touched his hand.

"I am beginning to remember what it is to be happy. The primary reason is because being here at Easby Hall, looking after Oscar, being welcomed into this family has allowed me to heal. 'Tis a special place."

. . .

A cryptic note in Mrs Lovell's tone left Adam with the sense she was going to say more. She didn't and changed the subject, but their conversation stayed with him.

~

Following this discussion, Kitty had pleaded with Prudence a number of times to be allowed to reveal her identity to Adam.

Thus far, her aunt had denied her petition. "Your presence is working wonders, Kitty. I know 'tis an ordeal to maintain the pretence but please do not give up. Adam has changed dramatically since your arrival. He is coming on in leaps and bounds, but there remains much to be achieved.

"Nightmares continue to plague him. I grant you they are lessening, but they debilitate him, a constant reminder of what he has lost. Melancholy lurks just under the surface. He is not yet the Adam who went to sea. Please, Kitty."

Shamelessly, Prudence appealed to Kitty's compassion and the ties of friendship which once bound her and Adam.

"I understand, but I wish to register my concern that this will backfire."

"I acknowledge your concern and pray it does not."

A prayer which, regrettably, went unheard.

~

September arrived in a blaze of glory. Long days under the unseasonal simmering heat left everyone crotchety.

One broiling Saturday afternoon, immediately after luncheon, and hoping to avert temper tantrums in small children unable to comprehend the vagaries of the English weather, Kitty and Mabel gathered up Oscar and Evie, a rug and a book and hunted down the coolest spot they could find.

There was an aged beech not far from the lake, where Kitty hoped they might be lucky enough to catch a breath of air off the water. Once there, the children settled in the dappled shade of the great tree whose leaves hinted at the kaleidoscope of colour about to overtake them.

Kitty was relieved when both children fell asleep before she had finished the first story. The nights had been too hot of late, with nary a hint of respite, making slumber elusive. Mabel excused herself, saying she had chores to finish.

Kitty waved her off with a grin and propped herself against the massive trunk. Her best efforts notwithstanding, several broken nights tending to fractious children overtook her and tired eyes refused to stay open.

She was disturbed by an obscure sound. Rubbing sleep from her eyes, she blinked and focused. *How long had she been asleep?* No longer clear and blue, the sky had darkened to a sullen grey.

Dense clouds billowed and rolled. The breeze was whining through the trees and the air had turned sultry. The back of Kitty's neck prickled a warning.

*Storm.*

They were quite a distance from the house, but not too far from the folly, which although little more than a ring of pillars with a roof, would offer a modicum of protection.

Kitty dithered. It was not just Evie and her, there was also Oscar. She had a responsibility to keep him out of harm's way. *Was she better trying to make it to the Hall?*

The whine became a howl, and a low rumble reached her ears. Waking the children, she slung the rug diagonally around her back, tied it across her chest, and tucked the book into its folds. Lifting Evie into her arms, she grabbed Oscar's hand.

"We are going to race the storm. Shall we beat it?" She smiled brightly, her voice steady, no panic in her tones.

"Ohhh a race. Where to?" Oscar, heedless of the swiftly encroaching tempest, jumped up and down.

"The folly, but be very careful on the stepping stones, they might be slippery. Are you ready?" Kitty shouted above the buffeting wind.

He nodded

"*Run*!" Kitty hotfooted it after the little boy who scampered off as though the devil himself was after him. They reached the huge slabs at the same time, and Kitty grabbed Oscar's hand. Lightning split the blackening sky and the first drops of rain pelted them.

"Faster," Oscar shrieked. They splashed off the stones and skidded into the folly.

Panting for breath, Kitty hustled the little boy into the farthest corner, where there was less chance of getting caught by the draught or the rain. The stone benches in the centre of the structure were of little use, but one section between two of the pillars had a solid wall rising to the conical roof.

Standing Evie down, Kitty removed the book from the rug which she rolled into a makeshift cushion against the wall. Oscar curled up on its warmth. Kitty sat alongside him — effectively creating a barrier between him and the weather — and wedged Evie in the middle.

"Cosy up. This is an adventure, and not one I expected this afternoon."

Oscar's bottom lip wobbled. "I want my Papa," he wailed, his thumb creeping into his mouth. He stared at Kitty, tears brimming under his wide blue-grey eyes.

"I promise we will find Papa as soon as the storm passes.

While we wait, I want you to tell me what pictures you can see in the clouds." Kitty gestured at the billowing grey mass scudding across the sky. "Hmmm… I think that looks like Minerva." Naming one of the very pampered kitchen cats.

This pulled a slight chuckle from Oscar. "No, it is just a blob,"

"No, see there are her ears." Kitty pointed. "And there is her tail. Granted 'tis fluffier than Minerva's…"

Oscar shook his head, but Kitty had diverted him and there ensued a ridiculous competition about who could spot the best picture. Evie, unperturbed, snuggled into her mother's side and drifted back to sleep.

The thunder boomed louder as the intensity of the storm increased. Oscar fell silent. His face was pale in the gloom and Kitty scoured her brain for a way to distract.

She remembered something Adam had said during a similar situation when they were children.

*"Did you hear that?" Adam asked, grinning at the scared faces in front of him. They stared back, jumping in fright at the hideous racket. "'Tis God pushing his old piano down the stairs."*

*"No, it isn't," Araminta retorted. "God does not play the piano."*

*"'Tis too, and of course, he does," Adam retaliated. "Listen…"*

*They had all listened intently, then Derek chirped up. "I can hear the keys tinkling."*

*"And there goes the wardrobe," Adam noted. "That's the doors banging." Beginning a litany of furniture being thrown down the stairs. Quite how half the pieces would have been upstairs in the first place was immaterial. It served a purpose.*

Kitty introduced it now and Oscar thought it great fun.

Hopefully, it would keep him occupied until the storm blew over.

~

Adam paced the library.

"I am sure they have found somewhere to wait out the storm, Adam. Please stop marching, you will wear a hole in the carpet," his mother sought to console.

"This is on your head, Mama. If you had not engaged her, my son would be here in the house, safe. Scatterbrains one and all."

Adam stopped to glare at his mother, continuing to gripe viciously about cork-brained fools and flighty chits without an ounce of sense. He was working himself up into a fury more violent than the storm raging all around them.

"Do not speak to your mother in that tone," his father interjected, mildly. "Be sensible, son, even with perfect eyesight, 'tis foolish to go out in this. You have no idea where to look." Reginald Marchmain studied Adam over his spectacles.

"Since there is nothing to be gained by being righteously outraged, pour us both a drink and sit down. Mrs Lovell has never shown any inclination to being bird-witted, and I understood, of late, you had come to terms with her presence, even to the point of involving yourself in Oscar's lessons."

His father's unruffled remark, penetrated Adam's anger. With unerring accuracy, he strode to the walnut cabinet nestled in an alcove and, feeling for the decanter, removed the stopper to sniff the contents. The pungent aroma told him it was whisky.

"Mama, would you like a glass of Madeira, Port?" Adam

asked, while he splashed the amber spirit carefully into two glasses.

"No, thank you, dear. I have rung for tea."

Adam gulped a mouthful of the liquor and topped up his glass. He handed the other to his father, then chose a seat by the fire. "Where are they?" he muttered.

"I imagine we shall find out soon enough," Prudence said, placidly.

"How can you be so calm? Oscar is only five."

"How many times do I have to remind you, Mrs Lovell is also a mother, and you know she would never intentionally let any harm come to Oscar. She loves your son, Adam. You might remember that before you rant at her," his mother reproved.

Adam grumbled, but conceded his mother was not erroneous in her assertion. He sipped his drink, trying to banish the scenarios playing around his head.

Kitty was starting to question whether the storm was in for the day. It was not cold, but the air was damp, and she did not want either child to get chilled. She tucked them closer, shielding them from the gusts of wind which drove the rain in under the roof of the folly, to splatter the back of her gown.

Evie was sleeping peacefully. Oscar, bored with looking at clouds, demanded a story. Loath to open the book in case it got wet, Kitty told her favourite tale. The one Adam had devised for her so many years ago.

Oscar was captivated, asking questions about the characters and their exploits. Kitty wove the weather into her narrative, creating a storm dragon who clapped his wings to make thunder and blew lightning out of his nose.

It did the trick and inventing new escapades for the dragon held Oscar's attention. Perhaps half an hour later, Kitty discerned a brightening of the sky, and the thunder had faded to a distant growl. A few more minutes and the rain eased, the sun breaking through leaden clouds.

Breathing a sigh of relief, Kitty woke Evie and gathered everything together. She waited until certain the storm had indeed passed and there was little likelihood of any more rain before setting off.

After so many dry days the world sparkled as though the drenching had washed away layers of dust. The dull and wilting trees skirting the lake looked taller, their canopy greener, and raindrops hung from the tips of the leaves like miniature crystals.

Once they had crossed the stepping stones, Kitty, unable to help it, pivoted slowly and stared.

"How beautiful," she murmured.

"Pardon?" Oscar piped up.

"I was saying how beautiful. Everything looks clean and fresh." That brought another thought and she glanced over her shoulder. "Look, a rainbow."

Oscar swivelled around. "Ohhhhhhhhhh." He angled his head in a most adult fashion and blew a sigh. "So pretty."

"Sir pwetty," Evie chimed in, drowsily,

"No, sweetheart, Oscar said the rainbow is pretty." Amused, Kitty managed to keep a straight face. "Come on, time to get you two home. I daresay your Papa and grandparents are worried."

She grimaced inwardly aware a rebuke was in the offing. *Maybe she could give notice?* A solution to all her problems. Well no, it wasn't, but *would* mean she could leave and put a distance between herself and Adam.

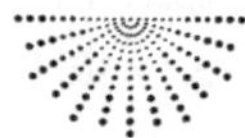

# CHAPTER ELEVEN

It did not take them long to reach the Hall. They slipped in through the domestic entrance, making sure to remove their muddy shoes. Kitty apologised profusely to Mr Wilderby, who brushed it aside.

"Naught to fret about, my la— Mrs Lovell." He smiled. "Best get along to the library. The family are there."

"Thank you." Kitty was about to head off when Mr Wilderby stopped her.

"Mrs Lovell, the back of your dress is soaked through."

"I know, but I would rather tell Lord Teasdale and their Graces that Oscar is still in one piece, first. 'Tis just water, Mr Wilderby. I am not cold." Ignoring the discomfort of her dress sticking to her.

Frowning, the butler nodded in acknowledgement. "Please do not linger, my lady," was all he said.

"I shall attend to it as soon as is reasonable," she placated, with which he had to be content.

Although Aunt Prudence had insisted she treat the house as though she was family, Kitty knocked on the library door. Barging in without invitation seemed… ill-considered.

"Come." Her uncle's voice summoned.

Kitty opened the door and, ushering in Oscar ahead of her, entered. Uncle Reginald and Adam were standing in front of the fire, the latter's expression grim. Aunt Prudence was in her favourite chair.

Hoping Adam would not vent his spleen in front of the children, Kitty rushed to explain.

"Please accept my sincerest apologies for our tardiness. I had no mind to cause anguish. Being some distance from the Hall, when the storm struck, I felt it prudent to take shelter in the folly, which was nearer. I appreciate you have been worried for Oscar, but at no time was he in any danger." She looked at each of the three, then lowered her eyes.

Oscar ran to Adam. "Papa, Papa, we played games and Mrs Lovell told a story about a storm dragon. I am not scared of thunder anymore. Did you know it is just God throwing out furniture?"

Adam swung Oscar into his arms and, in the guise of a hug, checked him over while the child prattled on about their soggy afternoon.

Oscar's words had Kitty cursing her wayward tongue, especially when Adam shot a suspicious glance in her general direction.

"Thank you, Mrs Lovell. I assured Lord Teasdale you would take the greatest care of his son and am glad to be proved correct." Aunt Prudence intervened before Adam could respond. "My dear," her tone became solicitous, "your gown is saturated. How is it you are wet, and the children are not?"

"Merely a result of the way we were sitting in the folly.

With your permission, your Grace, I shall change into a dry gown."

"Of course, Mrs Lovell. Be quick about it, you do not want to become unwell. I will ring for Mabel to assist."

"Thank you, your Grace." Kitty curtsied, not quite able to disguise a shudder when Evie's hand gripped the cold and sodden material.

"Leave Evie with us, Mrs Lovell," Uncle Reginald volunteered. "She is never a bother."

Surprised, Kitty looked at him to see his left eyelid droop in a slow wink. "You are very kind. I shall return directly." She smiled gratefully and, standing Evie on the floor, fled.

In her chambers, while Mabel helped divest her of the sopping article, Kitty pondered what was likely to happen. Undoubtably an interview with Adam, more so, given Oscar's remark. She massaged the back of her neck, a headache lurking.

Once properly dry, Kitty shrugged into a fresh gown, immediately feeling warmer. Mabel towelled her hair and brushed out the inevitable knots, removing the odd twig making them both chuckle, then whipped it into a bun.

"There you go. Much better. I hope as you haven't caught a chill standing around in wet clothes," Mabel worried.

"I am certain not to," Kitty soothed. "Time to find my daughter and pray she has been behaving. I am not sure his Grace knew what he was letting himself in for, offering to watch her."

"She's a good as gold, Miss and you know it. A credit to you and no mistake."

Kitty grasped Mabel's hand and squeezed lightly. "Thank

you, Mabel." There was no need to elaborate, the inference plain.

"Go on with you, Miss." Mabel blushed and shooed Kitty out, gathering up the dress to be laundered.

After checking to see whether Evie was in the nursery, which she wasn't, Kitty traipsed down the stairs, formulating and discarding numerous reasons as to how she could know about the game. In the end, if she was unmasked, so be it.

Swallowing her nerves, she rapped on the library door and, this time, walked in without waiting to be invited.

Adam was the only person there. Kitty stared around the room, as though expecting the others to pop out from behind the chairs. *Where was Evie?*

"Mrs Lovell?" Adam enquired.

"Yes, Lord Teasdale." She curtsied.

"Take a seat."

Kitty hesitated, unsure where was appropriate.

"Here by the fire, I imagine you might appreciate its heat." His tones were bland, his expression, unreadable.

'Thank you, my lord." Kitty slid into the closest chair and folded her hands in her lap.

"I should like a report on what happened this afternoon, including why you considered the folly, which offers insufficient cover, to be the sensible option."

"We were sitting under the old beech tree, the one by the lake. It has become a favourite spot during these hot days as any breeze off the water is cooling. The children had fallen asleep and I confess, I dozed off. Thus, I did not notice the storm was brewing until too late. It was a spontaneous decision. Either get two children, a book, and a rug to the Hall, aware we could not outrun the weather, or choose the best alternative. I know the folly is inadequate, but…"

Adam said nothing. He was standing next to the mantel-piece, propped on one elbow, holding a half-drunk glass of whisky.

Kitty had to force herself to remain seated, fighting an irresistible desire to leap up, to smooth his puckered brow, and kiss away his disquiet.

"My lord, I would never place Oscar at risk. Surely you know that?" She could not help but break the heavy silence, her tone containing mild reproach.

When he did not reply, she added, wistfully, "I thought you had come to trust me."

"I thought I had too." His deep voice resonated through her. "Now I am beset by questions. For instance, the game, Oscar mentioned. Where did you learn that? It was…"

Whatever Adam was about to say was interrupted by a loud clanging.

Somebody had rung the great bell at the front door. Callers on a Saturday were unheard of. What was so critical they had chosen to ride through a storm?

"The dickens?" he muttered.

His dark eyes bored into Kitty making her fidget. She swore he could see with acute clarity. She held her breath.

"I am not finished with you. Dismissed… for now."


Kitty was ascending the stairs when a familiar voice arrested her steps.

"Wilderby, good afternoon. Is his Grace home? I come with papers for his perusal. I am staying over the way and it was easier to hand deliver them than entrust them to the mail coach."

Kitty's jaw dropped. It was Emory.

~

Fresh from Oxford, Emory de Wilton, at two and twenty years old, had become apprenticed to Messrs Dunstan, Dunstan, and Fitch, Solicitors. Although based in London, the family firm had acted on behalf of the local nobility for generations.

Prior to attending university, Emory had informed his long-suffering parents that despite being enamoured of the military as a child, the war had changed his opinion. If it was all the same, might they permit a different path?

Lord de Wilton had acceded, on the proviso Emory found a calling suited to his status. Frederica agreed. The most important thing to her was that Emory was happy, secretly relieved he had decided against the navy.

While studying, Emory became fascinated by the law in all its branches and intricacies. Several lengthy and occasionally heated discussions later, Lord Grafton had endorsed his son's choice of career.

A private interview at the law firm had resulted in Emory being hired as a clerk between his university terms, and was now articled to the elder Dunstan, under whose expert tutelage he was thriving.

He found it absorbing, to the amusement of Ernest, his twin — older by fifteen minutes, heir to the earldom and currently attending more balls than parliamentary committees.

Their father, while proud of the young men his sons had become, struggled to comprehend they were of an age to be assuming their places in Society. *Was it not only yesterday they were carefree schoolboys?*

. . .

It was Frederica who had dragooned Emory into visiting Easby Hall the next time he was home.

"Surely you can concoct a reason to visit your uncle. Papers to sign usually works," she had urged, blissfully ignorant of the administration involved in running large estates.

"Mama, just because Uncle Reginald is a duke does not mean he is always signing papers, ask Papa." Emory had tried to demur. "Would it not be easier for you to pop in? You and Aunt Prudence often visit each other. It would not be unexpected given the proximity of the houses. They are close enough to walk there."

"I have paid more calls than might be considered courteous." Frederica had blushed a little.

"Kitty is in good hands. *Do* stop worrying, my dear." Her husband, Ernest, had glanced at her over the broadsheet he was reading.

"I am concerned she might be overdoing it," Frederica had fretted, knowing Kitty was liable to forget to eat if no one reminded her.

"Prudence will not let her waste away," Ernest had interposed, "and if members of our family keep turning up at random intervals, Adam is sure to suspect something is afoot. He is no fool."

"Nevertheless…"

"'Tis no problem Mama. *If*, and only if Mr Dunstan has anything requiring Uncle Reginald's signature, I will offer to deliver them." Emory had relented.

The discussion could become protracted and he would end up carrying out his mother's wishes anyway.

❦

That was a month ago. Reluctant for his arrival to appear contrived, this was Emory's first opportunity to 'pop around' to Easby Hall, unannounced.

The storm almost stymied his plans, but it had blown itself out, and he took the short cut, cross country, following the track linking the two estates.

"de Wilton? Is that you?" Adam poked his head out of the library door.

"Teasdale, well met." Emory beamed at his friend. "How goes it?"

"Admirably, all things considered." Adam opened his palms. "You are here to see Father?"

"Yes, I have some papers from Dunstan. I mentioned I was coming home, and he asked whether I would be so kind as to deliver these." Emory waved a sheaf of papers bound with red ribbon.

"Join me in the library? We can chat while you await Papa."

"Capital," Emory replied, sending a sunny smile to his sister who was gawking at him from halfway up the stairs.

They made polite conversation about how fortuitous it was that Emory had avoided the storm while they strolled across the hall.

"Comely chit that." Kitty heard her brother remark, somewhat irreverently. Adam's rumbled reply lost as the library door banged shut.

*Comely chit. What a cheek*, she mused, indignantly, simultaneously hoping she might orchestrate a few moments alone with him.

To her relief, Adam's plan to continue his interview was

foiled, or at least postponed in light of Emory's visit. The latter was invited to stay for dinner and, as dinner led to cigars, drinks and discussion, the night.

There was no plausible reason for Kitty to extend her presence in the drawing room after dinner, and excused herself straight after the meal, frustrated at being unable to snatch even a few minutes with her brother.

Oscar had a broken night and the next morning was disposed to be fractious. Kitty recognised an echo of Adam's initial demeanour in Oscar's grumpy attitude and black scowl; father and son sharing the same trait.

What perturbed her in Adam, she found endearing in Oscar, but was not about to allow him to get away with it. Surmising he was over-wrought from the previous day, by mid-afternoon, Kitty decreed a nap was in order.

"Might you keep an ear out for Oscar?" she asked Mabel. "I'll take Evie outside, that way she will not wake him. I have a bad case of the fidgets and need to walk them off. Perhaps it is because I get the sense my position is coming to an end."

She smiled, ruefully at Mabel's inquiring expression. "I spoke carelessly yesterday, and I doubt Lord Teasdale will let it lie."

"Mayhap 'tis no bad thing."

"Mayhap and, although relieved, I am also saddened because I fancy, I will lose a friendship over this. I have loved being here and helping, even in so small a way but, however good our intentions, I think his lordship will judge our ruse to be contemptible." Kitty shrugged, pessimistically.

"Come along, poppet." She lifted her daughter into her arms. "Let's go for a walk."

# CHAPTER TWELVE

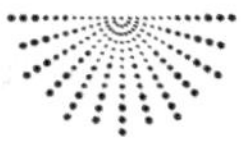

orn between attempting to see Emory and retaining her disguise as a lowly governess, Kitty chose discretion and left the Hall through the domestic entrance.

Reaching the edge of the lawns, she set Evie down and held the little girl's hand while they pottered at a snail's pace around the latticework of gravel paths interwoven through the flowerbeds.

Wrapped up in her own thoughts, Kitty's concentration wandered, and she loosened her grasp on Evie's fingers. At the same moment, Evie spotted a butterfly and decided to chase it. The little girl's eyes assumed her feet could keep up and, unsurprisingly, she took a tumble.

Evie's overly dramatic shriek yanked Kitty's mind back. *Lord but my head is skittish at the moment,* she lamented inwardly. *Yesterday I dozed off while in charge of two children, and now this. Tsk.*

Gathering her daughter off the path, Kitty hugged her, cooing, "There, there, precious, all better now. Did you hurt yourself or did you just get a fright?"

Evie mumbled something incoherent between doleful sobs. Making use of a convenient set of steps, Kitty checked Evie's knees and her hands. No grazes but they probably smarted. Carefully pressing each of the maltreated limbs, Kitty bent to kiss them, and blew softly on the reddened palms.

"Mama." Evie hiccuped, her face woebegone.

"A kiss makes everything better." Kitty emphasised each word with gentle kisses to her daughter's nose, cheeks, and tear-filled eyes.

Evie chortled, grabbing her mother's hair, pulling it out of its neat style.

"Cheeky girl." Kitty smiled and stroked the mop of curls off her daughter's flushed face. "You are tired too aren't you, my sweet?" Not expecting an answer, she rocked Evie, crooning a lullaby.

Evie drew a quavering sigh, hiccuped again and cuddled against her mother. Kitty sang on, unaware Adam and Emory, hearing Evie's yell, had bolted out of the library through the French doors and were crossing the terrace towards the two on the steps.

"Mrs Lovell?" Emory got there first. "What happened? We heard a scream."

Kitty twisted on her perch, and dipped an awkward half-curtsy, endlessly glad Aunt Prudence had remembered to introduce them the previous evening.

"My apologies, Mr de Wilton. I had no mind to disturb the peace of the afternoon. My daughter felt it appropriate to run after a butterfly, heedless of the fact she can hardly put two feet in front of one another without stumbling."

Her mouth curved upwards. "Thank you for your compassion. As you can see, she survived."

"I am glad there are no broken limbs or spilling of blood. Mind it would not be the first time, eh, Teasdale?"

Adam had joined them. "What are you wittering about, de Wilton?"

"Remember my sister gashing her knee when she was what… six or seven?" Emory clarified.

Kitty felt heat glide up her face and glared at her brother. "What are you doing?" she mouthed.

Emory sent her a puckish grin.

Adam chuckled. "I'm surprised you can remember that. My, but she near deafened us. There was blood everywhere. I could not stop it and recall being mightily relieved when Papa emerged from around the hedge. When the doc said it had to be stitched up, I thought she would bawl the place down."

He paused, in reminiscence. "They were happy days." His voice became practical. "Mrs Lovell, I take it Evie's knees are intact?"

"Yes, thank you, my lord. She is a mite drowsy now. Both she and Oscar have suffered broken nights because of the heat, and probably the reason she tripped in the first place. Too tired."

Adam pinned her with a grim gaze. "Is this why you fell asleep last morning while the children were in your charge?"

Kitty ignored the flick of anger his tone stirred. He made it sound as though she was inherently negligent.

"Almost certainly," she infused a cheerful note into her reply. "I have had less than two hours of uninterrupted sleep a night for a week but, had the storm not hit when it did, we would not be having this conversation. Oscar did not experience anything more serious than a longer than normal lesson, during which he overcame his fear of thunder. I got a little wet, and Evie recouped some of her lost sleep. None of us is the worse for wear."

Kitty bit her lip realising her voice had risen in her agitation.

"Mrs Love—"

"Once again, I must beg your forgiveness. My lack of rest has left me cantankerous." Kitty flushed with annoyance at her discourteous attitude.

"Ahhh, sleep. The great cure all," Emory sought to mollify. "We would all do better if we had more."

"Quite so," Adam observed, his tone flat.


Hearing the voice of her favourite man, Evie roused and interrupted with a jubilant cry, "Sir pwetty."

Squirming off Kitty's lap, she clambered up the steps, and made a beeline for the tall man, whose face she loved to stroke. She tweaked his trousers, then stretched out her arms, looking up in eager anticipation. Adam lifted her high in the air and rotated slowly.

"Wheeeeeeeee," she chortled, her fingers clutching at the air. "Bird."

Emory caught Kitty's eye and asked silently, "How are you?"

Kitty shrugged and, with a wry expression, wobbled her hand in a 'so-so' gesture.

Adam carried Evie over to one of the chairs and, as had become customary settled her on his knee. She chatted to him in her usual brand of infant babble mixed with the odd recognisable word, her fingers tracing the scars on his face and twitching the stubble around his jawline.

Far enough away that they would not be overheard, Emory spoke in hushed tones. "Are you sure? Mama is worried."

"I am fine, Emory, but I think Adam is beginning to work it out." She explained about the thunder game. "It never occurred to me Oscar would tell his father, although why I expected him not to, eludes me. Moreover, be careful, Evie knows your name. One word from her and the whole thing is ruined. Aunt Prudence would be so upset."


"Is something amiss?" Adam's question drifted to them.

"Not at all, I am asking Mrs Lovell about the roses." Emory snatched an excuse out of thin air, and Kitty gave a relieved smile. "She is as clueless as you."

Emory's banter deflected Adam from his train of thought, and the two men ribbed each other about their astounding lack of knowledge regarding the local flora and fauna.

"Do join us, Mrs Lovell." Adam indicated the adjacent chairs.

Hesitating — he was still holding Evie; she could not exactly walk away and leave him — Kitty did as he bade.

"Do you ride anymore?" Emory asked sinking into the chair at the other side of Adam.

With a *what on earth is wrong with you?* look, Kitty scoured her brain for another topic of conversation.

"Sometimes, with Papa. Juno is placid enough, but I cannot go alone, having no idea where I am most of the time."

"Juno, you still have Juno?" Emory asked, astonished. "She must be—"

"Elderly? Yes, she is, but in good health." Adam's voice took on a nostalgic quality. "Sometimes I want to saddle up and gallop off into the wild blue yonder. Leave all my cares behind and become a hermit."

"You mirror my sentiments, Lord Teasdale," the words blurted out before Kitty could stop them. She shut her eyes. *Heaven hush her contrary tongue. She **really** needed to get some sleep.*

"You wish to run away, Mrs Lovell?" Adam arched a quizzical brow.

"More than you could possibly imagine." She bent her head to hide her expression. A pointless exercise since Adam could not see, but it gave her a second to regain her poise

"May I be excused?" she entreated.

Adam gave a low chuckle. "Ahhh, finally, we have succeeded in flapping the unflappable governess. I thought it an impossibility."

"And not for want of trying," Kitty retorted, pertly. She stood, straightened her skirts and reached across to pluck Evie from Adam's knee.

"Thank you, my lord. It appears Evie considers you to be the consummate cushion." She knew her remarks exceeded the bounds of propriety. Plainly, her brain and her mouth had parted ways.

She swallowed and continued, "It was nice to see you again, Mr de Wilton." Kitty sketched a curtsy.

Balancing Evie on her hip, she fled with what remained of her composure.


"A tad feisty, what?" humour laced Emory's comment.

"Hmmm…" Adam rubbed his chin. Mrs Lovell perplexed him. Where once she had been reserved, remote even, she was now… *what was she…?* Candid with a dash of pepper? *A damned attractive quality whatever it was.*

Other than his immediate family, nearly everyone he met spoke around him rather than address him directly, and very loudly as though being physically scarred also meant he was deaf.

Mrs Lovell did not appear aware of his ruined features, or his impaired eyesight. She treated him the same way she treated everyone. Deferential, without being obsequious, but there was an underlying conviviality in her conduct, of a type generally found only among family or close friends.

A curious notion flitted into his brain… taunting him.

*It was as though she knew him.*

*No, that was absurd...*

He considered following the governess to ask whether they had crossed paths prior to her arrival at Easby Hall. He could not recall ever meeting a Mrs Lovell, but mayhap it was before she was married. *Did he dare ask her maiden name?* That might resolve the issue.

Mama had been certain this Mrs Lovell would be… *now what had she said...* 'I think she might be exactly what this house needs'. A statement which, in Adam's opinion, required elucidation.

*What was his mother up to?*

Ostensibly, Prudence Marchmain was the epitome of a duchess — refined, elegant, and dignified. Her family knew better. She was possessed of a playful disposition and, when her children were growing up, could be relied upon to foster rather than hinder their mad capers, even join in. Reginald had never quashed it or demanded she curb her fun-loving nature, hints of which still bubbled over with Oscar.

Was hiring Mrs Lovell a deliberate act to achieve a purpose as yet undisclosed? Adam toyed with the idea… it was feasible.

Emory spoke again and, although Adam pushed his thoughts aside, this time he did not forget.

When Emory and Lord Easby retired to the study to finalise their business, Adam ascended the stairs on a mission to find Mrs Lovell. They had an interview to conclude.

With resolute strides, he made his way to the nursery, coming to a halt a few steps from the open door. A blend of voices floated towards him and, slowing, he approached on silent feet.

Mrs Lovell was telling a story. At first the words were jumbled together but, on the verge of entering the room, Adam heard the word bluebell, and something made him pause. He listened intently.

*What...?*

It was *his* story, the one he had told Kitty when she hurt her knee. Yes, there were embellishments, including the storm dragon Oscar had been jabbering about yesterday, but the basic story had not changed for seventeen years. *Seventeen years... it felt like the blink of an eye and several lifetimes.*

Adam turned to lean against the wall, questions crowding his mind.

*Was it possible?*

*Was Mrs Lovell, in fact, Kitty de Wilton?*

*If she **was** Kitty, why had he not recognised her?*

*Why was she a governess?*

The questions kept coming, buzzing around his skull like a swarm of irate bees. Adam felt as though everything was tipping upside down. Scenes, conversations, odd remarks, those numerous perplexing moments, and impressions; suddenly, all of them made sense.

His mother's insistence they appoint a new governess — contrary to his wishes. The latter's immediate acceptance into the household. The reason she had brushed aside and was not upset by his churlishness. Her ability to soothe his discomfiture.

She *did* know him.

*Mrs Lovell **was** Kitty de Wilton.*

.   .   .

The realisation was like a punch to his stomach. He pressed his palms and the back of his head against the cool wood panelling. Closing his eyes, he willed his mind to quieten.

*What little imp had sparked **this** rash course of action, and who had initiated it? Kitty or his mother?* This scheme bore the hallmarks of his mother, Kitty merely a pawn. Soundlessly, he inched forwards until he could squint through the doorway. On the rug in the middle of the floor, he could make out two shapes. Kitty and Oscar.

He desperately wanted to see her face when he confronted her, but had no mind to upset Oscar, whose affection for his governess ran deep. This required careful handling.

A glut of emotions weighed Adam down. Exasperation, betrayal, disappointment, and an element of sadness, underpinned by a smouldering anger. *When would his family stop meddling?*

He pinched the bridge of his nose and made a concerted effort to quell his mounting ire. In truth, he knew his mother only wanted to ease his burden. He could not fault her, but this time she had involved Kitty... and why the *deuce* had Kitty complied?

Unbidden, an image popped into his head. The day he said goodbye to Kitty. No... she did not want to say goodbye, and he suggested they parted with 'until we meet again'.

She had looked so charming in her lilac dress, her green eyes sparkling, her hair an untidy mop, and the inevitable book clutched in her hand. Unable to conceal her anxiety at his news, she had remained uncharacteristically silent while the others plied him with questions.

He had requested a kiss. A reluctant smile tilted the corners his mouth in recollection of her shocked expression and subsequent response. *That had been... what? ...a decade ago?*

For so many years, their secure, sheltered, and cosseted

worlds were intertwined, only to cease virtually overnight. In his wildest imagination, Adam could not have predicted the course their lives would follow but listening to Kitty weave her tale, somehow, they had come full circle.

~

"More." Oscar exercised his most winsome wide-eyed smile.

Evie added her voice to his plea. "More, Mama,"

Kitty chuckled. "You two are never satisfied. If you promise to eat your dinners, and do as Mabel asks, I will read another when you are in bed. How about that?"

About to argue, Oscar peeked at Kitty's face, and whatever he saw persuaded him otherwise. He grimaced and, huffing a very grow-up sigh, got to his feet. "I s'pose," he said grudgingly, then squeaked with surprise when a voice from the doorway chided.

"Oscar, you cannot always get your way. You must learn to accept a postponement or refusal with grace."

"Papa." Oscar's cheeks reddened at the mild admonishment and he shifted from foot to foot, his face crinkled in bemusement. "What is popstern… posmentpop… poppenment?" Floundering with the unusual word.

"It means to put off until later," Kitty, who had scrambled to her feet, clarified. She performed a hurried curtsy, "Lord Teasdale…" she stopped, not quite sure what to say.

"Mrs Lovell, I believe we have a discussion to conclude. I expect you in the library forthwith." Walking to where Oscar stood, Adam ruffled his son's hair. "I know 'tis hard to be patient when you want something badly," he conceded, "but 'tis an important trait to master."

Father and son shared a look of understanding, then Adam inclined his head. "Mrs Lovell."

"My lord." She bobbed another curtsy.

Adam strode out.

Something had changed, Kitty was certain of it. Even the knowledge this day was inevitable did not alleviate her agitation. She had no time to alert Aunt Prudence. "Mabel, please will you ring for Mrs Wilderby, and ask her to inform her Grace, our pretence is exposed."

"Oh no, Miss. You must be mistaken. You have been so careful," Mabel replied, nonplussed.

"Evidently, not careful enough." Kitty checked her reflection in the mirror. She looked flustered, but at least her hair was still confined in its bun.

"You look perfectly presentable, Kitty," Mabel reassured.

Kitty gave a cynical harrumph and followed Adam.

# CHAPTER THIRTEEN

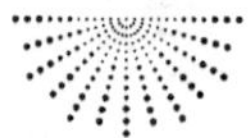

*B*randy in hand, Adam pondered the best way to introduce the matter. Circuitously or directly? The Kitty he remembered had been ingenuous, forthright, but was she still?

He had not recognised her even though she had been in his home for nigh on six months. *What had happened to change her so completely?* He rubbed his chin, his fingers touching the scars marring his cheek.

The knowledge he had been essentially hoodwinked, rankled. Ignoring the voice at the back of his head instructing him to remain impassive, Adam allowed irritation to supersede his better judgement.

A knock heralded Kitty.

He propped himself against the mantel.

"Come," he barked.

It was a command not an invitation.

At the other side of the door, Kitty's heart sank. She knew it. How many times had she cautioned her aunt that when

Adam guessed, he would be furious? Why had she allowed it to go on for so long?

*Because you found solace in being anonymous,* her conscience reminded, *you relished the challenge, and you liked being useful. You wanted to prove to those who pleaded with you to participate in this hare-brained scheme that their faith in you was justified.*

Squaring her shoulders, she opened the door.

The scene was a replica of the last time she was in this room. Adam was leaning against the mantlepiece, glass in hand, glaring at her. His focus did not waver, and again, she swore he could see right through her.

"Lord Teasdale." She curtsied, not quite able to prevent the quaver in her voice.

Adam watched Kitty's entry, a blur of pastel green which dipped low and rose again. She was still conforming to the expected protocols. Humour warred with umbrage.

*He must not let down his guard.*

All was quiet, but the air was thick with tension.

He let the silence drag out.

"Mrs Lovell. Of late, I have been plagued by disquieting notions. Notions which bring into question your suitability to continue as governess to my son," he began.

He heard a sound, like a hiss immediately smothered.

"So vexing are they, I believe my only recourse is to terminate your employment. 'Tis obvious you deceived my poor mother into engaging you under false pretences. You are not who you purport to be, and your duplicity must end today.

"That you used your daughter to gain a sympathetic ear disgusts me. I am not so callous as to expel you as night approaches, but I expect you and Evie to be out of Easby Hall by midday tomorrow."

Hoping to goad Kitty into confessing her part in the ruse, Adam instilled contempt into his voice. "I shall provide a coach to take you to the village, from there you can make you own way home."

His lip curled in distaste, and he swiped his hands together as though washing a stain off them.

Kitty shuddered, flayed by Adam's words. His dismissal, although merited and anticipated, cut her like a knife. Worse, his derision, the sneer in his tone, triggered bad memories.

What, on any other day would have produced a spirited response, today, the combination of fatigue, the uproar in her mind, and the festering dread of discovery, generated an entirely different reaction.

The life she had escaped, believed she had managed to consign to the past, reared up. It was as though she had gone back in time; that the previous two years had never happened.

Adam transformed into Godfrey. The cosy library became the soulless study at Asquith Place. Adam's indignation contorted into mocking insinuations, vile aspersions, and hateful gibes.

Oblivious to her surroundings, Kitty hugged her arms around her waist and bent slightly. "Please, Godfrey. On my oath, I was not seducing your steward. I was in the parlour sewing. You know I would never breach your trust." Her voice lowered to an inflection designed to mollify.

"Godfrey? Steward?" Adam was mystified.

His diminished ability to see, notwithstanding, it was clear she had not heard him.

There was a long pause. To Adam, it seemed as though Kitty was listening to an unseen person. Then she spoke again, exhorting him to cease his unfounded accusations.

Ashen, Kitty moaned, and she clapped her hands to her ears. Desperately, she shook her head. Her carefully modulated tones rose to a raucous scream, as her fingers speared into her dark-blonde tresses, rending them from the neat bun.

"**No**! You will *not* treat me this way, you odious… **whoreson**. I do not deserve it," she cursed. Her screech reverberated around the room, bouncing off the walls.

Like a creature possessed, she darted out through the French doors, hair streaming behind her.

And was gone.

Stupefied, Adam stood slack-jawed and motionless.

*What the devil…?*

Emory and the duke burst through the door, Prudence following on their heels.

"Adam… Teasdale," Emory demanded, sharply. "Where is Kitty?"

Adam swung to face the group. "Pardon?" Thunderstruck, he could scarcely comprehend who it was, never mind what they were saying.

"Where. Is. My. Sister?" Emory pronounced every word slowly and distinctly.

"She ran…" Stunned, Adam could not, for the life of him, rally his thoughts. He made do with pointing.

Emory shot off into the fading light of the afternoon.

. . .

"What happened, son?"

"Adam…" his mother's anxious tones overlapped his father's question.

Adam rounded on his parents. "What the hell made you think hoodwinking me was a good idea? Am I such a deplorable excuse of a father that you had to cajole Kitty de Wilton into play-acting? My vision may be impaired but the rest of me is as acute today as it was before that blasted cannon destroyed my life. I am not the bumbling fool you appear to think I am." He was trembling with shock and fury.

"*Adam*." The duke's bellow penetrated his son's wrath. "Do not *ever* speak to your mother with such disrespect."

"That works both ways, Father," Adam griped, pique overruling sense.

"Adam, my dear," Prudence interposed before Reginald lost his temper. She approached her son, her slender fingers enclosing his clenched fist. "Come, you know we do not think you addled or impaired. All I wanted was my son back."

"I'm back Mama, I've been back for five years." Adam shrugged off her hand and turned away.

"Look at me, Adam."

He ignored her demand.

"Look at me."

For all his mother's voice was soft, iron ran through it. Adam had never been disobedient and, current chaos aside, he loved his parents. He did as she bade.

Prudence stretched up to cup his face, her thumb smoothing over the pitted skin along his jaw. "No, you haven't. My son Adam, who went to sea, is buried under layers of loss, and sadness, and irascibility. There were traces, hints, but nothing substantial, and although Oscar lifted your spirits, it was not enough.

"Then I had this bright idea. Kitty was also mired in her

own misery. So much so, Frederica believed she would simply fade away. That vibrant girl we once knew might vanish for ever. I could not let that happen… to either of you. Kitty needed a lifeline, something to take her out of herself, to boost her confidence. You needed to let go of the past, to grieve, and to value your blessings."

Prudence offered a pensive smile. "You had scared off every other nurserymaid, and I was at my wit's end. One afternoon, while Frederica and I were chatting, we were watching Kitty play with Evie, and it came to me. There *was* someone who would not tolerate your nonsense but who would do so with courtesy and dignity. I took a gamble, deeming it a less brutal method than banging your heads together."

"What happened to Kitty?" Adam's outrage had dissipated as quickly as it flared.

"She ought to be the one to tell you. I know only what Frederica divulged, and that was in confidence. Suffice it to say, she has suffered as debilitating an injury as you, 'tis just her scars are invisible."

"She called me Godfrey. Who the dickens is Godfrey?"

"Her dead husband."

Adam walked to the nearest chair and slumped into it, his head in his hands. "I frightened her. I heard her telling Oscar the story I invented the day she hurt her knee. Suddenly I knew. So many inexplicable things fell into place and I knew. I ordered her to join me in the library, I wanted to trip her up. To coerce her to confess. I told her she had to leave. The next instant she called me Godfrey and cursed me. She actually swore."

He shook his head in disbelief. That Kitty even *knew* the expletive floored him. "She ran away, and you came in." He thumped one fist into his open palm.

"What have I become that I frightened a woman into running away?" He stared at his mother. "Oh God, Kitty."

Adam rose and made as though to follow the two already gone.

"Wait here, you cannot go wandering the grounds. You have no idea where she has gone," Reginald adjured.

Adam thought he might know but conceded his father's point. He paced the floor, walking in a wide loop, avoiding the furniture with proficiency.

Emory reappeared. "I cannot find her."

"I think I know where is. Let me go. I need to make this right."

"You can make it right when she's safely home," Emory retorted.

"No, this was my blunder. I need her to believe I care enough to seek her out, to beg her forgiveness. Sequestered here like some lily-livered coward, while everyone else searches the grounds, is not the way to persuade her."

Emory started to speak.

"Please, Emory. You are my friend, I hope. Trust me."

Prudence sent a wordless message to her husband. They both looked at Emory and nodded.

Emory bobbed his head in resignation. "All right, but if you make her cry, I will beat you to a pulp."

"Fair enough." Adam raised his palms in a conciliatory gesture.

"Where do you suppose she has gone?"

"The folly."

"Adam, it is dusk. You will lose your way, or worse, fall," Prudence wailed.

"'Tis a risk I am willing to take. I must do this."

"Come on then, Knight of the Garden." Emory harked back to their childhood. "Prove to Kitty that chivalry is not dead."

The two men headed around the house and across the lawns towards the lake. The day was waning, the early evening light, golden. Tiny insects flitted on the last eddies of warm air, their iridescent wings shimmering in the hazy glow. The pair walked in silence, but it was not uncomfortable.

Emory, sensing Adam was genuinely horrified by his actions, had no mind to add to his distress. Prior to this upset, Emory had detected a profound change in his friend.

During previous visits, Adam was never anything other than taciturn, unless Oscar was around. Now, there was a lightness about him, his expression no longer bleak. He had smiled, even laughed a couple of times.

Emory had the sneaking suspicion Kitty was behind the change, even if Adam had yet to acknowledge it.

A wry grin tugged at his lips. Despite being a man who had no time for romance, let alone love, Emory knew these two were meant for each other. He just hoped they would recognise it before it was too late.

They came to a halt at the edge of the lake. Emory spied Kitty huddled on the floor of the folly.

"Is she there?" Adam's question was naught but a whisper.

"She is sitting on the ground in the middle of the folly." Emory guided Adam to the stepping stones. "Here, the first stone is one stride in front of you." He watched until Adam had reached it and was facing in the right direction.

"Shall I wait?" Given the situation, Emory was hesitant to leave.

"Thank you, no. We will be fine. I promise to bring Kitty home in one piece."

"I am more worried she will shove you into the lake." Emory grinned, his teeth flashing white in the gloaming.

His remark caused a low chuckle.

"Thank you, Emory. I hope it doesn't come to that, but if it does, I can swim," Adam replied.

"If you are sure."

"I am sure. Go, pour yourself a large drink. I daresay you ought to stay here again tonight. No point riding cross country in the dark unless you have to. Aunt Frederica will know where you are," Adam said. "Wish me luck."

"Good luck." Emory turned for the Hall, glancing over his shoulder now and again to make sure Adam reached the other side without toppling in.

# CHAPTER FOURTEEN

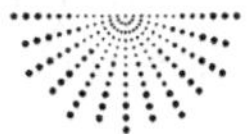

Adam padded across the cool slabs. Straight ahead stood the folly, the twilight adding a lustre to the slender white columns. He paused, gathering his thoughts, and calming his mind, which whirled like a sycamore key in a blustery breeze.

"Kitty," he called her name softly, as he entered the circular building.

Listening, he heard a muffled sob. "Kitty, please. I come to beg your forgiveness. I was trying to compel a confession, not scare the wits out of you."


Silence.


He took another step and saw her. A pitiful heap on the ground. He dropped to his knees alongside her. "Kitty…"

"Go away," her subdued reply ended on a hiccup.

Adam's chest pinched. Kitty rarely cried. His guilt at instigating this was bad enough, but the awareness someone else had treated her with such cruelty that a few rash words could incite so extreme a response, appalled him.

He inched forward and stretched out his hand until it came into contact with her shoulder. Taking a chance, he squeezed gently.

"Kitty, please don't cry. The last thing I meant to do was upset you. I was so shocked when I discovered what was afoot, the artifice I had not the sense to discern, I lashed out without consideration. Upon my oath, I only wanted to extract an explanation. I expected you to tick me off, and instead this…"

"I am s-so s-sorry…" Kitty's voice was empty, defeated.

Adam could not bear to hear her sounding so despondent.

He did the unthinkable.

Shuffling until he was sitting cross-legged, Adam slid his arms around Kitty and drew her slight frame onto his lap. She was shivering.

Nestling her head under his chin, he said, "Kitty, sweetheart, please tell me what happened to elicit so acute a response. Why did you assent to my mother's proposal?" He felt her stiffen at this. Ignoring it, he continued, "What caused you to change so drastically, that I did not recognise you? What happened to my princess?"

Adam's last words induced a fresh outburst of weeping. Kitty clung to him, sobbing wretchedly. She tried to speak but was less coherent than Evie.

Unable to make head nor tail of what she was saying, Adam didn't try. He simply held her, running one hand up and down her back in a soothing rhythm.

Gradually, the bout abated, and Kitty drew a tremulous breath.

"I b-beg your forgiveness, Adam. I j-just wanted to help." She lifted a tear-stained face. "Aunt Prudence h-has been s-so worried. I knew y-you would be upset w-when you f-found out, but I expected you t-to discover our scheme m-months ago. W-when you didn't, it became easier to p-pretend." Her words interspersed with little gasps as she strove to control herself.

"Mama told me why she asked you. I ought not be surprised by her chicanery, but this one caught me off guard, and I admit you bore the brunt of my indignation."

He felt Kitty angle her body to look up at him. She was so close, he could see her pale face, and damp cheeks, her green eyes luminous in the twilight. She scrubbed away her tears but made no move to extricate herself from his embrace.

Kitty's brain was careening off on several tangents. *Why had Adam come to find her? Why was he holding her? Oh, his arms felt so strong, so protective. Stop it, he is only being kind. But he called you sweetheart. His voice was so deep. She could listen to his voice forever. Not the time, Kitty.*

She tried to get her thoughts in order. Adam deserved the truth, however convoluted and humiliating.

"I agreed to Aunt Prudence's proposal because I had the insane conviction, I was the one to rescue you," Kitty spoke, haltingly.

"Rescue me? From what?" Visibly bewildered.

"From the darkness which your Mama believed had overtaken you. She insisted that because I knew you, I could get under the shields you had erected and make you smile again."

He let the last part of her reply go for now and instead asked, "Why did you not simply visit?"

"Aunt Prudence posited it would take some time. Five, six

years of desolation cannot be ameliorated in a handful of fleeting visits. To become Oscar's nursery maid and governess sounded like a sensible option. I was uncomfortable misleading you, but you know Aunt Prudence. When she gets an idea in her head…" Kitty's laconic tone had Adam nodding his understanding.

"I am not excusing what we did, just explaining why. Then I met Oscar. I was terrified at first. I was barely a mother myself, what did I know about teaching a little boy? Imagine my surprise when I discovered how much I love it, and I think I might be quite good at it. Oscar is a joy and so like you." She clamped her mouth shut.

Shaking her head, Kitty took a different tack. "I knew how ill-disposed you were to my presence, the day I arrived. You were standing at the top of the steps like a statue. I wanted to jump back in the carriage and beat a hasty retreat—"

"What made you stay?"

"Your expression, oh, and Oscar's words."

"Oscar's words?" Adam's brow creased trying to recollect what a five-year-old might say that was so persuasive.

"He said, 'Helping Evie is like helping Papa, if you are not careful, they will trip over or walk into something'. You were my knight, the boy who cared enough to find a cart to wheel me around so I would not miss out on the fun. The man who begged a kiss when he was going off to war. I could not let that man be subsumed by tragedy. Oscar deserves a father, not an automaton. A man who might trip over happiness, without even realising it was right in front of him."

She stopped again. *Her tongue was running away with her.* "Forgive me, that was unfair, but…"

Adam placed a finger on Kitty's lips. "Hush, you are not incorrect. I have allowed misery and frustration to overwhelm me. Strangely, it was Evie who yanked me from my introspection. Until that moment I had not realised how much of a curmudgeon I had become."

"She loves you…" Kitty spoke without thinking.

"She has certainly inveigled her way into my heart…" he paused and, closing his eyes, took a leap of faith, "…much like her mother."

Kitty gulped. She stared, searching Adam's face for mockery, and finding only honesty. Involuntarily, her hand cupped his right cheek.

"Adam…?" Her voice rose in hesitant question.


With a rapidity that left Kitty breathless, Adam changed or rather redirected the subject. Yes, he wanted to explore what his avowal might mean, but before they could consider romance or love or whatever was going on, he had to get to the bottom of his mother's meddling.

He shuffled them into a more comfortable position, propping himself against the nearest pillar, but did not relinquish his hold, cherishing the feel of Kitty in his arms. Pulling his mind from the sentimental to the prosaic, Adam asked his first question.

"Who is Mrs Lovell?"

"Me." The single word dripped with loathing

"Please elaborate."

"I was married to Godfrey Lovell, the Viscount Asquith. I could not call myself Mrs Asquith. That might have jogged your memory, neither did I want to provide a false identity. I hoped you might not recall his family name."

"Wait, isn't he the viscount who was…"

"…murdered?" Kitty finished for him. "Yes, about two and a half years ago in a squalid back-alley in London." The repugnance in her voice was unmistakeable.

"I think you may have to divulge all, my sweet. Am I

correct in deducing the reason I did not recognise you, relates to him?"

He felt her nod and heard a choked sigh.

"Godfrey swept me off my feet. He was charm personified. I suppose that ought to have been a portent, but I was starry eyed and, patently, addle-brained," Kitty said ruefully.

"He was everything a girl of ten and nineteen hoped for. Six years older than me, I thought him terribly sophisticated and erudite. He was tall, handsome, perhaps a trifle over-confident, and treated me like a precious treasure. He won over Mama and Papa, which gives you an indication of his silver tongue.

"He courted me, oh so properly, and when he asked for my hand, Papa could see no reason to deny him. My wedding day was one of the happiest of my life," she steeled herself to continue, "and one of the worst."

Needing some distance, she wriggled out of Adam's embrace, got to her feet, and walked over to the edge of the folly, facing out across the lake.

"Everything was marvellous until we left for Asquith Place, a lengthy journey." She pictured those ghastly hours confined to the carriage. *He is dead, Kitty. He cannot harm you.*

"We were barely out of sight of Foxgrove…" the de Wiltons' London residence, "…when it started. In a heartbeat, my enamoured suitor, my devoted husband, mutated into a monster."

In monotones, Kitty disclosed her nightmare. It was the first time she had revealed the magnitude of Godfrey's depravity, which also clarified why Adam had not recognised her voice. She had not wanted to burden her parents with every detail. Initially, it was too raw and, eventually the need to verbalise her distress, lessened.

"Then he was murdered. When I received the news, God forgive me, my principal emotion was one of relief. He was dead. Never again would I have to listen to his sordid accusations, worry about his volatile temper or vindictive behaviour.

"Four months later, I discovered I was increasing, just before I came home to Grafton Manor. To reside in any of the Asquith or Lovell houses…" She could not describe the aversion she held for the residences.

"I was going to sell them, but being titled estates, it is complicated. I have no idea whether there are other family members who may lay claim. As far as I am concerned, they can have them." Her lip curled in abhorrence.

"As I was saying, I came home. My parents know something of my life with Asquith, but I have never spoken of his… propensities in such detail. It was too hard, and my parents were already devastated because they had approved the match. To add to their remorse would have been unnecessarily harsh."

Adam wanted to whisk her back into his arms, to kiss away her sorrow, but refrained. The telling was not done.

Kitty's fingers interlaced over her stomach. "Nine long months." Her voice took on a faraway tone. "I did not want anything to remind me of him, but here I was carrying his child.

"It was a painful blow. Even in death, he did not have the decency to liberate what he considered to be his property. The notion of raising his child made me physically ill. I would never be free of him and, when I came to term, a part of me hoped I would die in childbirth…"

. . .

Adam flinched, opening his mouth to speak and, given what happened to Gwendolyn, possibly to admonish.


Kitty interrupted before he got a word in edgeways. "You wanted to know why I did what I did. In that case you need to hear it all — the bad and the worse." She smiled, sadly.

"My daughter… the moment they placed Evie in my arms, my equivocation evaporated. She was perfect. She opened her eyes and stared at me, her tiny fingers gripping one of mine and the ice around my heart splintered. She was my saviour, the reason I got out of bed, the reason I ate, the reason I remembered to breathe. A minute human being, completely dependent on me for life. 'Tis humbling."

She walked back to Adam, who had remained seated on the floor of the folly.

"So, you see, when Aunt Prudence proposed I help you, it was like a gift from God, although I do believe she was about to resort to blackmail by the time I consented." A grin flashed over Kitty's face remembering her aunt's pleas.

"I was uneasy with the idea of tricking you into something you would rather avoid, but I could not let you descend into a similar pit of despair. To help you, my Knight of the Garden, and your little boy, appeared to be heaven sent.

"I did not lie to you, Adam. I swear I did not. Yes, there was the occasional prevarication, and perhaps I steered conversations in a particular direction because I wanted to provoke you into an answer I already partially knew, but I did not lie."

She stopped speaking. Belabouring her point made her sound as though she was attempting to absolve her role, rather than clarify why she had participated.

. . .

The lull between them was broken only by the haunting call of a lapwing as it skimmed low over the lake.

Regardless of Adam's declaration, now she had imparted her innermost secrets, Kitty was dubious. Summoning up her failing courage, she knelt beside him. Repeating her earlier gesture, she curved a cool hand around his jaw.

He did not speak…

…nor did he pull away.

Her slender fingers ghosted over wrinkled flesh, delicately, tenderly. Unable to stop herself, she stretched across to brush her lips to his cheek. "Forgive me…" she beseeched.

Her hand fell to her side, her heart hammering in her chest at her audacity.


They were scant inches apart, and when Kitty withdrew her hand, Adam felt bereft. The caress of her fingers as they stroked his scars was divine. Taking his time, he studied her.

Kitty's nose was a little red from her bout of weeping, but her cheeks retained their pallor. Watchful eyes, her expression, wary. Errant blonde curls framed her face, and he wanted to bury his hands in the glossy tresses while he kissed her until she forgot everything that had come before.

The truth in his heart clamoured to be released but he hesitated. This step was not one to take lightly. They both suffered from a darkness which had yet to be vanquished.

*Was love enough?*

Her story wrenched at his soul. *How could someone who had taken an oath to love, revere, and cherish, do the exact opposite? What had possessed the man — to whom she had entrusted her heart, her body, her life — to treat her with such enmity?*

In two short years Godfrey Lovell had crushed Kitty's

spirit to the extent, her own mother feared for her sanity, perhaps even her life.

He could not fathom such inhumanity.

# CHAPTER FIFTEEN

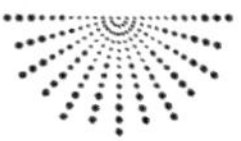

"*P*erhaps we ought not tarry. I have things to pack."

Kitty, intent on instilling some semblance of order to this tumultuous situation, got to her feet and brushed down her skirts.

Adam's lack of response spoke volumes.

Confusion reigned. Everything was off kilter. *Had she imagined those magical words? Did he still want her to leave?* It seemed improbable... *but...*

"Not yet, and you are going nowhere." Levering himself off the floor, Adam came to stand next to her.

"Kitty, you are not inaccurate. I did *not* want a do-gooding busybody interfering in my life, in Oscar's life. The previous nursery maids made my days a misery. 'Tis difficult enough to thwart the well-intentioned when you are *un*impaired, 'tis a hundred times harder when you are reliant on them.

"Thankfully, my family is compassionate without making me feel less of a man, but these women who thought I would succumb to their feminine wiles, drove me to distraction. Worse, they were in my home, supposedly nurturing my son, when, in fact, all they wanted was a husband. When Mama informed me of your appointment, I was furious." He rubbed his forehead.

"Your arrival was handed to me as a *fait accompli.* I protested, but Mama was adamant, and I acquiesced because, despite my objections, she would engage you anyway. Then you arrived and, my misgivings aside, I was struck by your reserve and the way you kept your distance.

"You did not worm yourself into my presence, nor did you interrupt the conversation at dinner with vignettes designed to ensnare me. It was as though you were trying to avoid me which, I surmise, is *precisely* what you were doing.

"To witness the changes you have wrought on Oscar has been a privilege. My son has thrived under your tutelage, your care. You have a knack for allowing him to be the child he is, while educating him to be the man he was born to become. 'Tis a gift.

"As the weeks unfolded, instead of trying to escape from you, I had to stop myself trying to find you. Your voice pacifies, while your perfume intoxicates. There was something frustratingly familiar about you, something which kept teasing, but for the life of me, I could not figure it out. All I could think was that we must have met at some Society function or other before I went to sea."

His hands found her shoulders and he turned her until they faced each other.

"Kitty, while the circumstances of our reacquaintance have been less than auspicious, I believe we share something profound. Something which has been brewing for more than the few months since your unexpected re-entry unto my life. Something which might just be our salvation, but I do not wish to rush into anything. We have both suppressed our emotions for an age, and there is more at stake here than our hearts."

Hearing his poetic turn of phrase, Adam pressed his lips together, shaking his head. *The deuce, but you sound like a damned fairy tale,* he groused inwardly.

"That said, I would be honoured if you might be so kind as to permit a kiss." The whispered words were out before he could stop them.

There was a long pause.

"I should be honoured to grant your request, good knight," Kitty replied, and he could hear the shyness in her voice.

Tentatively, Adam bent closer. They both angled their heads the same way and their noses bumped, drawing a muted chuckle from Kitty.

Inexplicably apprehensive, he curved his hands around her face. *This was Kitty, his friend, and one-time accomplice in mischief.*

His head contested they were about to step over an invisible line from which there was no going back, while his heart proclaimed the risk was worth it. Moreover, a herd of wild horses could not prevent him from taking that step.

He grazed her bottom lip with his thumb, following with his mouth.

It was the barest hint of a kiss and Kitty leant forward, wanting more. One of her hands came to rest on his waistcoat at the same time as Adam's arms came around her, bringing her flush to his body.

His face was inches from hers, and her nose caught the faintest trace of a fragrance: myrrh and calendula. Its subtle potency stirred something powerful… something elemental.

"Adam," it was an echo of her earlier plea.

"Kitty," her name slipped out on a sigh.

"Kiss me."

He captured her mouth, stealing her startled gasp. His lips moved over hers with sublime tenderness, as one hand slid up to her nape, fingers entwining in her silky hair.

Her arms circled his waist, fingers splaying across the fine wool of his jacket.

Kitty's heart drummed, and delicious tingles spiralled out along her veins. Adam's kiss was like nothing she could have imagined or had experienced. It was at once restrained and demanding, sweet and fierce, gentle and passionate. She would never tire of being kissed like this.


Adam was floored. Even as he wanted to retain some level of decorum, his body betrayed him. The instant their lips met, he was lost, drowning in sensations he struggled to interpret. He cradled Kitty's slender frame, gratified when he felt her mould herself to him, the faint pressure of her hands across his back, a brand.

Her innocent yet uninhibited response sent a thrill right to his toes, and his whole body ached for her. *Was this what it was like to be seduced by the laudanum he had declined so many years ago?*

In the cool of the evening, as the stars winked into existence in a darkening sky far, far above, Adam acknowledged there was nothing an apothecary could prescribe to cure him of this addiction.


It was Kitty who broke their kiss, trembling with the strength of the emotions tumbling through her. On a ragged breath, she tilted her head to study his face. His handsome features illuminated by the rising moon. To her, Adam's scars did not detract from his craggy good looks. She reached up to brush back his forelock.

"I never want this evening to end, but…"

Rather than step away, Adam drew her against him, tucking her head under his chin. He could feel the frantic beat of her heart and the heave of her chest as she tried to regain her equanimity.

*Mayhap it was time.* Here, now as they stood at a threshold. They had bared their souls, unveiled the demons kept at bay. Kitty was not a woman to give her heart frivolously, and her response when he kissed her was more telling than any affirmation.

The clamour in his heart was deafening and, for the second time when it came to Kitty, he ignored the voice of reason.

"I love you, Katherine de Wilton, my princess."


Kitty stilled.

All was silent.

Not even a hoot of an owl or the bark of a fox was heard.


*Was time itself suspended?*


Although she yearned to hear the words, when Adam confessed his love, Kitty was astounded. Yes, she reciprocated his sentiment one hundred, one thousand-fold, and in spite of what he had said earlier — *was it only that evening? It felt like an eon ago* — she had not expected so precipitous a declaration. Nevertheless, Adam was not a man to express his innermost feelings on a whim. If he said he loved her… he loved her.

She moved out of his embrace and dipped a low curtsy.

"I love you too, Adam Marchmain, my Knight of the Garden. I think I always have. An emotion, I did not have the perspicacity to understand a decade ago, has rekindled and is as exhilarating as it is overwhelming.

"While my heart aches for what you have lost, I am selfish enough to be glad your mother asked for my help. Had she not, this…" taking his hand, she lifted up on tiptoe to kiss his jaw, then his cheek, then his lips, "…might have passed us by, which would have been a travesty."

Adam gathered her close and his lips descended on hers with a fervour hitherto repressed. "God, Kitty," he husked when at last he raised his head. "I could kiss you 'til the end of time."

"Well, I would be a fool to stop you," she murmured against his mouth, revelling in the sensation of being cocooned in his arms. "That said, the evening draws on, your parents may be anxious."

"After what my mother has done…" He didn't finish his sentence.

"Adam," Kitty chided, fondly. "Aunt Pruden—"

"Yes, I know, it was for my own good, etcetera and all the rest. No doubt she will take credit for the outcome." He shook his head and hooked Kitty's arm through his. "Come, my love. "Let us assuage their worries. Emory was certain you would push me in the lake."

Kitty burst into peals of laughter, a golden sound which rang clear across the lawns. "Emory knows me too well."

Not easily, but as neither wanted to let go of the other, they navigated the stepping stones together, managing not to end up in the lake and strolled to the Hall chattering like magpies.

The constraints which had impeded previous conversations no longer bound them and they exchanged news and gossip in a manner reminiscent of their youth.

They entered the library through the French windows, to see matching expressions of stunned disbelief from the three therein.

"Adam?" Prudence's voice rose to a squeak at the sight of her son and Kitty arm in arm.

"Glad to see you did not push him in." Emory smirked.

"Adam, Kitty," Reginald greeted them with an arched brow.

"Mama, Papa. Mrs Lov… Lady… Kitty," he amended, recalling Kitty's tone, "and I have come to an… accord. One which I hope will flourish in the fullness of time, but one we prefer is not discussed beyond this room for the moment."

He smiled down at Kitty, perceiving the joy in her lovely face as she beamed up at him.

"As you know, neither of us is unscathed, and we have two children to consider. Thus, we would like things to unfold naturally, while we continue to come to terms with those matters which have… shall we say… left us a trifle debilitated."

"I am delighted at this turn of events." Prudence sailed across the room to envelop Adam and Kitty in a hug.

"You have shown fortitude in challenging circumstances and are deserving of a happy ending. I accept your wish to keep this between ourselves for the time being but permit me to request Champagne be served with dinner which, by the way, will be served shortly. We held it back," she clarified.

"Thank you, Mama, that would be splendid," Adam replied.

"Excuse me, please. I should like to check on the children." Kitty interposed, guilt niggling. She had neglected them for the whole evening, an unheard-of omission. She bobbed a curtsy and hurried out.

Amused by Kitty's strict adherence to etiquette, despite her sudden change in circumstance, Prudence gestured to those remaining in the room to take a seat until dinner was announced.

Their relaxed conversation continued throughout the meal and afterwards in the drawing room. The men did not retire for cigars and brandy as was they habit, and Kitty, for the first time since her arrival, did not leave for her own quarters.

The evening disappeared in bright chatter and, possibly, an extra measure or two of brandy. Kitty, who rarely indulged in anything stronger than a glass of wine, felt decidedly tipsy as she wove her way to bed, relieved when Adam offered to escort her to her chambers.

"Beg pardon, my body and my brain appear to have gone their separate ways." Her words were slightly slurred. "Oh dear, my mouth has forsaken me too." She giggled. "I might be in my cups."

Adam chuckled. "That you might, my love."

At the door to her suite, Adam bent to kiss her.

Kitty, uncaring who might come upon them, looped her arms around him and responded without reserve. Desire flared and, had Adam not been sober, their newly discovered ardour might well have spiralled out of control.

Hearts stuttered, hands explored, lips tasted, and tongues tangled. Minutes ticked by, and it was only the bank of a door closing on the floor below, which jolted them to their senses.

"Kitty…" Adam couldn't find the words to describe his emotions. They stood together, foreheads touching, breathing slowly returning to normal. "Find your bed before I take you here in the hall." His voice was hoarse. "I shall see you on the morrow."

"How," Kitty hesitated.

"How what?"

"How shall I, shall we… with the children, lessons?" Although losing her ability to concentrate, Kitty tried to infuse some objectivity into the situation. "I want to continue teaching Oscar. Is that going to be a problem?"

"I cannot see why it should be." His features creased in genuine puzzlement.

*Men*, thought Kitty, dazedly, *as long as their lives ramble along uncluttered by hazards, they are happy. Does he not see my dilemma?*

"'Tis only now with us… and me no longer being what I was, I mean because you know. My status." *My, but I ought to avoid liquor, I cannot master a single solitary sentence.* "Do you see?" She canted her head. Adam looked a bit swimmy. She squinted but that made it worse.

"Ohhhhhhh." She clutched his arm to steady herself.

"I am happy for you to teach Oscar as long as you choose to." Adam felt a grin pulling at his lips. Kitty looked decidedly woozy and delectably mussed.

"Good, excellent, thank you." Her words tripped over one another.

He chuckled, the sound rumbling though him. "Kitty, do

not overthink this, be yourself and everything else will fall into place. Trust me." He wound a lock of hair through his fingers. "Sleep well, my love."

She brushed her lips to his. "Goodnight, Adam," she said, and floated into her room on a cloud of euphoria and champagne.

The door clicked shut and Adam stood for a moment, his head against the dark wood, regaining his equilibrium. The day's events played on repeat in his head.

He thought he had loved Gwendolyn, and while he could not deny the depth of their affinity, the emotions he felt for Kitty transcended them by a prodigious margin.

As Adam made his way to his own bedchamber, another thought propelled itself forward. *Kitty Marchmain, Lady Teasdale sounded so much nicer than Kitty Lovell, Lady Asquith.*

The subsequent days were perhaps a trifle awkward at first, while Adam and Kitty adjusted to the change in their relationship. Prudence and Reginald reverted to the way things were, treating Kitty as the close family friend she was, rather than with the polite distance enforced because of her role as a governess.

Kitty persuaded the staff to continue as they had been. She appreciated the rapport they had attained during the preceding months and had no mind to lose their camaraderie.

Mabel did feel it pertinent to point out that if Kitty married Adam, she would, eventually, become a duchess and that really convention ought not be disregarded.

A remark Kitty had waved aside with airy insouciance.

"If I am ever granted the honour of becoming Adam's wife and subsequently a duchess, I hope I am humble enough to know the people who tend to my needs deserve the utmost esteem and cordiality." She said, imperiously, at which the pair gurgled with mirth.

"I am serious, Mabel, are we not friends? I do not wish to lose that." Kitty had pressed a hand on Mabel's arm and held her gaze.

"I think you are addled, but I will respect your wish." Mabel grinned.

That was over a week ago, and life at Easby Hall resumed its sedate routine. Kitty conducted Oscar's lessons, and played with the children, as she always had. The only obvious difference was that she accompanied the family to the drawing room or the library after dinner.

Had anyone peered along dim corridors or taken a stroll through the orchards at odd times of the day, they might have been shocked to spy an enamoured couple sneaking a moment or two of passionate intimacy.

# CHAPTER SIXTEEN

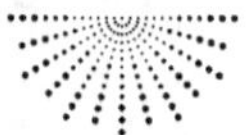

LONDON ~ SUMMER 1815

Sometime prior to this and a little over forty miles away, Silas Dryden — a man whose grim countenance could strike terror into the most courageous — slouched against a table, over which were spread sundry pieces of dog-eared paper. He kept shuffling the sheets as though by re-arranging them, they would make more sense.

What began as an odd note, marking a hint of foreboding, resulting from an intuition borne of experience, had grown considerably during the past months. Thus far nothing in the pile provided the answers he was seeking. Frustrated, he stood and crossed to the heavy wooden door.

Yanking it open, he shouted, "'Arold, get in 'ere."

A wiry, nondescript man of indeterminate age appeared. "Wotcha need, sir?" He bowed slightly.

"Pop 'round to Lovell 'Ouse would yer? See if you can find out where 'er ladyship is and when she's due in town. His nibs used to bring 'er down at the end o' summer, but I've had me lads watchin' and they ain't seen 'ide nor 'air of 'er since his funeral. Must be two year ago." Silas tapped his bristly chin, perplexed. *Who chose to stay in the wilds of the countryside?* He shuddered, *not him.*

"Lady Asquith?" Harold quizzed in surprise, before he could stop himself. "I thought you said she had no idea what he were up to?"

Silas scratched his head and pursed his lips. "I know, but…" he let that dangle. "However unlikely, I gotta check. I reckon he were a swine to 'er, and I doubt she were privy to his interests, but yer never know."

"Right you are, sir." Harold tipped his cap and scarpered. Working for Silas Dryden, even as his trusted second, meant you never questioned, delayed, or neglected an order. Well… you could, but it would be to your detriment, as anyone who had ever crossed him discovered.

Harold Simpkins, who had been 'found' by Silas at the grand old age of six while wandering the Rookeries, had no interest in being added to the list of unlucky ones.

Periodically, he worried what might happen if the Runners uncovered their business ventures. He trusted they could be bribed and, for the most part, cared more that he had a roof over his head and a hot meal at the end of the day, than a few useless constables.

Silas' current enterprise was high risk and, since his relationship with Lord Asquith had come to a sticky end, he was worried about loose tongues. Harold didn't hold with hurting women, but neither was he about to argue the whys and wherefores with Silas.

All he was tasked with doing was finding her whereabouts, possibly 'escorting' her to the office. There, his responsibilities ended.

Leaving behind the cheerless streets of St Giles, Harold wound his way across the city to the leafy suburbs of Mayfair and an elegant townhouse on Mount Street. He studied the façade.

Although pristine — the steps were swept, the windows clean and the garden tidy — the residence appeared encased in an air of genteel abandonment. More so than would be typical when the owners had simply retired to the country for the hot summer months.

His brow creased at the same time as his mouth distorted into a sly smirk. *This could prove a challenge...* and if there was one thing Harold had a partiality for… it was a challenge.

He strolled around the back and followed the mews to the domestic entrance. Ringing the tradesman's bell, he propped himself against the door jamb to wait.

Seconds ticked by. The door opened, and a jacket-less man holding a shoe brush peered out.

"What do you want?" he demanded.

"Is yer missus 'ome?"

"Why should I tell you?" The man, one of the Lovell's footmen, ran a knowledgeable eye over the scruffy lout on his doorstep.

"Me master would like a word wiv 'er. She'd do well to 'eed 'is invitation," Harold intoned loftily. Straightening up, he gripped the front of his open waistcoat, and endeavoured to look important.

"I cannot imagine her ladyship would ever have need to speak with your… err… master," the man replied with a sneer.

Quick as lightning, Harold was in the man's face, a blade pressed to his throat. "I asked nice like. I won't be so polite the next time. Where. Is. Your. Mistress?" The last delivered with malevolent calculation, spittle flying into the footman's face.

To his unending shock, Harold found himself flat on his back on the cobbles, winded.

The footman wiped his face with a kerchief. "Get out of here you louse," he barked. "Her ladyship would never associate with the likes of you or your evidently reprehensible master. Be thankful she is not in residence or I would march you to Bow Street myself. Go on, git."

The footman slammed the door and Harold heard him shoot the heavy bolt.

"Well, I'll be hornswoggled," Harold grumbled, under his breath at his spectacular lack of success. He sat until able to get his breath, debating his next move. So, she was not at home. That left the Asquith estates.

From Silas' dealings with the viscount, Harold knew one of them was Norfolk way. That was too far, but perhaps there was another closer to the city. Getting to his feet, he was about to leave when a rat-faced boy sidled up to him.

"Wotcha want 'er for?" The lad tipped his head in the direction of the house.

"Mind yer business."

"I might know where she is," he offered, slyly.

"And?" Harold arched a brow

"I can tell yer, if yer make it wurf me while." The boy folded his arms and puffed up his chest, maintaining a judicious distance between himself and the man with the sharp knife.

"I'll skin yer alive if yer don't."

"And then where'll yer be." The lad chortled and slapped his knee.

Sighing, and knowing this could go on all day, Harold withdrew a handful of coins from his pocket. "This do yer?"

The boy's eyes glittered. "Aye, that'll do nicely. She went 'ome, so I 'eard."

"Where's home? Norfolk?"

The boy scrunched his nose and shrugged — more in

incomprehension of the word than in any knowledge or otherwise of the place itself.

"Dunno where that is. Nah, she went somewhere called Grafton Manna." He nodded at the door. "Edith in there, she gives me a bit food when she can. She was wittering like a bird the ovver week about it being boring wivvaht her ladyship.

"I allus keep her talking, 'cause the more she natters the more food I get, so I asked where she'd gone. I didn't care much at the time, but I betcha glad I bovvered. Grafton Manna."

He nodded, importantly. "Dunno wot a manna is, but that's not a name easy forgot now, is it?"

Harold glared at the youngster until he squirmed. The lad was correct, however. Grafton Manor was an unusual word and not one a child of his ilk could fabricate.

"Thank you. Here." He tossed the money onto the ground. "Be careful who yer deal wiv. Not all is as understanding as me." Harold turned, took two strides then stopped and threw over his shoulder. "You ever want a proper job, come find me at the Creaky Wench." The local name for the Merry Widow, a seedy tavern on Long Acre.

The lad went white, a minuscule portion of his brain telling him he might just have done a deal with the devil, but coin overrode conscience. "Right you are, sir." He tipped his cap, grabbed the money, and fled.

Harold laughed as he strolled out of the mews, heading for the Rookeries. He treated himself to a pie on the way, well pleased with his morning's work.


Silas rubbed his hands together when Harold gave him the news. There had been numerous unsettling incidents… too close for comfort moments, during the last few months, which impelled him to consider the possibility someone had been tattling. Or worse, spying.

*Was it Asquith's wife? Had the viscount told her what he was involved in? Did she want to assume her late husband's role in the operation or expose it? Had she hired someone to follow him?*

In truth, he had not heard anything concrete to suggest this was the case and understood Asquith had been a boor to his wife, but one thing Silas never did was underestimate people.

*Moreover, if she was ignorant of the viscount's actions, why had she vanished? Bolting to the country like a frightened mare.* To his way of thinking, the only people who ran away were those who had come into information injurious to their health.

Grafton Manor, he jabbed his quill on the paper in front of him. Shouldn't be too hard to find. Might take a while, but in his game, patience was a necessary trait.

Initially, Silas' cautious enquiries — there was no need to alert the authorities he was taking an especial interest in the whereabouts of a member of the *ton* — came up against the proverbial brick wall.

He pondered the possibility Grafton Manor was a figment of Edith's imagination, but the man and his cronies were relentless and eventually, their efforts were rewarded. Grafton Manor, country seat of the Earl of Grafton was in rural Kent not far from the village of Chiddingstone.

Silas estimated it was a good day's ride from London, and if there was a coaching inn in the vicinity of his destination, he might overhear useful gossip about the local gentry.

As September drew to an end, his plans were made and, ensuring his empire would not collapse in his absence, Silas Dryden set off in pursuit of his quarry.

# CHAPTER SEVENTEEN

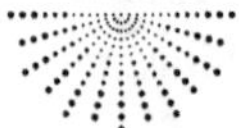

## EASBY HALL ~ OCTOBER 1815

Almost overnight, the season changed. The days became cooler and noticeably shorter, and the light softened from the brash glare of summer to the mellow hue of autumn.

The harvest was complete, and the fields had been ploughed. Trees, once cloaked in weary green, were adorned with shawls of yellow, purple, gold, red, and bronze, their brilliant display — breathtaking.

Smoke from the numerous bonfires dotted around the estate created a haze, as though the world was shrouded, poised on the cusp of something extraordinary.

Kitty loved everything about autumn. The myriad colours, the smell in the air, the chill of early morning, and the crystal-clear night skies full to bursting with stars. Often up with the dawn, a childish habit she had never shaken, Kitty took every opportunity to indulge in a solitary walk.

Besides the staff — who thought her addled for choosing to leave the warmth of the house before even the birds were up but were too kind to comment — Kitty was the only soul abroad. She valued this time when she could sort through her thoughts without worrying, she was neglecting Evie or Oscar or even Adam.

*Adam.*

This particular morning, wrapped in a heavy wool cloak, Kitty strode out along the gravel pathways towards the Great Park, pondering the enigma that was Adam.

He was attentive when among family, and gratifyingly passionate if they chanced a private moment, yet Kitty sensed a cloud lurking, a vague reticence. The flash of something marring his features, gone before she could be sure she had seen it. An odd inflection in his voice.

*Why was he withdrawing?*

*What troubled him?*

*A lingering resentment for her participation in his mother's scheme?*

*What was she missing?*

Not foolish enough to suppose, simply because they had become romantically entangled, that their burdens would miraculously evaporate, neither did Kitty think Adam petty or a man to bear a grudge. She trusted they were in concord, *perhaps not entirely.*

She huffed a weighty sigh, little insecurities pestered. *Did it have anything to do with her being a widow with a child, and therefore not the innocent maiden she once was?*

The wife of a nobleman was expected to be untouched prior to their nuptials, but Kitty could not turn back the clock. She was who she was and, until this recent turn of events, had resigned herself to a life alone.

Of course, she wished she had never met Godfrey. That he had not asked her to dance that fateful night four years ago, or feigned his attraction, or pursued her so diligently. Moreover, regardless of the debacle which was her marriage, Evie had resulted from their union, and Kitty would not be without her daughter for anything.

She scuffed through the profusion of leaves on the ground, kicking them up, partly to vent her frustration, and partly because they looked so attractive gliding down to earth.

Reaching the edge of the Great Park, she found a convenient tree and leant against its weather-beaten trunk to watch the rising sun shoot ribbons of radiance across the grey ground, reviving the land for another day.

*Revive... to bring something back to life, to reanimate, to rejuvenate.* This was what Aunt Prudence had wanted... for Kitty to revive Adam...

...and she believed she had.

Did Adam love her, genuinely love her? Or was the emotion he felt for her, gratitude? Kitty's ability to distinguish nuances of affection, once finely honed had been dulled by circumstance.

This was the crux of the matter.

*Love.*

Although it was quickly doused, Kitty had believed herself in love with her husband. That paled in comparison with the emotions Adam had awoken.

With hindsight, she acknowledged what she bore for Godfrey was naught but girlish infatuation. One which likely would have dwindled naturally into an amiable rapport, had Godfrey been a true gentleman.

Then there was Adam.

Kitty had lost her belief in love, or rather it had been unceremoniously destroyed. Thus, it was the last thing she wanted or was looking for when she undertook this mission. To help her friend overcome his demons had been her sole aim. Inadvertently, Adam had lit a fire, which could not be extinguished. It might not always blaze fiercely, but it would burn forever.

*Was his love for her the same?*

*Or was it the memory of once upon a time?*

*Was the knight simply following the time-honoured tradition of fairy tales?*

*Who was rescuing who?*

A loud crack in the undergrowth snapped her attention to her surroundings. In the sunbeams glimmering through the trees, she spotted the flick of a bronze-red bushy tail as a fox scurried through the undergrowth. Overhead, the avian chorus was tuning up.

The world was waking; time to make tracks.

The turmoil in her mind in no way addressed, Kitty trudged home to the Hall, greeting the staff already busy in the domestic quarters, when she passed.

"Good morning," she hailed those therein.

"Isn't it a mite cold for you to be outdoors so early?" Mrs Wilderby asked.

"'Tis wonderful. Cool, calm, and quiet." Kitty poked her head around the door and winked.

"Breakfast is still a ways off. Would you like some hot buttered toast?" Alice, the Marchmains' cook offered.

"That would be most welcome. I confess my stomach is protesting at its emptiness." As she had done regularly when officially the governess, Kitty began preparing the toast herself, to be shooed to the massive table by Alice.

"Go on with you, my lady. Take a load off and Mary here

will see to it." Alice nodded to the young maid who did as she was bidden with alacrity.

Shortly thereafter, Kitty was munching through thick wedges of crispy toast, dripping with butter, and smeared with Alice's famous gooseberry preserve. Thanking the cheery cook and Mary, Kitty went to check on Evie and Oscar, who would be rousing. Peeking into the nursery, she saw Evie sitting up, rubbing her eyes.

Kitty carried her daughter to her own bedchamber where she washed and dressed the little girl. By the time this task was completed, Oscar had woken. Consigning Adam's peculiar behaviour to the far recesses of her mind, Kitty began her daily routine.

For a while, it worked.

Along with the three stewards, Adam had been busy for the last week or so. Once the harvest was gathered in, the priorities around the estate moved to the multitude of jobs requiring completion prior to the onset of winter.

Checking fences and walls where applicable, ensuring the various smallholdings were weatherproofed, felling of trees, maintenance of trails and pathways, the list went on.

Upon his return to Easby Hall, Adam had assumed much of the estate's administration. In the main as a tacit thank you to his parents for their love and support.

Teasdale Mallow, being much smaller, was easily managed by Messrs Fotheringham and Hathaway. While both men were eminently capable, Adam acknowledged they might appreciate their employer's presence more than the once a year he currently visited— if he could not put it off.

Shoulders protesting from stooping over the desk, he pushed back in his chair, stretched, and glanced out of the window; the daylight was waning. *My but the hours had flown.*

Fighting a nagging headache, Adam stared at the glass, wishing he could see more than smudges of colour. He conjured up an image in his head of the view from the office, which was part of a collection of free-standing buildings situated across the rear courtyard from the main house. To his right, the wood, to his left, beyond the kitchen garden, the newly ploughed fields.

He needed fresh air.

"Please excuse me." He swung his gaze to the three dark shapes around the table. "I find myself losing focus, so to speak." He smiled at the irony of his words. "Perhaps we could finish this on the morrow?" He looked at them questioningly.

Chairs scraped on the stone floor; the stewards stood as one and bowed. "Of course, your lordship."

"We have made good headway today, thank you for your diligence."

After summarising the following day's requirements, Adam left them to it. Going out into the cool afternoon air, he paused and drew a long slow breath, identifying the faint aroma of woodsmoke from the ubiquitous bonfires.

He walked over to the edge of the courtyard and leant against the corner of the stables, the dull ache moving to the back of his head.

Kitty's face drifted into his mind. Her puzzlement not masked quickly enough. He knew he had been pulling away, he couldn't help it. She deserved more than he could offer.

He was due to travel to London the following week. He had an appointment at St Bart's to review his progress. His lip contorted into a sneer. *What progress?* If he told Kitty prior to his departure, it provided a legitimate excuse for her to go home to Grafton Manor.

He rubbed his forehead, his fingers running over the mutilated skin, and growled under his breath. Adam gave himself a mental kicking; what a fool, allowing sentiment to countermand acuity. He would invite Kitty to take a stroll around the grounds with him that evening, whereupon he would extricate himself from their liaison before it was too late.

*Too late?* His heart remonstrated. *It was too late the day she arrived at Easby Hall.*

~

By mid-evening, the two children were tucked up in bed, under the watchful eye of Mabel. A sumptuous dinner eaten, four adults retired to the library, where a warm fire and a digestif awaited.

As they were crossing the hall, Adam posed his question. He missed the look Kitty exchanged with his mother, in whom she had confided less than a week ago.

*"Adam is going to tell me he cannot continue with his courtship,"* she said flatly, while the two were partaking of a late luncheon.

*"Don't be so dramatic, Kitty,"* Aunt Prudence tsked.

*"'Tis naught but the truth. I can see it in his gestures, his demeanour. Something has prompted him to retreat. No doubt he will apprise me of his decision when he feels it appropriate. Probably immediately prior to his departure for London."*

*Piqued at Adam's volte face, Kitty mused over whether she had the energy to argue her case. She loved him but was not going to grovel. If he was afraid to commit to her, for whatever ridiculous reason, then so be it.*

*She was not the same guileless girl who Godfrey had so easily dazzled. She was older, wiser, and had no intention of abasing herself... ever again.*

"Kitty?" He repeated her name, his expression quizzical.

"My apologies, I was wool-gathering," she murmured. "A walk sounds lovely, my lord. Pray permit me a moment to fetch my wrap."

Wilfully formal, Kitty sketched a curtsy, and hurried out, taking the stairs two at a time, her heart drumming. She grabbed her woollen shawl, and slung it around her shoulders, only just avoiding getting her feet tangled on the corner of the rug in her rush, nerves making her clumsy.

If Adam was perplexed by her deference, he made no comment, merely offered his arm. Shortly thereafter, they were following their customary path to the lake. Twilight was giving way to nightfall, the moonrise creating unearthly shadows which formed and faded as the couple passed.

The tranquillity of their surrounds, in stark contrast with the disquiet brewing between the pair despite outward composure.

Neither spoke as they walked, each lost in thought.

# CHAPTER EIGHTEEN

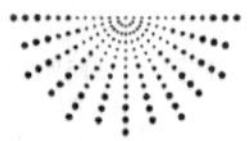

Upon reaching the little island, Kitty unhooked her arm from Adam's and went to stand at the water's edge. The reflection of the pale columns gleamed in eerie splendour on the black, mirrored surface of the lake.

The beauty of the illusion induced unexpected sorrow; it emulated her romance with Adam. Ephemeral and finite.

It was too dark for Adam to see where Kitty had gone, but her fragrance wafted towards him on the evening air. He breathed it in, his chest pinching with the knowledge he was going to cause her pain. *It is better this way,* his brain insisted. *Rubbish* scoffed his crestfallen heart.

He opened his mouth, but before he could express his remorse or spell out his reasons, Kitty spoke from somewhere off to his right.

"Do not cushion your decision with prevarication or excuses, Adam, just tell me." Her voice was hard, emotionless.

Adam prayed for the strength to let her go.

"Kitty, I love you, but I am not the man for you. After

what you have endured, you deserve someone whole in mind and body, not a disfigured shell. It is not fair either to you, or Evie.

"You need a man who can be a proper husband, and father. Someone who can take an active role in your days, be engaged, involved, not lurking on the periphery, inhibited, a liability. You, both of you, deserve light and laughter, and a life overflowing with happiness. I can only bring you sorrow."

Pleased with his speech, which he had worked on diligently, and then practised for an hour, Adam waited for Kitty to — perhaps with a soupçon of regret — acknowledge the logic of his argument.

He heard a sniff and a kind of strangled gulp. *Well, he **had** upset her. To weep was predictable.* He stretched out his hand but, with no idea where she stood, it fell back to his side.

As ever, he had underestimated Kitty.

A swish of movement and Kitty was right in front of him. Even given the gloom and his own limitations, Adam read the wrath on her face, saw her glorious eyes fairly spitting green sparks. *Wait... anger? He had not predicated that.*

"You, selfish cad. How *dare* you presume to know what I do or do not deserve. I believe *I* am the best judge of my own happiness. *Not* involved? A *liability*?" she berated, throwing up her hands in exasperation. *Where **did** he come by his preposterous notions?*

"Do you suppose Oscar deems you an incompetent father? I, for one, know he does not. The child worships you.

The right husba…" She stopped, registering his words. *He had said husband.* When Adam made to respond, she raised her palm. "No, you have made your point. 'Tis *my* turn."

Side-stepping him, she stomped around the modest interior of the folly, bristling with fury.

"What makes you think I do not deserve you? What makes you a lesser man than *any* of our peers? We are none of us perfect, Adam. My own experiences leave me sorely lacking. The question is, do we allow those imperfections to rule us, to determine our future, to extinguish what we truly desire, or do we show our mettle and seize control of our own destiny?"

She made a valiant attempt to moderate her tones.

"You, Adam Marchmain, are the most courageous man I have ever met. I cannot begin to comprehend the obstacles you have overcome, obstacles by which most would be defeated.

"Setting aside the *ludicrous* conviction you are somehow saving me from yourself, take a moment to consider this. You are here. You are alive and loved, standing proud and tall, doing everything a good son and father ought. *Please*, tell me how that makes you undeserving?"

Kitty continued to pace, weighing up the ramifications of doing what her brother thought she might do all those weeks ago, and shoving Adam into the lake.

"'Tis your choice, your life and — if you are unable to lower your guard to take this risk — your loss. I will **not** prostrate myself before you, to beg for the few morsels of affection you deign to sprinkle my way.

"Neither of us was looking for this, and I for one, fought it quite vigorously. Against the odds we found each other. So, perhaps it was pre-ordained, either by God's hand or a twist of Fate."

She came to a halt less than two feet from Adam.

"The joy you bring to my life is indescribable. The slightest touch of your hand makes my heart beat faster. Your too rare smile elicits *the* most irresistible tingles. Unwitting though it was, your first kiss stole my heart, your second ensnared my soul, and that will never change.

"Happiness should never be treated carelessly, for she can be a fickle mistress. Toss it aside once and you may never find it again."


Adam stared, his expression inscrutable.


She gazed at him, imprinting him into her mind. His chiselled face, his wayward hair, his broad shoulders, long legs, beautiful hands. An image of them tangled together, naked, popped into her head, which did not help one jot.

Her dream fading, and distraught at his apparent detachment, her temper spilled over.

"This is not chivalry, Adam. It is cowardice." Kitty spat, and turned to go.


She did not take a single step.


Dumfounded that what he had intended as selfless gallantry could be perceived thus, Adam reacted on instinct.

His hand shot out to grip Kitty's arm.

He hauled her against him, pinning her to his body as his mouth descended on hers, bruising in its intensity.

. . .

Kitty went rigid, refusing to succumb to the delectable frissons tumbling down her spine. She wriggled and jerked her head backwards.

"No," she gasped. "You cannot snatch away everything only to compensate with a crumb."

He did not loosen his hold and she pummelled on his chest with her fists, with little effect. She was *not* yielding.

"Do not trifle with me, Ad—"

His lips cut short Kitty's diatribe. This time with an achingly sweet tenderness. A quiver rippled through her and she felt herself melting, opening to him. Never slackening his hold, his tongue skimmed hers, while one hand cupped her nape, fingers weaving into her hair.

Her fury dissipated.

Her grief eased.

A soft mewl escaped, and she tilted her face, craving more. "Adam." His name a question and an answer. She felt the brush of featherlight kisses along her jawline to the sensitive spot behind her ear and on, down her neck.

"Adam," she repeated.


He lifted his head, so close he saw the glisten of tears in her eyes. Sending a silent prayer of thanks, he retained some sight, he muttered, "Forgive me, Kitty." He kissed her nose. "Forgive me, Kitty," then each of her eyelids.

"Forgive me, my darling. I thought I was being a gentleman, behaving as a true knight ought. Setting aside my feelings to release you from a life which would be, in so many ways, as fettered as your marriage. I had no mind to clip your wings when you have just learnt how to fly. I…"

A slender finger hushed his defence.

"Clipping my wings? *Releasing* me? Adam," she reproached.

Taking the initiative, she wound her arms around his neck and, bringing his head to hers, kissed him soundly.

With a groan he responded.

Seconds ticked by.

Desire simmered. The very air seemed to vibrate with it.

Breathless, Kitty broke their embrace. "I am no fool. I am witness to you surmounting the challenges thrown at you… admirably, I might add… every day. I know you suffer from bouts of temper and want to lash out. 'Tis human nature to retaliate thus, more so given your past."

Lowering her hands to his chest, her fingers splaying over the rich brocade of his waistcoat, she studied him. "Why should that force you to sacrifice your happiness? Why do you think yourself unworthy? What do *you* want, Adam? Be honest."

*If will alone could persuade him…* she thought, on tenterhooks.

"You." His simple reply gave them a lifetime.

Once again, Kitty surprised him.

"So, take me." She grinned suddenly, her fingers tweaking at the silk covered buttons.

"Beg pardon?" His eyebrows shot up to his hairline, his heart rate increasing. *Did she say what he thought she said?*

"I said, take me." Her hands slid beneath his waistcoat, to clutch at the crisp cotton of his shirt.

*She did.*

Hesitating, uncertain quite where this was going, Adam felt his shirt glide out from his buckskins. The stroke of cool fingers made his heated flesh prickle. The whole of his body pulsed with need.

"Kitty?" he husked, questioningly.

"Adam?" she replied, distracted by his torso.

She glanced up and, seeing the crease across his forehead, her fingers stilled. "'Tis impolite not to assuage a lady's desires, especially when offered so freely." She gave a wicked smile and shimmied against him.

He inhaled sharply. "Here? Would not a bedchamber be… more suitable?" He felt it gentlemanly to recommend, but without giving her time to answer, his fingers tiptoed down the back of her dress, unfastening the tiny buttons.

"Who wants suitable?" She stifled a moan as his lips seared a line from her shoulder across her collarbone, to the swell of her breast. "I want reckless spontaneity. I want wildly impetuous, wanton lovemaking and I want it here, in our folly."

She divested him of his waistcoat and tugged at his shirt until he gave in, pulling it over his head.

"Lord be praised," Kitty sighed at the magnificence that was Adam. His broad chest heaved slightly, his muscles flexing. In the moonlight, the pattern of gnarly scars enhanced rather than diminished the sculpted beauty of his body. Inexorably, her fingers were drawn to trace each one.

"I am endlessly glad you became a crotchety old marquis," she said, pertly.

"Because… and less of the old," Adam countered, tackling the last button.

"Another might have stolen your heart." Her gown slithered to the floor, and she shivered in the chill evening air.

"Unlikely, and the bedroom is warmer," he growled.

"No." She fiddled with the fall of his trousers. "Here, now."

"I do not recall you being so demanding." His chuckle became a hiss when her fingers captured him.

"Woman…" he croaked.

Releasing him, Kitty stepped away and unhurriedly pulled her petticoat over her head and flung it to one side. Preferring not to wear stays, she stood in naught but her stockings, and chemise. The fine material doing nothing to hide her svelte figure.

"Kitty," adoration in his tone, Adam caught her hand and drew her to him.

"Love me, Adam," she whispered.

"Always." Requiring no second bidding, Adam removed the last of Kitty's undergarments, taking especial delight in rolling her delicate stockings down her leg, chasing after the silk with his lips. He kissed the scar on her knee, recalling the day it happened. They had been entwined for nigh on two decades.

Beginning at Kitty's feet, he explored every inch of her body with his hands and his mouth, drawing her to the precipice again and again, without allowing her to tip over the edge.

Kitty, starting to think she had died and gone to heaven, tugged at the waistband of Adam's trousers.

"Get these off." She huffed, trying to push them over his hips, with little success.

Amused and aroused by Kitty's audacity, Adam stood. Kicking off his shoes he shrugged out of his trousers.

Kitty stared, unashamedly. Adam was a masterpiece. His upper body was riveting enough, but now she could see all of him. Powerful legs, honed from his military training and the hours of walking since his discharge from hospital, supported taut hips, tapering slightly at his waist only to widen into the inverted v of his chest.

There was no doubt he wanted her, the sight of which unleashed a primitive hunger.

The last vestiges of decorum fled.

A split-second's hesitation, then they came together in frenzied haste.

To touch, to feel, to inflame, to revive...

...to rescue.

The smouldering ashes ignited.

# CHAPTER NINETEEN

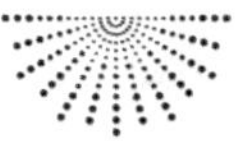

$\mathcal{A}$dam's jacket became a makeshift rug onto which they tumbled. Neither was a stranger to sex and how to satisfy their partner. Adam and Gwendolyn shared a bed, regularly; even Godfrey had been a skilled lover when he chose. Nothing could have prepared the couple in the folly for the potency of their passion.

At once they were seducer and seduced. Their love-making savage and tender, fierce and reverent, enticing and beguiling; each taking the other to heights unequalled.


Holding himself above Kitty, Adam was momentarily trans-fixed by the beauty of the woman beneath him. Her adorably dishevelled hair, billowed around her in golden abundance.

Her slightly parted lips, swollen from his kisses. Her cheeks a becoming pink. The sheen on her porcelain skin, luminescent in the moonlight. The dark green depths of her eyes glinting with the strength of her emotion.

. . .

Kitty could feel the tension in Adam's body as he strove to maintain his rapidly evaporating restraint; stunned and elated that she had this effect on him.

Cupping his jaw with one hand, she smoothed her thumb along the ridge of his lip, while her other described leisurely patterns across his body. His eyes glittered like polished obsidian and she swore he could see without hindrance.

His shock of dark hair framed a ruggedly handsome face, the scars on which she no longer noticed.

To Kitty, Adam was perfect.


Her eyes on his, she arched upwards, applying slight pressure to his back.

The urgency to possess her, outweighed Adam's ability to contain his ardour, and he sank into her heat with a muffled roar.

Sensations running rampant through her, Kitty hooked her legs around Adam's thighs driving him deeper. Impossibly, her body appeared to recognise this exquisite joining for, as they began to move, their rhythm although torrid had a familiar harmony.

Hands caressed, lips meshed, and cries mingled, as Adam controlled the tempo, letting the pleasure build, carrying Kitty inexorably to the crest.

She writhed underneath him, a hint of the ecstasy awaiting her hovering tantalisingly out of reach. Her gyrations undermined Adam's resolve to take his time, to stretch out the euphoria.

"I love you, Kitty," he rasped.

They crashed over the cliff together, hearts pounding, breathing erratic, bodies slick.

. . .

Her body thrumming, Kitty savoured being enfolded in Adam's arms. A tiny corner of her brain was hell bent on scolding her for being unconscionably brazen, while the majority basked in the glory of being utterly satiated.

She stretched like a cat, desire kindling back into life when Adam's hand trailed over her nakedness.

"I want to do this every day until we are too old to recall our names." She lifted over him, the shining swathe of her hair creating a curtain around their heads.

"I can find no fault with your proposal," Adam replied, weaving his sorcery.

Her breathing hitched, his fingers stoking the fire. She bent her mouth to his. "Again, my knight? You are insatiable."

He bestowed on her a wolfish smile. "I think you will find when it comes to you, my princess, I am voracious. My appetite will never be slaked."

To which he attested without delay and to Kitty's bliss.

Under the ethereal lustre of the harvest moon, Adam embraced his fate.

"Would you be amenable to accompanying me to London?" Adam asked while they wended their dilatory way home, looking decidedly tousled, despite their best efforts.

"I should like that very much, but are you sure you can be bothered with an entourage?" Kitty suspected the appointments with his doctor would be enervating. "After a long day of tests, you might desire solitude."

He squeezed her hand resting on his arm. "Your presence would be more soothing than being alone."

"You say that now, but I will have to take Evie. She is too

young to be left for the duration, and what about Oscar?" She nudged his shoulder. "I ask again, are you sure?"

"I am certain. My assumption, prior to asking and were you agreeable, was to take the children. Undoubtedly, they will find the journey boring, but the city has parks and sights aplenty to keep them occupied. It is new to Oscar. We left when he was a babe."

"As long as you understand what you are letting yourself in for. Two children in an enclosed carriage for two days can be, at best, taxing."

She heard Adam's soft laughter. It was the most captivating sound.

"You can distract them with a story. I know of one Oscar is partial to hearing." He adopted an innocent expression.

Astonished, she twisted to stare at him. "Was *that* what gave me away?"

He nodded. "I overheard you, the afternoon of the storm. You were narrating our story, and a number of apparently unconnected factors coalesced."

"I thought you had guessed when Oscar told you about thunder being God tossing out old furniture," Kitty said ruefully. "It never occurred to me, he would mention that, although why escapes me."

"That did take me by surprise, but my brain told me I was imagining it. The only people who could know, were far from Easby Hall. I had to assume it was pure coincidence. Until that afternoon."

"That was a trifle imprudent," she conceded. "Perhaps subconsciously I wanted to get caught. It was getting harder and harder to maintain my equanimity when you were near. Thank goodness you disliked the idea of a governess. It kept you at a distance far longer than I anticipated."

She chuckled. "Oh, what a tangled web we weave…"

"...when first we practice to deceive." Adam finished for her.

"Oh, you know of Scott?" she quizzed with a rapturous sigh.

"It is a tale Mama insisted on reading to me while I was in hospital. It was a recent publication, and she decided my mind needed edification. 'Tis a very long poem." He rolled his eyes dramatically. "How did you come across it?"

Amused at his disgust, she said, "I read it at Asquith Place. Fortuitously, *he* had an extensive library and liked to purchase any newly published novels. He aspired to be considered educated and philanthropic, a supporter of the arts in all their forms.

"He did not like me to read them, a well-read wife was not acceptable. Risking his wrath by flouting his directives, I used to sneak as many as I could when he was in the City. Luckily, none of his staff was disposed to betray my transgression."

She shook her head banishing unpleasant memories. "'Tis an odd tale, not wholly dissimilar to ours, which might be why the line popped into my head... thankfully, without anyone being walled up in a convent."

The couple spent the remainder of the walk discussing the merits of the poem and other such stories.

The Hall was in darkness. As they slipped in through the side door off the terrace and crept along the dim corridors, Kitty was prone to giggle.

"I feel like a naughty child who snuck out to play, after being sent to bed without any dinner." She gurgled. "Oh my, what if we are discovered?" She clapped a hand over her mouth.

Adam stifled his mirth. "Kitty, we are both adults and widowed to boot. That said, I am fairly certain our protracted absence has been noted by the entire household. 'Tis glad I am they are discreet."

They climbed the stairs, heading first to the nursery. Peeping in, they saw their respective children fast asleep. The moonlight through the unshuttered windows, illuminating faces angelic in repose.

"How adorable," Kitty murmured. "Look at them. Who would guess how these two frolic about when awake?" A fond smile curving her lips.

Adam drew her out onto the landing, closing the door with a muffled click.

"Come." He led her in the opposite direction to her bedchamber.

She hurried to keep pace, as ever amazed by how easily Adam navigated the Hall. "Where are we going?"

The clock at the bottom of the stairs struck the hour.

"Gracious me, 'tis one in the morning. I have not been up this late since…" she stopped.

Insomnia had been her companion for much of the past four years. Initially because of her husband, and then it became entrenched. It was only latterly she had enjoyed an undisturbed night's sleep.

"Since when?"

"Not important. Where are you taking me? My bedchamber is the other way."

"Sleep with me?"

Kitty came to a halt so abruptly, Adam almost tripped over her foot.

"B-beg p-pardon?" Shock making her stammer.

"The thought of saying goodnight and sleeping alone after… is unappealing. I want you by my side every night. I know it flouts convention, but I do not want to wait until we are wed."

Kitty stared. To share his bed... her body thrilled to the idea, while her head tried to slap some sense into her. *Wait... did he just say wed?*

"Wed? Adam you have not asked for my hand. Never mind that, what of your parents? Of propriety?" She huffed a sigh, only to add ingenuously. "Although to sleep next to you is a most inviting prospect." That image of them tangled together naked popping back into her mind. Heat rushed up her cheeks.

He brushed his lips to hers. "Please." His hands began their dance, extinguishing rational argument. "Sleep with me tonight, and on the morrow, I will speak to my parents and explain my reasoning. I do not expect them to deny my petition."

"The children." Kitty could feel herself capitulating. *My, but he could turn her brain to porridge with a single kiss.*

"Are safe under Mabel's care. You do not sleep in the nursery. They cannot miss you. I wake with the dawn as, I understand, do you. None will be any the wiser."

"You are rather devious." Kitty angled her head, lured by the illicit nature of Adam's plea as much as his sinfully sensuous kisses.

"I had a good teacher," he replied, archly. "Please."

Grasping his hand, she pressed a kiss to his knuckles and echoed her earlier words.

"Take me to bed, Adam."


Adam's suite was a larger version of Kitty's. Masculine in its décor, the dark wood and materials of muted hues reflected its owner. Blazing logs crackled in the huge hearth. Interesting shadows, created by the leaping flames, cavorted over the textured wallpaper.

The room was suffused with a soft glow given off by two candelabra, one in the centre of the mantelpiece and the other atop a table tucked into a corner.

Through an open door to her left, Kitty spied a dressing room complete with bath. There was another door, currently closed, which, she discovered later, accessed a private study.

Focused on admiring the space, she did not notice Adam retrieve something from the ornate cabinet by his bed.

Returning to where she stood, he swept a bow, dropped to one knee and, in a gesture befitting knights of yore, proposed.

"Katherine de Wilton, my princess, my heart, my soul, my beginning and my end, please grant this lowly knight the honour of your hand in marriage. I hereby swear my allegiance to you and vow to love and cherish you 'til the end of my days."

Had she been irresolute… which she wasn't… his old-fashioned language would have won her acceptance. Kitty's heart was pounding so hard she was certain he could hear it. She opened her mouth, nothing came out, not even a squeak. She swallowed and marshalled her capricious brain.

"Yes, yes, yes, *yes*, **yes!**" She fell on her knees beside him, flung her arms around his neck and kissed him with a fervour which escalated so swiftly, they ended up making love on the rug, in front of the fire.

Adam requested a moment of his parents' time as they were finishing breakfast the next morning. Out of their son's line of sight, Prudence and Reginald exchanged knowing glances.

There was little the couple did not discuss. Prudence had

disclosed Kitty's unease regarding Adam distancing himself, generating concern as to what had kept the pair out so late last evening.

When Prudence brought Adam home to Easby Hall five years previously, she was resolved not to squander the progress achieved when he was in St Bart's, and dedicated herself to ensuring he did not regress into the darkness. This included counselling her son to express his feelings, emotions, thoughts — anything at all relating to his wounds and his grief.

Unusually for families of the *ton*, the Marchmains preferred their children to talk about whatever they chose, rather than bottle things up. Prudence was unobtrusive but indefatigable in her endeavours, aware how easily he could shut down.

Witness to Adam's increasing devotion for Kitty, Reginald and she rejoiced but remained cautious. Adam's tendency to second guess everything following his injury, meant his apparent change of heart was not unexpected.

When Adam and Kitty took their walk the previous night, Prudence had warned Reginald of the consequences, should Adam reject Kitty. Their son was not the only one who was vulnerable and fragile.

Thus, his parents were primed for the worst, only to be surprised when Adam announced his betrothal. Their congratulations mildly tempered by his added solicitation that they turn a blind eye to who slept where. Among polite society, sharing a bed prior to marriage was outwardly forbidden, irrespective of what might go on behind closed doors.

Kitty and Adam were both widowed, meaning their constraints were perhaps less strict. Reginald did feel moved to suggest, the couple consider marrying with minimal delay, to stave off spurious tittle-tattle. While their staff was discreet, rumour inevitably found a way to leak out.

# CHAPTER TWENTY

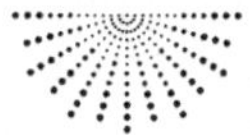

itty was eating breakfast with Oscar and Evie when the duke and duchess swept into the nursery, Adam on their heels.

"I am very pleased, my dear," Prudence spoke in Kitty's ear, enveloping her soon-to-be daughter-in-law in a loving hug. "I knew my plan would have a felicitous ending." Blithely dismissing the recent upheaval.

Kitty lifted a sceptical brow.

Prudence raised her palms. "I admit there were a few hiccups, not least that Adam might be unable to forgive our, my," she amended, "interference, but he is not my son for nothing." Her impish wink revealing a hint of her headstrong youth.

She grasped Kitty's hand and reached for Adam. "If you two are half as happy as your father and me, your marriage will be blessed. Permit me to offer a few words of advice. Never go to bed angry, and never let pride come between you. Communication is vital, if you fall silent, you have failed.

"To love someone is only one part of marriage. Of equal

importance is supporting, respecting, and understanding each other. Be patient, be kind, and be generous of spirit. These qualities are what sustain a union when the first flush of passion fades.

"When you argue, for you will argue and there is nothing wrong with healthy debate, be as quick to apologise. Make the effort to see the other's point of view and, if your opinions continue to differ, agree to disagree. To be in accord on every little thing can lead to boredom."

She swung her gaze between the two.

"As for your children, always show a unified front. Any sense of disharmony can undermine their trust, their confidence in themselves and their family as a whole, as well as adversely affect their approach to life. Last, but not least, while I concede certain boundaries are essential, you must also love them enough not to hold on too tightly."

Oscar and Evie were listening to all this with varying degrees of confusion. Too young to grasp the significance of this moment, Evie's attention soon reverted to her breakfast, most of which she was wearing, but Oscar was possessed of a canny intelligence.

Unbidden, he was reminded of the fairy tales he pestered Kitty to narrate over and over again. Nearly every story concluded with something called a wedding which was always followed by a happily ever after.

"Papa, are you going to wedding Mrs Lovell?" His piping tones slicing through the air.

Smothering a grin at Oscar's misinterpretation of the word, Kitty looked at Adam. In some ways, telling Oscar was harder than apprising Aunt Prudence and Uncle Reginald. His world was about to undergo a drastic change, one at which he might balk.

Crouching, so she was eye level with the little boy, Kitty crooked her finger. Sidling over, he leant against her.

"When two people have a wedding it is called getting married. Yes, your Papa would like to marry me, but we wanted to ask your permission first," she said.

Oscar folded his arms and scrunched up his face, unsure what she meant. "'S'plain, please."

Adam sat cross legged on the floor next to Kitty and pulled Oscar onto his lap. "Do you think it is a good idea for me to marry Mrs Lovell? If I do, she will become my wife and your mama."

Oscar looked at his father, then Kitty, then back to his father. "I would have a mama, like Evie?" His eyes and mouth grew round.

Kitty nodded, blinking back tears at the child's hopeful expression. "Would you like that, Oscar?" She held her breath. Kitty believed Oscar and she had formed a loving bond but, if the child was uncomfortable with her being a more permanent part of his life, she had no intention of forcing it upon him, however heartbreaking it would be.

"Ohhhhhhhhhhhhh." He pressed his hands together as though praying, a beatific smile spreading across his face. "You would be my mama?" He pinned Kitty with an exultant gaze, his grey eyes gleaming with excitement.

"Yes," she affirmed, exhaling slowly, the knot in her stomach easing.

"Oh, goodie." Oscar hurled himself at her, squeezed her tightly, and landed several sticky kisses on her cheeks.

"Me too, me too." Not one to be left out, Evie slid out of her chair and toddled over to join in. Kitty disappeared under a swarm of arms and legs, chortling voices, and the smacking of kisses.

"I am going to take that as approval." Adam grinned, relief making him slightly giddy. "Come now, you are squashing

Kitty." Standing, he looped a hand around each wriggling child. Lifting them off Kitty, he hugged both to him.

Evie immediately stroked his cheek. "Sir Pwetty." She beamed at her favourite man.

"That means Evie will have a new papa," Oscar trilled. This news was getting better and better.

Another thought struck him. Without overwhelming the child, Kitty had begun to teach him about his family and had drawn a simple family tree as a visual aide.

He canted his head to study his father. "If you are my papa, and Mrs Lovell is my mama does than make Evie my sister?"

"It does." Adam nodded.

"Lawks!" Oscar exclaimed to the hastily masked hilarity of the adults in the room.

"Perhaps a quiet word in Mabel's ear," Reginald lamented, his expression pained. "Not even six years old." He shook his head in resignation.

Kitty chuckled. "Regrettably, unless we cover his ears all the time, overhearing the odd expletive is unavoidable. Best ignored, soon forgotten. If he thinks 'tis a naughty word, he will repeat it in gleeful ad nauseam."

"True, true," Reginald conceded, "and on that note, my dear." He looked at his wife. "'Tis time we left these four to their day. Adam, when you are done here, please join me in the study with regard to London." Reginald nodded to his son, offered his arm to Prudence, and the two strolled out


Kitty and Adam spent the next little while with the children, answering Oscar's eager questions, which ranged from the expected to the nonsensical, reducing the two adults to gales of laughter.

Shortly thereafter, Adam went off to the appointed

meeting with his father, Mabel gathered up Evie, and Kitty began Oscar's lessons.

In the event, Kitty persuaded Adam to move into her bedchamber, rather than the other way around. The decor was brighter, the rooms airier, and she was closer to the children.

A connecting door, now unlocked, linked Kitty's suite to a reasonably sized and currently empty room. Purloining it as a dressing room, Adam asked Elias and Ben — another of the Marchmains' footmen — to transfer everything across. He had to agree with his betrothed; there was cheeriness in her chambers, lacking in his own.

Adamant she would continue teaching Oscar, Kitty had discussed the matter at length with Adam — and in a far more sober fashion than her first attempt — who had no objections. Kitty teaching his son, and including her daughter when Evie was old enough, was a far more favourable option than repeating the excruciating rigmarole of hiring yet another governess.

Oscar, with Kitty's thrilled permission, immediately began calling her, Mama. Evie, to the amusement of her mother and her soon-to-be father, continued to refer to Adam as Sir Pwetty in spite of Kitty's coaxing.

One and all, the staff of Easby Hall congratulated Adam and Kitty on their betrothal. Mabel alluded to a friendly wager being held behind the baize door, but they had been laying odds on when rather than if.

Kitty thanked them for their good wishes, assuring them nothing had changed. She was still just Kitty; the girl from next door who used to run amok, a governess who just happened to be a viscountess.

Her loyalty to those in the domestic sphere was appreciated and reciprocated from the lowest scullery maid to the butler. A sentiment about to be put to the test.

~

Preparations for the trip to London began apace. Trunks materialised. Autumn in the capital could be cold, so clothes and shoes were picked over for suitability and, if chosen, cleaned.

Shortly after dawn five days later, the Teasdale town coach rattled down the long drive, beginning the journey to London. A veritable mountain of luggage was strapped to the back, six black horses harnessed to the front, the smartly liveried driver and groom sitting up top.

Their inordinately early start was to avoid an overnight stop; Kitty being disinclined to expose either Evie or Oscar to the dubious attractions offered by a coaching inn.

The weather was kind and the journey uneventful, if tedious. The carriage kept good time and drew up outside The Laurels, not long after nightfall. Nestled in a leafy street off Grosvenor Square, the elegant town house was a welcome sight to the four weary travellers, two of whom were fast asleep. After being assisted down, they were ushered into the cosy hall.

Mr Pembroke, the butler, greeted them, as maids and footmen scurried about fetching luggage. The driver and groom pointed the coach in the direction of the mews, where they saw to the needs of the horses before hunting down their own meal.

A thorough wash to rinse off the dust of the day, followed by a scrumptious dinner and the four were tucked up in bed. Slumber claimed them before the clock struck ten.

*A Coaching Inn not far from Chiddingstone, Kent*

Silas Dryden was annoyed… no that was too polite a term… he was infuriated. A boring horse ride, a night on, what he swore was, a louse infested mattress, and meals he could only describe as slop, for what? A big fat nothing. The bloody chit was not even *at* Grafton Manor. Which begged the question, *where the hell was she?*

With practised guile, he had tried every trick he knew to extract information from the estate workers scattered across the Manor grounds. Without fail, they remained tight lipped, even under threat of violence, something he generally avoided when alone.

One sharp jab with a pitchfork and he'd be buried under a pile of cow dung without anyone being the wiser. He acknowledged a reluctant admiration for their allegiance; he could use people like that in his business.

Back at the inn, he deliberated over his next move. He felt like he was stuck in a bad dream or one of those Drury

Lane farces where all the characters kept missing each other.

*Was it really worth all this effort?*

He mused over the likelihood Lady Asquith had been oblivious to her husband's business dealings. In this instance, his gut instinct was no help.

The rumours about Godfrey Lovell, the less than esteemed Viscount Asquith, painted him as a bounder of the first order. As far as Silas knew, the man had treated everyone with equal contempt. This trait had precipitated the course of action which led to his death.

*Was the viscountess cut from the same cloth, or was she as much a victim as he?* To Silas, Godfrey's actions were an egregious betrayal, justifying the latter's brutal demise, while conveniently ignoring his own depravity.

While supping a well-deserved pint of ale, he caught an odd word about the movements of the local nobility. His ears pricked up. At the far side of the tap room, a handful of farmhands were chatting about their day.

Candid conversation often provided useful information, and Silas edged closer. Propping himself against a wooden upright which formed part of the interior framework, Silas pulled his cap low over his face, and tried to make himself invisible.

"Ay, 'twas this morn they left, barely daybreak." One of them answered another's question I was 'eading to Home Farm when this 'uge coach thundered past, six horses. I had to skip out the way smartish like. Spotted the Arms, it was Lord Teasdale's carriage. I 'eard they was off up to London for at least a fortnight. Poor bugger that."

There was a collective mutter of agreement.

Silas, with no idea who the 'poor bugger' was, prayed they

might elaborate. To his undying and tacit gratitude, their conversation continued in this vein, including mention of Lord Teasdale's war wounds and that, recently, he had become betrothed to the elder of Lord Grafton's two daughters.

"Aye, but that'll be a spirited union. Lady Katherine was a rare one for fun when she were growing up. Din't she marry that Lord Whatisname who were killed?" The first man quizzed.

In the resulting debate, each threw out names until one of them recollected it was the Viscount Asquith. This was followed up by mention of one or two of Kitty's more fool-hardy exploits as a child, which led to a discussion about their own offspring.

As nothing else useful was forthcoming, Silas — amazed men such as these gave any thought to members of the *ton*, never mind be able to recall their titles — tuned them out. He meandered casually through the patrons to an empty corner, where he mulled over their words.

The Lady Asquith they were talking about did not match his recall. He had seen her intermittently, when spying on Godfrey, but everything about her appeared drab and colourless. It was as though she was trying to fade into the background, a wraith of a person. The antithesis of the woman these people knew.

His own hypothesis regarding Godfrey's behaviour gave him momentary pause. It was over two years since the man's death. Had she been cognisant of, or inadvertently uncovered, his business affairs and wanted to become involved, would she not have made contact?

If she intended to apprise the Runners, or even enlist her own investigator to take a closer look into her husband's murder, why delay? It would make sense to do so upon his death. Her waif-like figure and downcast visage drifted through his mind again. Perhaps it was time to renounce his quest.

Then those unsettling incidents reared up, and his resolve stiffened. He would discover the truth, whatever it took. He had no time for sympathy. If she was trying to undermine his venture, to steal his profits or worse, denounce him and all he had worked for to the authorities, she would pay.

The next morning, Silas spent fruitless hours scouting around Easby Hall, hoping to solicit extra fragments of information relating to Lady Katherine, Viscountess Asquith.

As with Grafton Manor, he came up short. In fact, the staff and estate workers here were even more circumspect about the woman in question. Had he not known better, Silas would swear she was a figment of his imagination.

She was fortunate indeed to engender such fealty.

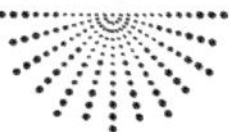

# CHAPTER TWENTY-ONE

LONDON ~ OCTOBER 1815

For Adam, the first few days in the city were taken up with hospital visits. Doctor Latham — under whose care Adam had been while at St Bart's and every six months since his discharge — examined his former patient meticulously, in consultation with his colleague Dr Napier.

All too familiar with the gruesome variety of wounds they ministered to with depressing regularity, the two medical men were endlessly relieved the war appeared to be over.

Scarred skin often lost sensation, meaning infection could lie undetected, if not checked regularly. Thankfully, Dr Latham had instilled into Adam the importance of applying a balm to his ruined flesh. A blend of calendula, flaxseed, honey and myrrh, the ointment — the aroma of which had so bewitched Kitty — protected his skin and kept it supple. Neither doctor observed anything to cause them concern.

While Adam's skin had strengthened and some of the scarring was less distinctive, the disfigurement was permanent, as was his diminished eyesight. There was definite improvement since his admission to St Bart's, five years previously, but Adam had been cautioned, as kindly as possible, not to anticipate a full recovery. The damage was simply too extensive. The doctors *were* encouraged by Adam's ability to distinguish details at short range for, if nothing else, it meant he could build a picture in his mind of his surrounds and the people in it. Conversance was key.

The comprehensive series of rigorous examinations and tests concluded, Dr Latham affirmed Adam was as healthy as an ox and, to continue with the regimen already instituted.

"I think a year unless you experience any problems," the doctor said with a smile. "Go, make the most of your time in the city. Take your betrothed to the museum, or one of the art galleries. Wonderful places to spend quality time together."

Adam's lip curled. "What point is there in visiting either? Totally wasted on me."

"Yes, but I expect Kitty…" as she had asked both doctors to call her when she accompanied Adam to the hospital for his second appointment, "…would gain an inordinate amount of pleasure from visiting them and, I daresay, be more than happy to describe what you struggle to see."

The doctor cocked his head, contemplatively. "'Tis essential you try to live as normal a life as possible, Adam. I accept you chafe against your limitations, but you have changed markedly since your last appointment. You are at ease with yourself, even jovial, a far cry from the sullen lieutenant I saw six months ago." Dr Latham paused. "I can only assume Lady Asquith is responsible."

Adam flushed, and bowed his head. While personal discussions had become the norm with his doctor, especially when he was at his lowest ebb, this was different. "I… err… hmmm…" he prevaricated.

"Take it from me, ladies relish an afternoon with their

swain, and I imagine Kitty has had little opportunity to benefit from such enlightening pastimes of late." Dr Latham, not incognisant of the late viscount's reputation, suggested delicately. The *ton*, disgusted by Godfrey's dishonourable behaviour, had been less than diplomatic, and rumour had spread far beyond its usual confines.

Leaving it at that, the two men chatted about other matters for a few more minutes and shortly thereafter, Adam was sitting in his carriage, savouring the fresh autumn breeze on his face.

Kitty did not sit by idly while Adam was otherwise occupied. Although she favoured the serenity of the countryside, she had to admit it was fun to be in the bustling capital once more.

She took Oscar and Evie to Hyde Park, treated them to a hot chocolate at Gunter's, took the second and much smaller carriage to the embankment and showed them the Thames. Oscar was rapt to see the ships sailing up and down the busy river, perfectly happy to watch them for hours.

While the children were under the watchful eye of the staff at The Laurels, Kitty indulged in a little pampering, in the form of an afternoon with her modiste.

It was at least four years since Kitty had visited Madame Renaud's boutique, and the latter declared herself elated at being able to dress one of her favourite customers. Her Gallic accent becoming more pronounced in her delight.

"Ah, but you 'ave filled out a little, my lady and your 'air, she is shiny once more. I think you are 'appy *non*?" She gave a sly smile and Kitty blushed.

"You were too, *too* thin, and melancholy. I 'ear 'e is dead, *non*?" She arched a finely shaped brow while measuring; an assistant amending the precise notes the dressmaker maintained.

"Yes, he died more than two years ago and, you are correct, I *am* happy. Thank you, Madame Renaud."

"A beau?"

Kitty blushed again. "I am newly betrothed to Lord Teasdale. He was someone I knew when a child and we met again recently, after many years. He is a widower—"

"Wait, 'e is the marquis who was married to Lady Gwendolyn, *oui?*" Madame Renaud interrupted. "Oh, that was a sad business." There was a pause. "She was one of my ladies, eh, Celeste?" The modiste nodded at her assistant who looked suitably sorrowful.

"Still, you 'ave found each other, and no more grief." She shrugged, a fatalistic gesture and changed the subject, banishing the spectre of Adam's wife with the flick of a bright blue ribbon.


By the end of the afternoon, Kitty had been tempted into a dozen new gowns of various styles, matching shoes, boots, gloves, and hats, plus two cloaks. This, unheard of extravagance, was justified because Madame Renaud had tsked and reminded Kitty how long it had been since she last bought anything from her boutique. Moreover, being betrothed, she should consider this part of her trousseau.

While Kitty's new wardrobe would be made from the finest fabrics and in a rainbow of hues, she had chosen practicality over frivolity; favouring day dresses and limiting ball gowns to two. Frugality aside, she was thrilled with her purchases.

Throughout Kitty's short marriage, Godfrey had alleged any garments were purely to titillate her supposed lovers. Refreshing her wardrobe would only fuel his distrust. She had become thrifty and, already clever with a needle, made do with what she had.

To spend without being afraid of the repercussions was liberating, even more so because Madame Renaud had persuaded her into a particular ensemble, Kitty hoped would turn Adam's head to mush.

Silas arrived back in London and went straight to his 'office' — a grand title for the shabby room on the third floor above Dryden's Den, a gaming hell and brothel. He and three of his men had mediocre accommodation on the same level. It provided a useful cover for his operation and he did not have to look far for entertainment.

Harold, who was sampling the charms on offer in a convenient alcove, heard the thunder of familiar boots. Pushing off the buxom woman, he yanked on his britches and scarpered up the stairs. Silas had returned alone. *Was that good or bad news?* Harold was not going to dally in finding out.

"Success?" he asked, praying the answer would be in the affirmative. A wasted journey boded ill.

"Not exactly, but not a complete failure." Silas was in his chair, resting his chin on steepled fingers. "The chit left for London the day I got there," he grumbled.

Give him his due, Harold kept his features schooled, banking down the laughter rising up at the series of images this evoked. "Bugger," was all he said.

"Mind, I over 'eard a good tip. She's courting a certain Lord Teasdale. Apparently, 'e were wounded in the war, can't see too well *and* 'e 'appens to be the son of the Duke of Easby. You know, him who 'as that massive place on Berkeley Square."

He ruminated for a few seconds, then snapped his fingers. "Marchmain Court, that's it. Werf going for a look-see."

"Want me ter go now?" Harold tried to sound eager, his chance for an evening with his favourite whore, dwindling.

"Nah, tomorrow's fine."

Visibly, Harold relaxed.

Silas grinned.

"Go on wiv yer, I saw yer straddlin' Sadie. Best go make sure she 'asn't 'ad a better offer." Silas chortled at the speed with which Harold fled. "Ten sharp," he yelled after his second, before calling for his own evening's entertainment.

After discounting Marchmain Court as their quarry's place of residence, Harold discovered Lord Teasdale had retained his own house, The Laurels, and decided to try his luck there. When he saw a gentleman whom he assumed was the Marquis of Teasdale, step out with Lady Asquith, he almost crowed his success.

Loitering in the bushes, Harold, who considered himself a ghost when he was tracking someone, was not quite careful enough.

Small children often notice things adults miss, without recognising the significance. Oscar liked to watch the comings and goings of the street and spent hours sitting at the nursery window.

It was all movement and colour and noise. Horses, carriages, children driving hoops, elegantly dressed couples taking constitutionals. Scenes far removed from his life at Easby Hall.

Arm in arm, his father and Kitty strolled down the street, chatting animatedly, turning to wave before disappearing around the corner. As the little boy's gaze swivelled back, he spotted an unkempt figure lurking in the private garden across from the town house.

Despite his young age, Oscar registered that this person did not fit the surroundings. Unsettled by the stranger's furtive demeanour, the child watched until Hettie, the maid assigned to the children in Adam and Kitty's absence, called him over to play a game… and, for a while, he forgot.


Pleased with his day's work, Harold — who had no idea his movements had been witnessed — reported his findings. His target located, Silas ruminated over how to extort a confession. He needed to catch her unawares and alone. Lord Teasdale might be impaired, but Harold's description was of a man capable of inflicting harm if challenged. It might take a little vigilance, but he was too close to stop now.

On a cold, grey, damp morning, his plan — and he believed it infallible — in place, Silas summoned Harold. Splurging on a hackney, for concealment and speed of getaway, the pair set off for the gentrified streets of Mayfair.

Three days of surveillance had indicated his lordship, in company with another man —Harold guessed he was either a man of business or, possibly, Lord Teasdale's guide — departed the house each morning around half after ten. He returned at midday and, unless with Lady Asquith, did not leave again.

This meant they had a window of about an hour and a half to interrogate Godfrey's widow.

Silas had not apprised Harold of the entirety of his scheme, knowing his second's opinion with respect to hurting women unnecessarily. He sighed inaudibly. Once the chit had seen his face, she could identify him, and he never left a trail. The biggest hurdle was how to get her to come outside… alone, when customarily the butler or a footman greeted callers.

Between them, they had decided that, while Harold caused a commotion just out of sight, Silas would bang on the door and beg for assistance. Should one of the male staff answer the knock, he would surely make all haste to help the kerfuffle. If it was a maid, she could be silenced and then 'encouraged' to lead Silas to her ladyship.

For a man who had orchestrated hundreds of schemes in his life, this one contained a *lot* of holes. In his defence — if one was inclined to grant him an excuse for what he was about to do — this was the first time Silas had found it germane to confront a member of the nobility within their dwelling. Normally, he had them brought to him, deep inside the Rookeries.

To the relief of both men, this convoluted and fraught scenario was not required. Leaving the hackney with the driver, who was under strict instructions to wait or else, the two strolled casually towards The Laurels discussing their next move.

Upon their approach, they saw the front door opening. A woman dressed for the chill morning, came out; a little girl on her hip and a small boy holding her hand.

Harold pushed the gate.

"Mama," the little boy said in a loud whisper, "'tis him."

"Who, sweetheart?" Slightly distracted, the woman took no notice of the people walking up the short path, and bent low to listen.

"That man." The boy pointed at Harold. "I saw him."

She pivoted on her heel, spotting the two men who had come to a halt half-way between the gate and the bottom of the short flight of steps.

Nobody moved.

In undertones, the woman said something to the child who fled inside, banging the door behind him.

"May I help you?" Her question was polite, but her gaze narrowed.

"I 'ope so, yer ladyship." Silas came forward. "'Cause, it'll be the worse for you if yer don't." Menace clear in his tone.

"Do I know you?" Her voice was cold enough to freeze a blacksmith's forge.

"No, Silas Dryden at your service." Removing his cap, he swept a bow. "I knew yer dearly departed 'usband." Silas replaced his hat.

Her expression was disbelieving. "I sincerely doubt that but, do please enlighten me."

Aware he had to tell her or leave and risk her informing the Runners, Silas lounged against the stone pillar at the foot of the steps and outlined the business he was in.

He and a handful of his most trusted men, 'sourced' women from all over the city. Once selected they were subjected to a vigorous examination to ensure they looked to be healthy, had good teeth, and were lice free.

They were taken either to a wharf along the Thames or — if perhaps a little past their prime, or not attractive enough — removed to one of a selection of brothels spread around the Rookeries.

# CHAPTER TWENTY-TWO

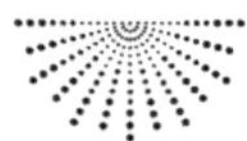

*I*n appalled fascination, Kitty stared at the pair of reprobates on her doorstep. "What does any of this have to do with me?"

Silas tucked his thumbs under the flaps of his jacket and rocked on his heels. Trying to sound cultured, he intoned, "Your 'usband financed me ventures and the cash is running dry. Furvermore, I fink yer know abaht it and either want a cut of me profits or 'ave been trying to set up yer own business. I don't like competition. Mind yer'd bring a pretty penny."

He raked his eyes up and down her willowy figure.

His gaze made Kitty's skin crawl, while she regarded him slack-jawed.

"My husband paid you to steal women?" Her voice rose at least one octave, shaking her head in an attempt to make sense of his words.

*Godfrey? Smuggling people? How had she missed that?*

. . .

Unbidden, a comment her solicitor had made when discussing the Asquith assets popped into her head.

'For the last five years, there was a regular monthly withdrawal. The same amount on the same day. Your husband was meticulous with his accounts except for this particular transaction, and it was a considerable sum. We have no idea what it was for. It stopped at his death, implying a possible connection, but that is mere supposition.'

She coaxed her brain back to the more crucial matter. "How did my husband finance your… errr… operation?" Temporarily, Kitty's curiosity overcame her panic.

"It was 'is money set it all up, including me expenses for the office and me lads. I 'as to 'ave trustwervy accomplices yer know. We met by accident at the races," he reflected, stroking his chin. "Must be six year ago now. We got to talkin'. Seems he required someone of my calibre to 'andle 'is business, because 'is previous lackey 'ad done a runner. He paid me to take the risks. We met once a month. I showed 'im me book, 'e gave me the money."

*That explained the undocumented outgoings.* A terrible suspicion gnawed at Kitty's consciousness. "Wait… wharf? Why take them to the wharf?"

"To put 'em on the ship?" He scoffed as though that was blindingly obvious.

"A ship to where?" she pressed, faintly.

"Europe, the Americas, or India." Silas shrugged carelessly.


Once the damn wenches were aboard, Silas didn't much care where they ended up. His end of the bargain was complete. The payment he received from Godfrey went towards the upkeep of the women prior and during their voyage. Godfrey had secured a ship, whose captain and crew were willing to transport the *cargo* anywhere in the world, no questions asked.

An overseer accompanied every shipment to ensure the women were treated properly; a dead chit was worthless. Essentially the middleman, he was the one who collected payment when the women disembarked, and the minimal legitimate cargo sold at their destination was a bonus.

The ship's hold was packed with genuine merchandise for the return journey; silks, spices, tea, furs, hemp, and tobacco — to name but a few. Every voyage garnered appreciable income, and the management of revenue was tightly monitored.

Silas knew the overseer would be tempted to skim a proportion of the proceeds and always adjusted the price to allow for such an eventuality. It was a highly lucrative arrangement; the profits earned, substantial enough to keep the business flourishing long after Godfrey's death.

"Why?"

"Gawd but yer nosy. To be wives to them as need 'em. Evidently, there's not enough decent women out there, and I 'elps ter fill the gap like." Silas cocked his thumb over his shoulder.

Harold nodded his agreement. "Them'll 'ave a better life than 'ere. We're doin' 'em a favour really." He boasted, his pride in their accomplishments, undeniable.

Kitty was floored by their candid dismissal of human life. *What about the women's families? What if they had husbands, children? People who were looking for them.* Her stomach rebelled and she swallowed repeatedly to control rising nausea.

"Fill the gap? Better life?" she croaked, looking at the two men, blankly. *She was dreaming... this was some bizarre dream. Too much rich food last evening.*

"And pray, *how* do you persuade these women to do as you ask?" Unable to credit she was actually having this conversation.

*Where was Adam?*

Silas laughed, a mirthless sound. "I 'as me ways. Nuffin yer need to worry yer lovely 'ead abaht, s'long as yer pay up." He rubbed his hands together.

His words bounced around Kitty's head. How many poor gullible women going about their daily business had been lured — *or were they snatched?* — into a life which might easily be worse than the servitude they were trying to escape.

The lucky ones, if anyone could call them lucky, might, just might be fortunate to find a sympathetic husband who treated them with some kindness. It was conceivable the odd one might find love, but given the circumstances of their 'appropriation,' unlikely.

Evie fidgeted, jerking Kitty from her musings. Unwilling to draw the men's attention to her daughter, she hugged her close, settling the child more comfortably on her hip. The little girl snuggled in, oblivious to the alarm surging through her mother.

"Stop askin' questions. Pay up or it'll be the worse for yer. Do you want ter end up like 'im?" Silas growled in sinister tones.

Feeling the last vestiges of colour leach from her cheeks, Kitty gritted her teeth. She was *not* going to swoon. *This was the man who killed Godfrey.* Abhorrence of her husband aside, the last thing Kitty expected when she got up that morning was to come face-to-face with his murderer.

Kitty's stunned reaction was not feigned, and corroborated Silas' initial inkling she had no clue about Godfrey's activities. Too late now. She had seen his face; she knew too much. She had to go.

He slid his left hand into his pocket and fingered the knife secreted therein. His thumb tested the blade; it was nicely sharp. He patted the other pocket feeling the outline of his pistol.

Shame really. Not the best place to kill someone. Then there was the child. As Silas studied Kitty and Evie, the cogs began to grind in his brain.

*A handsome chit and a little girl. Lady Asquith would bring a decent price no matter where she was dispatched. Foreign parts would be better, reduced the chance of anyone tracking her down.*

"'Arold," he muttered under his breath. His second leant close. "You grab the babe. I'll get her ladyship."

"Errr... s-sir... I-I... m-maybe..." Harold stammered. He might be a bad lot, but he didn't hold with harming babies.

"I'm not gonna 'urt either of them," Silas interrupted, placatingly. "But look, she must be worth extra coin and the little one will be useful. Sadie'll look after 'er and they are best started young."

Harold was becoming less and less convinced by this scheme. As far as he could tell, the viscountess was in the dark about her husband's relationship with Silas, and the child was an innocent. "Silas, I don't think..."

"Yer not paid and 'oused and fed to think, 'Arold. Yer paid to follow my orders." Silas snarled. "We cannot walk away now. We kill 'em or we take 'em."

. . .

Silas had forgotten to keep his voice lowered and Kitty overhead his last remark. Terror roiled through her.

*Adam, where are you?* she pleaded, wordlessly.

He was still at home, somewhere. She had sent Oscar to find him and, although the Teasdale residence was sizeable, it should not be taking this long.

~

Unbeknownst to Kitty, Oscar had been diverted by Hettie. Unaware of what was unfolding on the doorstep and presuming his parents deemed it too inclement for a walk, the young maid had chivvied him upstairs to the nursery.

Precious moments ticked by before Adam who was passing the nursery heard his son chattering away with Hettie.

"Hettie? I thought Oscar was coming for a walk?"

Hettie leapt to her feet and curtsied. "I came upon him on the landing, my lord. I supposed you had decided to forgo your walk on account of the weather. Her ladyship was nowhere to be seen. I just assumed... forgive me... I..." her brow furrowed.

Something was not quite right. "My lord."

"Mama is talking to the man I saw from the window?" Oscar said, coming over to slip his hand in his father's. "She asked me to find you, and here you are." He beamed.

"Hettie, stay here with Oscar." Adam rang for Mr Pembroke and, taking care not to miss his footing, hastened down the stairs.

~

Kitty was frozen to the spot. These men who were apparently in the business of slavery, albeit couched in less brutal terms, were sizing her up, worse they wanted Evie too. The notion there was a significant likelihood she was about to be added to the next shipment, heightened Kitty's senses.

Straining her ears, she caught the sound of muffled footsteps from within the residence. *Were they coming to her aid, or was it just a maid running down the stairs?* She scanned the street. It tended to be quiet at this time of day, but she noticed a hackney waiting nearby. The impatient horse stamping its hooves.

Silas never missed an opportunity to gain the advantage. Noticing Kitty's gaze had swung away from him, he darted up the steps to seize Evie. It happened so quickly, Kitty barely registered him moving until her arms were empty.

He thrust the child at Harold, who, not expecting this, squeezed the little girl rather more tightly that he ought. Evie squeaked in surprise.

Twisting around, she fixed Harold with a disgruntled and very adult stare. Her face contorted. A sign she was about to make an ear-splitting fuss.

Kitty bit back an oath. *Do not panic,* she exhorted herself.

"Mama," the little girl wailed.

"Hush, precious, Mama's here," Kitty soothed, hoping to pacify her daughter, while her brain worked furiously. She was *not* about to stand aside while they took Evie.

Some, up until now latent, instinct prompted Harold to rock Evie, murmuring nonsense words under his breath in a bid to settle the child. Evie, hearing the comforting sounds, looked up at Harold and clutched at his beard.

"Hullo," she warbled and planted a kiss on his cheek. "Pwetty."

Harold stared, an ineffable emotion unravelling. Blinking, he swivelled his gaze to Silas, and even he was shocked when he registered the man's intent.

To Kitty's unadulterated horror, Silas drew a gun and levelled it at her. "This mite will make a splendid assistant," he crooned, reaching out to stroke Evie's cheek.

Evie was having none of it and batted at him, pulling away to bury her head in Harold's shoulder.

Patting Evie on the back, Harold muttered under his breath that this was lunacy. "Silas, we're in the middle of Mayfair, not Seven Dials. This is not the place to stage a kidnap or commit murder. On the path. In plain sight. In broad daylight."

Ignoring Harold, Silas chuckled. "When she's old enough, I'll dress her up and train her the ways of the street. No one will suspect a sweet blonde child to be a pickpocket. When she has exceeded her usefulness, I'll ship her off to the Americas."

His tone suggested Kitty ought to be grateful for his generosity. *The man was addled.*

Kitty closed her eyes, fury and fear battling for dominance. There was no time to succumb to either emotion, nor could she wait for Adam, or anyone else for that matter. It was up to her. Kitty had grown up among a gaggle of boys who took gleeful pleasure in teaching the girls in their coterie a rowdy assortment of pursuits, generally frowned upon.

Climbing trees, skimming stones across the lake, swimming and, most importantly, how to fight — with wooden swords and with fists. Had they known the full extent of their cherished daughters' escapades, their parents would have been aghast, but they never found out.

The girls, ecstatic to be included, practised whenever an occasion presented itself and had proved surprisingly proficient. Never had Kitty been so glad of the skills she learnt all those years ago.

Mentally straightening her back, Kitty glared at Silas. "If you think I am going to let you take my daughter, you are a stupid, stupid man," she snapped.

"I am not sure you have any choice," he retorted.

Several things happened, throwing the already tense scene into total chaos.

Wresting Evie from Harold, Silas commanded his second to ready the hackney.

Frightened, Evie squealed and tried to catapult herself out of Silas' arms.

Kitty hurtled down the steps, launched herself at Silas, and grappled for the gun.

The door burst open and Adam appeared.

# CHAPTER TWENTY-THREE

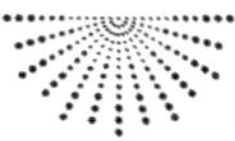

"*K*itty," Adam bawled, unable to discern who was who, or where they were standing.

"Adam, get Evie," Kitty screamed. Recalling her childhood scraps, she wrestled with Silas, managing to wrench the gun out of his hand.

Silas realised he had made a mistake by grabbing Evie. He could not fight off Kitty and keep hold of the child. *You fool*, he castigated himself, as Evie wriggled like an eel. Silas was hard pushed not to drop her.

He saw Kitty aim the gun at his chest and shifted Evie, so she became a shield.

Adam bellowed an order over his shoulder into the house and descended the steps at a run.

"Give me the gun, Kitty." He urged, skidding to a halt alongside her, his hand finding her arm.

"**No**, he is in my sights, and I am a good shot. He will *not* take my daughter," she hissed, an anger greater than anything she had ever experienced blazing through her.

Acceding, Adam edged towards her target, keeping out of the firing line.

Cursing, Silas recognised he was outnumbered and over-encumbered. Evie in his arms, intent on keeping her as leverage, he wheeled around, hearing the click of the hammer being pulled back. Presuming Lady Asquith was faking her ability to wield the weapon, Silas ignored it and began to run.

When she realised Silas was not going to relinquish her daughter, Kitty gave a shriek worthy of a banshee, and pulled the trigger, aiming low to avoid hitting Evie. The muzzle flashed and she saw Silas sag when the bullet grazed his right leg.

"'*Arold*," Silas roared, agony slicing through his thigh. "Get that bitch."

Harold leapt to do his bidding.
Evie was crying for her Mama.
Silas hobbled towards the hackney at a speed which belied his injury.
Kitty sprinted after him, Adam following behind.

Mr Pembroke and two footmen barrelled out of the house in hot pursuit.

Harold dodged around his boss and stepped in front of Kitty, barring her way.
She clawed at him, frantically.

His grand plan evaporating into pandemonium, Silas needed to escape as fast as possible. He glanced at the child in his arms and those giving chase.

In that split second, dread of the noose overrode sense, and he did the unimaginable.

Silas tossed Evie as though she was naught but a sack of coal.

*"Evie... Adam!"* Kitty scrabbled to extricate herself from Harold's grip, to reach Evie before she hit the ground, even knowing it was futile. Tears streamed down her cheeks. Her sobs hysterical.

Against his better judgement, Harold delivered a heavy blow to her cheek and she crumpled in his arms, unconscious.

Abruptly, everything fell ominously silent.
The next few minutes seemed to unfold in slow motion.
The players fanned out, each with a different goal.

Adam peered at the blur of movement heading his way and lurched forward, his arms outstretched. To the stupefaction of all who witnessed it, Evie landed against Adam's chest. He clutched her to him, and slumped onto the street, sucking in lungsful of air.

Harold hauled Kitty to the hackney, dumped her on the seat, swarmed up top, next to the driver and shouted at Silas to get a bloody move on. The latter narrowly managed to heave himself inside before the driver flicked the reins and the carriage barrelled off at a breakneck pace.

The two footmen chased after the cab but, despite being fleet of foot, when they turned the corner, the hackney had gone.

Dejected, they traipsed back to The Laurels, where Adam was consoling a distraught Evie.

∼

A man, looking forward to luncheon with his wife, rounded the corner and strode along the street towards the huddle of men, offended by so loud a rumpus in his peaceful neighbourhood.

"What the *deuce* is going on here?" he barked, preparing to upbraid the scoundrels who had caused it.

"*Teasdale?*" His tone became one of surprise. His nephew was at the centre of the group, holding a distraught child.

Over Evie's sobs, Adam recognised the voice. "Uncle David?" He reverted to his childhood greeting without thinking.

"Adam, what happened?"

"They took Kitty. Oh God, they took Kitty."

"Who took Kitty, where?" David Wells, 7th Marquis of Clarence and older brother of Prudence, was perplexed.

With no answer forthcoming, he assumed charge of the situation.

Ushering everyone inside, the marquis asked Mr Pembroke to pour a brandy for anyone who needed it, staff included. Then he dispatched one of the footmen with a message to his wife explaining he would not be home for luncheon after all.

Shortly thereafter, David was sitting by the fire in the

drawing room, Evie on his lap, listening to Adam's somewhat sketchy description of the morning's events.

"Let me see whether I have this straight. A few days ago, Oscar saw a strange man loitering near the house. Today this man and one other turn up here, threaten Kitty and try to kidnap Evie. Kitty shoots one of them, but they somehow kidnap her instead of Evie and now they've gone to ground?"

Adam nodded. "Basically yes."

"You could not make this up," David observed, mildly. "Why would they want Kitty?"

"I can only assume it is related to Asquith," Adam opined. "Uncle David, we have to find her, I… we are… I cannot…" he struggled to articulate his trepidation. He could not lose Kitty.

"Did you hear anything of value in all the commotion?" David quizzed.

"Not a thing." Adam thought back. "It was utter mayhem by the time I knew something was amiss. No wait, I think the one who hit Kitty, was called Harold, and the other man, Silas." He stood up and, after touching the back of the chair to get his bearings, paced the room.

"I have a friend, who I think might be able to offer an insight. Give me an hour or so."

"We do not have an hour." Adam came to a standstill.

"Without help, we have nothing." David rose from his chair and passed Evie to Adam. "Here take Evie and go up to Oscar. He is probably scared and confused. Tell him what happened. I'll be back as quick as I am able." He hurried from the room and seconds later, the front door slammed.


Adam did as his uncle bade, relived to have something to distract him. Oscar was pale. The ruckus outside had terrified him, despite Hettie's restful presence. Still holding Evie,

Adam sat on the floor, and drew Oscar onto his knee. He gave an abridged version of events, trying not to exacerbate the boy's fright. Oscar burst into noisy sobs, which set Evie off again.

Banking down his own consternation, Adam, with Hettie's help, soothed the two children and diverted them with a story. In the midst of this, luncheon arrived and Hettie shooed Adam out, affirming she would call him if necessary.

"They'll be fine, my lord. Children are more resilient than we give them credit for." With a kind smile, she curtseyed.

"Thank you, Hettie. I shall be in the study."

Adam traipsed down the stairs, and rang for Mr Pembroke, asking for his meal to be served in the study rather than the dining room.

He hated feeling so impotent. *Where was Kitty?*

Groggily, Kitty opened her eyes. She had half-woken for brief periods, but any movement made her dizzy and it was easier to stay asleep. This time, she felt less sluggish and succeeded in shuffling into an upright position.

Wherever she was, it was murky and damp and cold. Feeling as though she had been run over by a carriage, Kitty risked pressing tentative fingers to her throbbing face. It was swollen and would doubtless bruise. *Thank you very much, Harold.*

Running her tongue around her mouth, Kitty tasted blood, and guessed she had bitten her cheek, thankful to note her teeth felt intact. She tried to move, only to discover her ankles were clamped in irons.

*Damn, this just got better and better.*

To counteract the scream bubbling up, Kitty released a string of curses. She had amassed an impressive array during her marriage, learnt when in the earshot of heedless farm hands. Striving for calm, she emptied her mind of everything else, and concentrated.

In the distance, the chime of a church bell. She counted. Four o-clock. Nearer to where she sat there came an occasional shout, and she could hear water lapping gently. It reminded her of the lake at Easby Hall.

*Evie, Adam, Oscar.*

Her eyes grew misty.

*Not the time to weep, Kitty,* she lectured. *Godfrey is the cause of all this, the good for nothing villain. Even dead, he does not deserve your tears.*

She used her repugnance to counteract her fear. She was *not* going to be bundled onto a ship and transported to some faraway land. She had a daughter who she was going to watch grow up, marry and have children of her own.

*Evie,* the image of her child being tossed carelessly into the air, whipped up her rage. *Had Evie been saved or had her tiny body slammed onto the unforgiving cobbles?* That rogue would pay for his actions if it was the last thing she ever did. His behaviour was beneath contempt.

All she had to do was escape.

Not easy when you have metal clamps around your ankles.


Cautiously, Kitty turned her head, and squinted into the gloom.

"Hello," she called, softly. Her voice echoed in the stillness, leading her to surmise she was in a large space.

No reply. Nothing except silence, which was both disconcerting and a relief.

Patting around her, she came to the conclusion she had been placed on a pile of sacks. Her gown was dry, and she was still wearing her cloak and boots. *Small mercies.*

Stretching forward, Kitty felt the manacles. They were not tight, but she was unable to get them off, no matter how hard she tried. She could not even unlace her boots to see whether that helped.

The lack of light prevented her from seeing anything beyond a few feet. *Why was it so dark?* A thought came to her. *Was it four in the morning? No, surely not.*

The pounding in her head increased. In fact, everything hurt, even her eyelids.

To make matters worse, as far as Kitty could tell, she was the sole occupant of what appeared to be an otherwise vacant building, size to be determined. She rued the day she had met Godfrey bloody Lovell.

*Ah, but then you wouldn't have Evie.*

She propped herself, more or less comfortably, against the rough wooden panelling.

Now, she was the one who needed rescuing

Which presented a bit of a problem, given no one knew where she was.

"Sadie," Silas yelled, hobbling into the Den. "Get your arse over here."

Slightly flushed, Sadie peeked around a curtain half-way down the wide corridor. She nodded towards the heavy material in tacit indication she was serving a customer. Silas cursed in annoyance. His leg hurt like buggery and the wound had to be cleaned.

He limped along to the kitchen, finding Nancy — ruler of the meagre domestic sphere — busy concocting what he hoped was a hearty stew.

"Nancy, give us an 'and will yer?" He plonked down onto

one of the rickety chairs, unbuttoned his trousers, and slid them off where they puddled at his feet.

Glancing across, Nancy was about to toss a saucy remark, when she saw the blood running down his leg.

"Sir?"

"Water, salt, cloths," he bit out.

Nancy rushed to follow his orders. Reaching for a bowl, she filled it with warm water from the pan on the stove. Throwing in a handful of salt, she added a splash of vinegar for good measure. The older women at all of Silas' premises, possessed a little basic medical knowledge. Essential, given some of their clientele. Swilling the water to dissolve the salt, Nancy grabbed a couple of greyish rags.

Soaking the first cloth in the mixture, she dabbed at his thigh, fastidiously.

"What the 'ell 'appened?" Nancy asked, more to distract him while she cleaned the wound than out of any real interest. Silas dead would not upset her; she could govern the Den with her eyes closed.

"Bitch shot me," he bleated.

"Which bitch would that be, and why?" Wiping away the blood, Nancy could see it was a flesh wound, nothing too serious. *Shame, a nice festering laceration might be enough to carry 'im off.* She kept her face bland. Silas was adept at reading expressions.

"Lady soddin' Asquith, that's who. Stupid trollop wouldn't listen to reason. There was me, pointing out why she should support me endeavours, as 'er old man used to do and she took offence." Silas said, morosely, confounded by Kitty's reaction and the resulting fiasco. Women of the elite were reputed to be simpering milksops, not feisty, gun-brandishing harridans.

Nancy, who knew far too much about Lord Asquith,

made no comment. Inwardly, she praised whoever had been brave enough to stand up to Silas.

"She'll be docile as a lamb after ternight… tssss," he hissed. "Watch it woman."

"Why's that?" Nancy took no notice, inspecting the wound to ensure there were no slivers within — fibres from his trousers, dirt.

Silas gave a derisive snort. "She's locked up in yon Shed. A night in there without food and she'll be on her knees begging me. A good place for what I 'ave in mind. She'll do anything I want, including scratching me itch," he leered, unattractively.

Nancy felt a stab of something akin to sorrow for his hapless victim. Any insubordination in Silas' stable was usually quashed after a night… or two… in the 'Shed'. A ramshackle building on an unused quay where there was naught but rats and spiders.

Tales of uncooperative whores being stripped naked, gagged, and strung up by their bound wrists, so they had to stand all night, were rife around the Den. True or not, it served to keep Silas' girls in order.

*If this chit, a lady no less, who dared shoot Silas had been treated similarly…* Nancy stopped and hardened her heart, thankful she wasn't the one in Silas' bad books.

Tying a cleanish binding around his leg, Nancy picked up the bowl and walked to the back door, throwing the bloodied water out into the alley.

"You'll do," she said, dropping the dirty cloths on the fire.

Silas muttered his thanks and stumped up to his office.

An odd sense of unease prickled at Nancy as she watched him go.

# CHAPTER TWENTY-FOUR

The afternoon had begun to fade into a cold, late October evening, when David Wells knocked on the door of The Laurels.

The tall and much younger man to his left was possessed of a military bearing. Although the latter's countenance was solemn, closer examination would have revealed laugh lines crinkling at the corners of his eyes and a mouth pre-disposed to smiling rather than frowning.

Mr Pembroke admitted the pair and showed them through to the study as requested by Adam.

"The Marquis of Clarence and Major Withers," he introduced.

"Thank you, Pembroke. Please arrange for coffee and perhaps a plate of Mrs Milward's cakes. I daresay some light refreshments would be appreciated." Adam stood upon their entry and smiled in the direction of the butler.

"Yes, my lord." Pembroke backed out and the door closed.

. . .

"Welcome, make yourselves comfortable. Thank you for coming, Major Withers. As you can see, I am rather limited when it comes to chasing kidnappers across London." Adam flicked a hand at his eyes, and his lips twisting into an ironic grin.

"I am honoured to be approached." The major responded in kind. "Lord Clarence has given me a vague précis, but I would like to hear the details from you."

"Just today, or do you think some background might help?"

"Anything you deem relevant, and please call me Lucas," the major invited.

"On the proviso you are amenable to returning the favour and call me Adam."

"I should be glad to, thank you."

Pleasantries over, Adam mustered his thoughts, and furnished Lucas with a succinct account of everything he could think of regarding Godfrey Asquith, concluding with what he had heard when he had arrived on scene.

Lucas listened intently. He did not take notes, nor did he interrupt.

"I believe the situation had been going on for some time. In my opinion the man, Silas, was the one in charge and his accomplice was called Harold. They had a hackney waiting, and the driver must either have been in the pay of or was under threat from this Silas character, because he never moved until ordered and then sped off as though the hounds of hell were after him."

Adam spread his palms in an apologetic gesture. "I am sorry, that sounds pathetically paltry. As I said to Uncle David, it must be related to Asquith. There can be no other reason for them to accost his widow in so overt a fashion. I know nothing of him personally, and Kitty, Lady Asquith, has spoken only a little of her marriage. It was an… unhappy union."

With this massive understatement, Adam leant back in his chair.

Pembroke came in bearing a tray laden with tasty looking treats and three steaming coffees. The men mulled over Adam's words while the butler served the drinks.

"I am not incognisant of Lord Asquith's business dealings. His murderer has never been brought to justice. We have no leads, nothing, not even the slightest hint of a name. With Lady Asquith targeted, perhaps we are closing in, finally," Lucas said, once Pembroke, ensuring nothing else was required, had left the room.

"Before we go any further, perhaps I ought to provide some background of my own. Currently, you know nothing of me and what I do, besides the fact, your uncle recommended my services."

"If Uncle David considers you trustworthy, I need no further evidence, but I am interested to hear your story," Adam replied.

"Until last year, I was with our forces first on the Peninsula and then in France. After my discharge, I was approached by the representative of a group within our government who asked whether I would be interested in establishing a covert organisation.

"Initially, my orders were to hunt down French spies whom, they believed, were infiltrating Society at the highest levels. I confess I was wearied of war and glad to be on English soil again. I will not bore you with the details, suffice it to say, I agreed.

"My operation has expanded, and we investigate a variety

of illegal activities, most especially cases requiring absolute discretion. Although we are, by necessity, a clandestine group, we work alongside the Runners, and are able to access information from a diverse and broad range of sources."

Lucas leant forward, his elbows on his knees. "I have eyes and ears all over London, my lord, we *will* find your betrothed."

The men began a serious discussion which lasted into the early evening.

Lucas was the first to leave. He stood and bowed. "I shall begin forthwith. My men know the places people like this Silas person patronise. I do not believe it will take much to track him down. He cannot be without enemies and coin is a great incentive."

"Thank you, Lucas, I am in your debt." Adam rose to shake the major's hand.

"We find Lady Asquith, there is no debt." Lucas bowed, said his goodbyes and was gone before Adam could summon Pembroke to see his guest out.

Adam looked at David. "Thank you, too." He smiled although it didn't reach his eyes. He rubbed his forehead, and grumbled, "I wish I could do more."

"Do not fret, Adam. Lucas will find her. Trust him. He and his men are exceptionally diligent. I would not be at all surprised if she was home safe and sound by morning." He patted Adam's shoulder sympathetically.

The ormolu clock on the mantel chimed seven. The sound reminding Adam, Kitty had been missing for almost eight hours. It was going to be a long and sleepless night.

"Time I was going." David walked to the door. "Don't call Pembroke, I can find my way out."

"Please apologise to Aunt Louisa…" Adam had no need to finish his sentence.

"I have no doubt she will want to come and mother you." David grinned, glad when Adam reciprocated. "Eat something, and even though I know you will ignore this, do try to get some rest."

Adam promised to try, hearing the swish of the door closing when David left.

In an attempt to adhere to their normal routine, Adam went to check on the children, pleased to see both were fast asleep. In the rather oppressive silence of the dining room, while he ate his meal in solitary splendour, Adam reflected on Kitty.

Her vitality, her innate sense of fun, and the wonder she found in the simplest of things. Her flashes of temper, her fiery passion. Her love for Evie and Oscar. His enhanced awareness when she was near, his sense of melancholy when they were apart, as though she was the very reason his heart continued to beat.

*She possessed him,* he mused whimsically, *in fact, arguably, she had always possessed him.* An ownership to which he gladly surrendered.

In truth, although Gwendolyn and he were an affectionate couple, once the shock of her death diminished, he had to acknowledge, he did not miss her unduly. They had enjoyed each other's company, but neither felt compelled to seek the other out during their days, each pursuing individual interests.

A gregarious soul, Gwendolyn revelled in lively afternoons, gossiping with her friends. He sought the quiet of an hour or so at White's or Brooke's. Looking back, except for Society events, they were rarely together until the fortnight prior to Adam re-joining his ship.

He assumed this was a habit they had fallen into because of their mutual understanding he would spend most of their married life at sea. Now he realised it was simply that they did not need each other.

With Kitty, he hated going more than an hour without seeing her, yearned for the touch of her hand, or to breathe in her fragrance. To hear her voice or brush his lips to hers and feel her quake with the fierce desire echoed in his own body.

Without Kitty he existed.

With her... he lived.

Kitty despaired. The gloom had been subsumed by a darkness, black as pitch. She had yelled, bawled, banged on the walls, broken off a wooden slat and used that to make more noise. This had yielded nothing but a sore throat and sore hands.

Huddled into her cloak, she took stock.

Three things...

...she was trapped,

...she was alone — expect for the odd rat scurrying about. Unnerving, but at least they had not tried to nibble her — yet.

...it was reasonable to presume she was to be included in Silas Dryden's next 'shipment' — suppressing the spasm of alarm *that* engendered.

She *had* to escape. Somehow, she had to escape. Even if it meant Silas would make good his threat and kill her. *Surely better than the alternative.*

Throughout the interminable hours, she invented and rejected numerous scenarios by which she evaded Silas and he ended up at the bottom of the Thames. To be fair, most were ludicrous in the extreme, but it served to keep her panic at bay.

After what felt like the longest night of Kitty's life, dawn broke. The impenetrable obscurity lessened marginally. Here and there, fingers of light stole through gaps in the walls, and she could see dust motes dancing in the pinkish glow. The church clock struck seven.

Her stomach rumbled, she had not eaten since breakfast the previous day, and she was very thirsty. *Did Silas intend to starve her? To imprison her here until she was naught but bone?*

Kitty shivered. Even wrapped in her thick cloak, she was cold, her breath hung like gossamer clouds on the frigid air, reminding her that winter loomed. *Perhaps she would freeze to death first. Again, a preferable option.*

As it grew lighter, she was able to distinguish the interior of her prison. Wooden walls cracked and split. A stone floor strewn with rat droppings. The underside of an ageing shingle roof liberally adorned with massive cobwebs. Heavy chains with vicious-looking hooks on the end, hung from the rafters; some with ropes looped over the hooks. Glancing around the walls, Kitty spotted more iron manacles.

This time her shiver was nothing to do with the cold.

Kitty battered on the wood in her frustration, resuming her efforts to attract someone's, anyone's, attention. To no avail. Defeated, she slumped, kicking out with her feet as though magically the irons would come apart. All that did was hurt her ankles.

An ugly thought reared its head. *What if her calls were heard by those with less scruples than Silas? If that was* ***remotely*** *possible.* Shackled, she was defenceless against anyone who had a sudden craving to satisfy a basic… urge… as it were. Nausea churned and she drew several long slow breaths to settle her recalcitrant stomach. *She was **not** going to be sick.*

Plucky she might be, but Kitty was a daughter of the nobility, cushioned from the dregs of society. Even her execrable marriage had played out in relative comfort.

Her current situation was far removed from anything she had or ought to encounter, and the skills she learnt as a child playing with her brothers in no way equipped her for this.

Kitty could see no reprieve from her predicament and, hard as she tried to stop them, weak tears brimmed over.

Lucas' night had been more fruitful. Employing enough men to operate twenty-four hours a day across three shifts, his office never closed. Crime did not stop when the sun went down, in fact, generally it increased during the hours of darkness. Once the team on duty had been apprised of the situation, they slipped out into the shadows.

Tracking people down, whether they be offender or victim was one of their specialities. They knew people, who knew people, who knew people, a ripple effect which flowed both ways. Lucas and his men did not discriminate. Those who inhabited the slums of the city were treated with the same respect as those living in the genteel neighbourhoods.

In the early days, their efforts had been met with mistrust and the proverbial brick wall, but Lucas persevered. Soon his anonymous organisation became associated with integrity. Any investigation was conducted with dignity and civility regardless of status, motivating those who would normally remain tight-lipped to become garrulous.

# CHAPTER TWENTY-FIVE

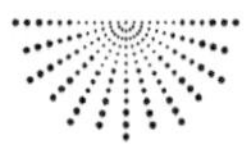

onight, while they walked the streets, spoke with contacts, and bought the odd round of drinks, the team began to make progress.

Whispered allusions relating to a smuggling operation were winnowed out until Jack Parsons, a recent addition to the unit and brother-in-law of Lucas, heard the name Silas Dryden.

Some artful probing earned him an address in St Giles, and the name of a public house on Long Acre where Dryden's crew were known to drink.

Satisfied he had obtained all pertinent details, Jack flipped the inebriated man enough coin to cover rent for two weeks and melted into the crowd.

Hurrying through the dank lanes and alleyways, he arrived at the office on Bow Street shortly after midnight. Another of their number, a burly chap known as Bulldog — more owing to his ruthless tenacity than his size, although he *was* huge — had also ferreted out a mass of disturbing information.

As they pieced everything together, it was evident Kitty's

kidnapping was connected to a labyrinthine enterprise spanning three continents. They needed to isolate someone in Dryden's crew who would snitch on his boss given the right inducement.

Lucas studied the men around the table. "This is bigger than we can handle. We'll have to bring in the Runners. To transfer that number of women, agreeable or not, from wherever they are barracked to a ship, unseen, is a laborious undertaking. It can only be done at night.

"We need a quick chat with the customs officers, find out which of the smaller ships ply trade regularly to India or the Americas. It is unlikely to be an Indiaman, too big and therefore noticeable. A brig or a barque perhaps, an older vessel, probably also carrying enough legitimate cargo to fool a quick glance in the hold. I do not know how many women each ship transports, but I would imagine twenty-five to thirty as a minimum, otherwise there is no profit."

Lucas stopped and ran his hand around the back of his neck. "Listen to me discussing women as a commodity. Have people sunk so low?"

There was a unanimous murmur of assent. Regrettably, certain members of the population *had* sunk that low. Their despicable actions a constant justification of why Lucas' organisation existed in the first place.

Lucas concentrated on the matter at hand; the ignoble traits of their quarry could be discussed another day. Finding Kitty was their first step. Hopefully, Silas would lead them to her, after which the blackguard would be dealt with in a manner befitting his crimes.

"Right, Bulldog take Ned, Hawk, and Jack, and follow up those addresses. Do not make contact unless you have no choice. I want to know how many are involved before we take them on.

Lucas swung his gaze to his second in command. "Tom,

take Matt and locate the customs officers. Tell them you are there on my orders, if they show any hesitancy. The rest of you, keep looking. Maybe pop down to the smaller, less frequented, even officially disused quays, see whether anything looks out of the ordinary.

"I'm going next door to have a word with Ted Slater." Watch Commander of the Runners. "I think he's on duty tonight. It's cold out there, I reckon we'll have a frost before morning. Wrap up warm." He waited until his men nodded their understanding, then stood to leave the room.

Two small groups of men peeled out, en route to complete their assigned tasks. The mood was sombre but optimistic. They believed they had garnered enough information to hunt their prey, the only question was whether they would be in time.

Moments later, peace descended on the office, with only one man remaining on watch.

~

The day began.

Adam, who had not slept a wink, trudged upstairs to wash, and change into fresh clothes. He felt utterly impotent, raging at being hindered by his lack of sight. *What use was he as a protector when he couldn't see?* He banged his fists on the dressing table, scattering brushes and ointments onto the floor.

A knock heralded Mr Pembroke. Placidly, the butler picked up the items replacing them on the table in their correct order.

"I'm certain her ladyship will be home afore dark," he reassured, helping Adam with his jacket, brushing the shoulders.

"What if she is not?" Adam posed. "What do we do then? We have no idea where to look. London is a sprawling city. People could wander it their whole life and never be seen. 'Tis the ideal place to vanish."

"Now, now, that Major Withers sounds like a canny chap. I hazard he will be indefatigable in his investigation. Do not lose hope."

"Easier said than done, Pembroke." Adam offered the ghost of a smile. *Where are you, Kitty?* Pulling himself together, he made his way to the nursery, pleased to see Oscar and Evie eating their breakfast. Oscar looked up eagerly when he heard his father.

"Mama?"

"Sorry, son, not yet."

Oscar's face fell.

Evie, too young to understand the full impact of what had occurred, was eating her breakfast with gusto, swinging her chubby legs against the chair. The previous day's uproar forgotten.

Adam remained with the children for a while but found he could not sit still. He needed to be doing something, anything to aid the search. Jumping to his feet, he padded through the house to the kitchens where he found his staff preparing the day's meals.

"Adam Marchmain." Flustered at her master's precipitous entry, Mrs Millward, who only used his title when she was about to upbraid him, expostulated, "You can't be in 'ere."

"Milly." His use of the diminutive generally guaranteed him anything he wanted. "May I have breakfast here," Adam asked in his most engaging manner.

"Go on with you, you oughtn't..."

"I know, but 'tis lonely and it saves lighting the fire in the dining room," he replied, unaware the fires had been lit all over the house an hour ago, to banish the chill.

Milly, tsked and tutted and banged around at the stove, but shortly thereafter handed him a platter piled with eggs, ham and fresh toast.

"Get that into you." She gave him a tolerant grin. Adam was her favourite of the Marchmain children, and she went to great lengths to spoil him whenever he visited his London residence.

It was also obvious to Milly and all the staff at The Laurels exactly how much Kitty Lovell, who the majority had known almost from her birth, meant to Adam. The woman was a breath of fresh air, unfailingly bright and cheerful. Her effect on Adam, evidenced by his optimistic demeanour; a buoyancy which had long been absent.

Milly sighed inaudibly and sent up a silent prayer that Kitty would be home soon.

~

Straight after breakfast, Silas Dryden went to inspect his cargo. Twenty-six women, enticed off the streets with promises of a better life, had been sequestered in a row of derelict houses not far from the docks.

Away from prying eyes and nosy constables, the whole area was due to be demolished, but its secluded position meant it was low priority and thus, ideal short-term accommodation.

Provided with the basics, the women were guarded by three of Silas' retainers and 'mothered' by a blousy woman known as Marge. The latter's presence reassured those cloistered within that they hadn't made a grave mistake by accepting Silas' terms. Marge explained away the guards, saying it was for their safety, and talked up the voyage, making it sound like an adventure.

The hope they might escape the drudgery of the slums, however slim, was enough to conquer the women's qualms, and eminently preferable to the brothels where the less fortunate had been sent. A dash of laudanum added to their meals kept them quiescent, and Marge assured Silas there had been no problems overnight.

Unbeknownst to Silas, he was followed. It was a rare day when he missed someone monitoring his movements, but he had overslept, his leg pained him, and it was freezing cold, causing his customary vigilance to lapse.

With the stealth of cats, Bulldog and Jack tailed Silas all the way to the dilapidated terrace. Jack inched closer, using the early morning shadows to mask his movements.

Some of the houses had no doors. These he discounted. Coming to one which had a large bolt on the *outside*, he stopped and motioned to Bulldog. His colleague closed the gap.

"Who puts a bolt on the outside of a door?" Jack muttered.

"Them's as what's up to no good," Bulldog replied, under his breath.

"Wait here." Jack edged to the adjacent house, pointed to the door, and nodded. Angling his head, he saw the same thing on the next one along the row.

Creeping back to where Bulldog was hiding in an open doorway, the two conferred. Jack would head to Bow Street, while Bulldog secreted himself in one of the empty houses to keep watch.

Ensuring he wasn't seen, Jack legged it.

~

While Bulldog and Jack followed Silas, Hawk and Ned introduced themselves to the inhabitants of The Den.

Hearing the commotion, Harold nipped out of a window, across the roof and down an outside staircase to the street below. He had recognised Bulldog and, if he was at their door, the operation was in danger, if not already uncovered.

Harold was irked and, in his opinion, righteously so. He had *told* Silas it was lunacy to kidnap Lady Asquith. The whole damn *ton* were probably hunting for her, not to mention the Bow Street Runners. He could see everything they had worked so hard to achieve evaporating like the autumn mist under a warm sun.

Partial to his neck, Harold didn't fancy it being elongated any time soon. In his mind's eye he saw a tiny child, one who called him *pretty* — no one had ever called him pretty — sailing through the air and prayed someone had caught her. He did *not* hold with harming innocent babes.

Harold pondered the notion of releasing their captive and escorting her to one of the city's more salubrious neighbourhoods. He reckoned she was canny enough to find her way home. He could persuade Silas to take their business to a new town, Plymouth or Manchester. Far from London, where no one knew them. The idea took root, and Harold made a decision.

~

Kitty herself, of course, had no idea of the trenchant measures being employed to find her. Unpinning her hair, she combed her fingers through its heavy length in a fairly futile attempt to make it look less like a bird's nest.

Plaiting, then twisting it into the semblance of a bun, she

jabbed in a few pins to secure it. It felt a bit skewed, but that was the least of her worries.

Daylight would undoubtedly bring Silas unless he had indeed decided to leave her here to starve. *Was she to be shipped abroad or sent to a brothel?* Hmmm… the choice between serving one man or hundreds. *Pitiful options.* Abroad sounded like the lesser of two evils, but neither was an attractive proposition by any stretch of the imagination.

Her sheltered upbringing had shielded her from the seedy side of humanity, but Kitty was an astute woman. She had no illusions about life as a whore. Typically, and mercifully short.

She huddled into her cloak, trying not to succumb to the cold, and the terror slowly eroding her hope.

Harold, not a stupid man, avoided tearing down to Newell Street to alert Silas. If those hunting for Lady Asquith had found The Den, it was likely they had followed Silas to the halfway house.

Instead, he headed for a secluded wharf nestled off Narrow Street, between Limehouse Basin and the East India Dock. Far enough from either and the Pool of London, to avoid notice.

The last thing they needed was a dead member of the nobility of whom they had to dispose. Asquith had broken the cardinal rule and tried to circumvent Silas. His death was justified, and in Harold's mind, the viscount deserved all he got. His widow did not.

She was a victim in all of this, twice over. Once, duped by her husband. Twice because Silas, unable to forgive or forget Asquith's treachery, could not accept his widow was oblivious to his activities.

Silas had his cargo. Twenty-six women who would board a ship this evening bound for the Americas. To subject Kitty to a life away from her daughter, presuming the latter had survived, was a cruelty Harold could not condone. He had a plan.

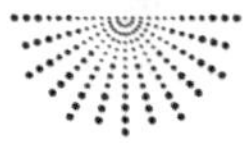

itty heard the thunk of a bolt being shot and straightened her shoulders. Whatever happened she refused to cower. She was the daughter of an earl, the widow of a viscount. She would *not* give her kidnappers the satisfaction of seeing her crumble.

Difficult to be stalwart when hampered by leg-irons, nevertheless, Kitty rose to her feet and faced her future with no sign of fear.

Harold walked towards her.

He held a huge knife.

Kitty's heart plummeted. He was here to kill her.

Paralysed by mind-numbing dread, images of those she loved filled her mind. She prayed the knife was sharp and Harold knew how to wield it.

"My lady, I am here to release you,"

Harold's words were so shocking, Kitty plumped back onto the pile of hessian.

"B-beg p-pardon." Speechless, she gaped at him.

"Whatever your husband's misdeeds, you are not responsible or to blame. I cannot allow Silas to ruin your life, or that of your daughter."

Relief began to tease at the edge of her mind. *Did he mean it or was this another trick?*

"Your sentiment is all well and good, but there is a reason I am tethered like a lamb waiting to be slaughtered." She rattled the irons. "How am I supposed to get out of these?"

With a dramatic flourish, Harold produced a key.

Kitty's heart fluttered.

Hope fought back.


Bending, Harold unlocked the metal clamps. They opened and fell onto the stone floor with a loud clang, which reverberated around the building.

Kitty rubbed her aching ankles, flexing them to counteract the stiffness.

"Come on, me lady. We need to hurry and get you out of here afore Silas works out what's going on."

Gratefully, Kitty hooked her hand through his proffered arm, the soles of her feet stinging as the blood circulated.

"Why? Why are you helping me? You were quick enough to knock me out yesterday." Kitty quizzed, fixing him with a baleful frown.

Harold grimaced. "I'm sorry, me lady. Twixt you and 'im." He jerked his head. "'E's the scarier. Silas'll kill me soon as look at me. I doubt you'd 'urt a fly. That said, yer didn't arf give 'im a scare when yer shot 'im."

Harold chortled, and slapped his leg. "Never thought I'd see the day a proper lady could fire a gun wivvout fallin' over or blowin' off 'er own foot."

Her plight aside, Kitty felt a grin tug at her lips. "Regrettably, I missed," she quipped, dryly. "Had my aim been true, I would not have spent the night in this hovel. You have not answered my question."

Harold took off his cap and scratched his balding pate. "I don't 'old wiv kidnap, nor do I 'old wiv stealin' babes." Apparently ignorant of the irony of his statement.

"Is not your entire business predicated on kidnap?" Kitty challenged.

Harold stared at her in bafflement.

"You seize vulnerable women off the streets and ship them overseas. How is that not kidnap?"

"Nah, we don't steal 'em, they come of their own accord."

"I think on that we must agree to disagree. You may believe your claim, but I suspect their compliance comes under duress.

Harold opened the door and scanned the quayside, glad the Shed was off the beaten track.

"We offer a service, simple as that." He shrugged and changed the subject. "Tek care where yer put yer feet. It's a mite frosty this morning."

Kitty spied patches of ice where puddles had frozen and the tell-tale rime on the flagstones. Gingerly, she stepped out into the fresh air, inhaling deeply, surveying her surrounds.

In front of her, the wide expanse of the Thames. With no breeze, the river was smooth as glass, its dark surface sparkling under the rays of the rising sun.

Using her hand to shield her eyes from the glare, she could make out the silhouetted skyline of London. It looked so far away. To her left, the river snaked around towards the huge docks at Rotherhithe and the Isle of Dogs.

Above, the sky was cloudless. The golden pink of dawn giving way to vivid azure. The only sound was the keen of the gulls wheeling high overhead.

"Why, 'tis breathtaking," Kitty murmured. Harold glanced

at her in surprise. She waved her hand at the panorama and he paused, turning to look.

A fatal error.

~

Pleased to see the women were concluding preparations for their long voyage, Silas spent a few minutes chatting with his men before telling Marge he'd return within the hour.

"I'm off to collect an extra special piece of merchandise. Be sure to treat her with the utmost respect," he smirked, nastily.

"Silas," Marge remonstrated. She was the only one who could get away with questioning the boss. "What 'ave you done?"

"Nowt that need trouble yer, any of yer." He pointed a threatening finger at the group. "I'll be back shortly."

With that, he pulled up the collar of his jacket and stepped out into the chilly sunshine.

~

At the Den, Nancy and Sadie were singing like canaries, information gushing out of them at a speed rivalling a river in full spate. Nancy told Hawk what Silas had divulged about the Shed adding she believed the woman to be the widow of a dead business partner.

"He's been wittering about that bloody Lord Asquith for weeks, blaming his widow for everything from sour milk to the cost of spuds." Nancy shook her head. "She'll be wishing she were dead too, like as not."

"Where is this Shed?" Hawk pressed.

"Narrow Street, by Ropemaker's Fields right on the quayside."

Hawk yelled for Ned and the two men took off.

~

From his hiding place four doors down, Bulldog observed Silas exiting the house where they now believed he was holding numerous women.

Hunched into his jacket, and heedless of the man tailing him, Bulldog's quarry strode down the street, turning right into Oak Lane before following Rope Walk and weaving through the alleys to Narrow Street.

~

At the same time, Jack, in company with Lucas, the rest of the latter's team and several Runners who were hastening to Newell Street, came upon Hawk and Ned.

Their individual reports given, the group adjusted their plans and set off in the direction of the Shed, hoping to get there ahead of Silas.

~

Bulldog rounded a corner to see Silas approach two people who appeared to be admiring the view. Momentarily perplexed, he dodged back into the alleyway, and evaluated the scene.

To his right, a sizeable wooden building, not in the best state of repair, but solid enough. This must be where Silas had imprisoned Lady Asquith. *Was she the woman of the pair?* It was a fair bet.

Disgust at the man's behaviour gnawed at Bulldog, and the yearning to beat Silas to a pulp had his fists clenching in readiness.

He steadied himself. Rescue the viscountess first, deal with Silas second.

Stealthily, he crept to the side of the building closest to him. Using it as cover, he pressed his back to the wooden wall and cocked his head to listen.

~

A grating voice from behind them, prompted Kitty and Harold to whirl around. Kitty's stomach knotted. *Why had she pointed out the view?* Precious seconds wasted when they should have been fleeing the wharf.

Harold took a step, so he was slightly in front of her. An honourable gesture she would have found hard to fathom prior to his actions this morning.

"Well, well, well, what do we 'ave 'ere? 'Arold Simpkins, after everyfing I've done fer you, you would double-cross me? There was me, finking you was a loyal comrade, but yer a bloody traitor," Silas jeered, hefting his knife from hand to hand. "And yer knows how I deal wiv traitors." The threat in his sibilant tone left nothing to the imagination.

Relieved to note Lady Asquith appeared unharmed, Bulldog, guessing the second man to be Harold, swore under his breath. This was not going to be easy.

In a bid to avoid detection, he padded soundlessly around the far side of the building, trying to conceal his bulk behind a convenient post at the right-hand corner. He could see Silas' knife glinting in the sunlight. It was an evil-looking blade.

He weighed up his odds. He too carried a knife and, while

quite prepared to use it, preferred not to unless he had no alternative. He was alone.

If he got near enough to throw his blade with accuracy he would be seen, reducing the chance of rescuing Lady Asquith without her being hurt or worse.

Unless events precipitated his involvement, all Bulldog could do was pray the team found them soon.


"Silas, I told yer we shouldn't 'ave tekken 'er," Harold retaliated, hotly. "The authorities is onto us. Couple o' bruisers searched the Den, the girls couldn't spin 'em a yarn fast enough, bloody blabbermouths. I hared it over 'ere to free the chit, then was comin' to Newell St to alert yer. 'Onest, I was. 'Tis 'er they care about."

He waved his hand at Kitty. "We've got time to get the others to the ship, afore they track us down, but we'll 'ave to hurry."

"Might be easier for me to kill yer both right here, then drop yer bodies in the Thames. By the time anyone finds yer, I'll be long gone," Silas brooded.

"Don't care what you do to me but let 'er go. She dun't deserve this."

"Hark at you, concerned for a piece o' skirt. Oh." A sly smile curled his lip. "Wait, did yer give yerself a little treat did yer?" Silas quipped, ignoring Kitty's outraged exclamation and Harold's furious denial.

"Yer going soft in yer old age. Yer'll pay fer this. Both of yer'll pay fer this. *You.*" He jabbed the knife in Kitty's direction. "You, I was going to be kindly and send yer to America. Now yer'll see out yer days serving the worst of me customers."

Silas tapped his chin with the point of the blade. "I 'ave them as like it, shall we say, rough. Men who have a propensity for restraints and sharp implements and leather whips. Sometimes they like to share... and watch." He gave a fiendish smirk.

Kitty's already pale face turned ashen and she swayed on her feet. Harold put out a hand to steady her and muttered something in her ear.

"Oh dear, have I upset your sensibilities? Forgive me, my lady," he mocked, sweeping a bow. "'Arold, tie 'er up." Withdrawing the length of rope from his pocket, brought for the purpose, Silas tossed it to his second.

"No." Harold defied his boss. "Sorry, Silas, I refuse. Yer crazy. Yer'll never get away wiv it. Let 'er go. Don't yer understand?" His voice rose in his desperation to make Silas comprehend the danger they were in. "The people searching for 'er are not idiots. They could be watchin' us as we speak. Let 'er go and we have a chance. Keep 'er and we're doomed."

"Never," Silas snapped, ferociously.

The two began to argue.


As slowly as possible, Kitty gazed around. Out of the corner of her left eye, she spied a figure lurking behind a post at the corner of the Shed. Swallowing a startled squeak, she peered into the sun. It was a man. *Was he friend or foe?* Trying to become one with the air, she moved almost imperceptibly sideways.

Harold and Silas were cursing up a storm. Insults, accusations of perfidy, and dire threats flew back and forth, neither giving the other any quarter. The pair were all but bouncing in their vehemence, and Kitty deduced a brawl was in the offing. A deduction well founded seconds later when Silas threw a punch. Harold retaliated with an uppercut and it was on.

This was her moment.

Lifting her skirts, Kitty turned to run.

Bulldog, realising her intent, abandoned his hiding place to intercept and protect her.

Silas saw the flicker of colour and roared his fury. Delivering a savage thump to Harold's belly, he gave chase.

Fear spurred Kitty on, but she had forgotten about the ice and missed her footing on the slippery cobbles. She pitched headlong onto the unforgiving stones, winding herself, scuffing her knees and palms.

Incensed beyond reason, Silas was on top of her in a trice, hauling her upright by her hair. Slinging one hand around her waist, he yanked her to him, pinning her back against his chest.

The knife in his other hand, he brought it up under her chin, the blade digging into the soft skin of her throat, cutting off Kitty's terrified scream.

Spewing a volley of expletives, Bulldog slithered to an abrupt standstill.

Now there were four.

Harold, gasping for breath, implored Silas not to hurt Kitty.
Bulldog waited, silent but watchful.
Silas cackled, the eerie sound echoing off the buildings.
Kitty remained motionless. Too scared to move. Too scared to breathe.

~

This was the tableau Lucas and his team came upon. Hurrying along the same alley, through which Bulldog had followed Silas, they heard muffled shouts and the unmistakeable sounds of a scuffle.

To a man, they sprinted the last few yards, skidding to a halt when they burst onto the wharf, temporarily blinded by the bright sunshine.

Quick on the uptake, the team flanked the four, but kept their distance. Clearly, Silas was unhinged, and they had no mind to exacerbate the situation.

# CHAPTER TWENTY-SEVEN

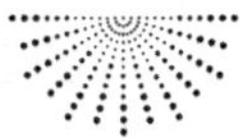

"Silas Dryden, my name is Lucas Withers. You are under arrest for murder, smuggling, kidnap, and false imprisonment. Release Lady Asquith." Lucas stepped forward, speaking in modulated tones.

"Don't make me larf. Why should I release me leverage?" Silas took two steps backwards, dragging Kitty with him.

"You will not escape, Mr Dryden. The Runners are rounding up your… lackeys, and we are looking forward to a quiet chat with a certain ship's captain, later today."

Silas crowed with laughter. "Which all sounds very interesting, *Mister* Wivvers, but I have the wench. Yer'll not hurt her so yer can't touch me." He tightened his hold, squeezing Kitty who bit her lip to suppress another scream.

"It's Major Withers," Lucas replied, mildly.

"*What?*" Silas countered, rudely.

"I am a major not a mister."

"What difference does that make?" Momentarily taken aback by the man's courteous tone.

"None, save you understand my men and I are a match for your cunning."

"We'll see about that." Silas spat on the cobbles. *Mister Major Bloody Withers.*

"Silas, let her go," Harold interjected. "We're done."

Pivoting, Silas pointed the knife at Harold.

"You, pathetic weasel," he snorted. "When you are rotting in jail, think of me being serviced by the lovely Sadie. For I will not be taken alive and I will not be taken today," he retorted, emphatically.

Silas gesticulated with the knife at the men advancing inexorably closer.

"Stay back. I am more than happy to slice her throat. She is no longer of use, except as a means to an end." He walked backwards until his heel came into contact with one of the timber sleepers marking the edge of the quay. A glance over his shoulder affirmed the water was high enough to risk the jump.

Unsurprised Silas had no qualms about killing her to affect his escape, Kitty forced everything else out of her head, and focused on his increasingly volatile behaviour.

Emboldened by the patently stalwart efforts of this Major Withers and his men, an inexplicable calm settled over her. That a group of people who did not know her, cared enough to save her, revitalised Kitty's flagging spirits.

*She was not going to die today.*

She had shot him. *Which leg was it?* She visualised the scene when she had fired the gun, identifying his injured leg. When Silas twisted, she felt his grip slacken slightly. Without pausing to consider the consequences, Kitty seized the advantage and drove her fist hard into his right thigh.

Silas bayed his agony, immediately releasing her. Her own

anger momentarily clouding her judgement, Kitty spun around and jabbed her knee hard into his groin. Howling in pain and fury, Silas doubled over.

A flurry of movement ensued as Lucas and his team closed in, trying to separate Kitty from her captor.

There was a loud click.

The report of a gun being fired, boomed around the buildings.

Kitty felt someone shove her, roughly.

Blood mushroomed out, coating those alongside the victim.

Appalled, Kitty saw a red stain bloom over Harold's chest; his astounded expression would have been amusing at any other time.

He locked eyes with Kitty as he crumpled to the ground.

"Run," he mouthed.

Realising it was he who had pushed her, she shook her head, stubbornly. "No, I am not leaving you to bleed on the ground, you saved my life."

Impervious to the chaos exploding around her, Kitty fell to her scuffed knees, lifted Harold's head onto her lap and tried to staunch the blood. Her hands became slick, but she continued to press them against the gruesome and obviously fatal wound.

"You will be fine, tis naught but a nick," she crooned.

"You are addled." Harold gave a lopsided smile, his breath coming in shallow gasps. "You cannot save me, Lady Asquith—"

"Call me Kitty," she interrupted, making him smile, just a little.

"Kitty." He dipped his head. "Do not waste your time on me. I've done nowt to be proud of, or to redeem meself since the day I was found by 'is nibs. I am not worthy of your charity. Go, get away before Silas finishes the job," Harold croaked.

Kitty lifted her head.

The light of battle and probably mania glittering in his eyes, Silas was dodging around the wharf. Nimbly, he avoided everyone's grasp, slashing the knife at anyone who got close.

Lucas' orders were to hold fire in hopes they could garner further information from Silas once he was in custody, in exchange for a lesser sentence. Also, Silas made sure no one had a clear shot.


Kitty's brow creased. Then she saw it.

Lying in a puddle of blood was the gun.

"That's as maybe, but I do believe you redeemed yourself today, and I *will* avenge you," she vowed, her fingers snagging the weapon. It was heavier than the one she had fired the previous day… *was it only yesterday?* It felt like a lifetime ago. *How many guns did Silas own?*

"Avenge me?" Spying the gun in her bloodied hands, Harold managed a feeble chuckle. "'Ow do yer propose to do that, m'lady? He's already fired," he wheezed.

Kitty watched, horrified, as blood bubbled out of his chest, and trickled over his waxen lips.

She studied the gun. "'Tis a double barrel," she muttered. "'Tis weighty, but…"

"You will end up shooting yerself, which I do not recommend, it hurts." Harold's voice was weakening.

"Hold on, Harold, please do not die. Help is coming." Kitty had no idea whether that was true but for reasons she could not explain, wanted him to survive.

"Forgive me, for being unable to grant your request. If yer

promise to live a long and happy life with that pretty daughter o' yours, I can die in peace." Harold spoke in as formal a tone as he could muster, but his words were little more than a whisper.

"I promise, Harold," Kitty pledged. Tears for the man who in the blink of an eye had gone from enemy to saviour, poured down her grubby cheeks.

"Don't cry, lass." Harold reached for her hand and brushed his lips to her knuckles.

With a weary sigh, he died.

Sobbing, Kitty swept her fingers over his eyes, closing them for the last time, leaving red smears across his face. Using her gown, it was ruined anyway, she dried her hands. Doing the same with the butt of the gun, she gripped it, getting comfortable with the weight.

Silas continued to bait the other men. Each time one of them grabbed him, he wriggled free. He was a master of evasion, which probably explained why he had never been apprehended before. Thus far, all they had prevented him from doing was jumping in the river. If he did, he was gone.

Laying Harold gently on the icy cobbles, Kitty got to her feet and rolled her shoulders. An unpleasant realisation skittered across the back of her mind. This was all Godfrey's fault. The varlet *still* controlled her. Even now, nigh on three years since his death, she was no less dominated than when he was alive, as shackled as she had been in that awful shed.

His intimidation of her ended today. She would only be free when she had severed every single solitary connection to Godfrey, to her marriage, and it started here. It started now. The last thing she had ever anticipated was *wanting* to kill another human being. The emotion scared but did not deter her.

*Adam. What was Adam doing? To be in his arms, oh to be in his arms.* She conjured up his face, picturing his cherished features one at a time. It helped steady her nerves, and thus her hands.

A quick glance to pinpoint each of the players, Kitty straightened her back and entered the fray.

~

Adam was wearing a path into the plush carpet of the library. He was torn between staying at The Laurels, in case Kitty came home, or taking Pembroke and joining the search. He muttered as he paced, talking himself in and out of various options.

A sweet voice broke into his cogitation.

"Adam, do stop for a moment and have a cup of coffee with me." It was Louisa Wells, David's wife.

"Aunt Louisa, when…?" Adam frowned. *What time was it?* He walked over to squint at the clock on the mantel. It was nearly eleven. Kitty was abducted twenty-four hours ago, and he knew the longer a person was missing, the less likely they were to be found alive.

"Pembroke showed me in about fifteen minutes past. You did not even hear him announce me, and I have been listening to your grumblings ever since. Come and sit by me, Adam." Louisa patted the adjacent chair.

"Stewing over the whys, wherefores and what ifs, does not help. Kitty will need to you be strong of heart and mind when she is returned—"

Adam started to speak but Louisa raised her hand.

"Yes, she will be returned. I have every faith in Major Withers, he is good man."

"How can you be so certain," Adam quizzed, doing as she

bade. He picked up his coffee, the robust aroma helping to cure his aching head.

"I know him, I believe in him. He helped a friend of ours. He is ethical, respectful, discreet and dogged." Louisa's confidence touched something in Adam, and he allowed himself a brief smile.

"That's better." She beamed. "Now, I want to hear all about how our scamp of a Kitty became a governess."

"That was Mama's madcap idea." Adam sipped his drink and told the tale.

Louisa studied her nephew while he talked. He looked haggard, possibly more so than after he was released from hospital.

Determined not to let him wallow, she engaged him in lively conversation, mostly related to the four families who had been friends for so many years. They exchanged snippets the other did not know, and the easy chatter soothed Adam's anxiety, for a time.

Silas did not see Kitty approach. He was intent on avoiding arrest by any one of the dozen or so men circling ever nearer.

With a mind to the ice scarcely melting in the autumn sunlight, Kitty marched towards her nemesis. Godfrey's vile torments, along with his and Silas' despicable deeds, swirled around her head, fuelling her anger and her determination. This time she would not miss.

When Lucas spotted Kitty holding the gun, his heart missed a beat. "Lady Asquith, Kitty." He dared use her name, in hopes of getting her to look his way.

She shot him a sidelong glance. He held out his hand, but she shook her head.

"No, he is mine, I want this finished," she objected, bitterly.

"Kitty," Lucas wheedled, "we need him alive. We need him to talk."

"About what? You know what he has done. What else is there?" She slowed her steps.

"Names, businesses, other brothels, anything that helps us terminate his operations in their entirety. Leave this to us, Kitty, please. He will not escape."

Lucas' words struck a chord.

"He does not deserve to live," she fumed.

"No, he does not, but to spend the rest of his days in Newgate is a fitting punishment."

"Should he not hang?" Kitty deplored capital punishment but today, she was a proponent of the noose.

"Yes, he should but, if he talks and the information is credible, he might be spared the drop. Do not take his life, Kitty. You do not want that on your conscience. 'Tis a burden from which you never recover. Silas Dryden has already destroyed enough. Do not allow him to ruin your peace of mind too," Lucas cajoled.

Kitty pondered this, ignoring the shouts of the men.

Her anger evaporated as quickly as it had erupted. The hand holding the gun wavered and sagged. She turned to face Silas.

"Silas Dryden." Her voice rang over the hubbub. "You are the spawn of Satan and I hope you rot in hell."

"Only if you come with me, bitch," Silas sniggered and hurled the knife.

Like a ghastly parody, the men tried to intercept the blade as it whistled through the air towards Kitty.

Silas chortled and, seeing his pursuers otherwise occupied, tried to make good his escape.

*No, he was **not** getting away.* Oblivious to the imminent danger of being filleted, Kitty raised the gun and fired. The bullet ripped through Silas' shoulder as, simultaneously, his knife sliced through Kitty's cloak.

With an agonised screech, Silas staggered backwards. His heel caught on a sleeper and he toppled into the river with a resounding splash.

Grimacing — the Thames was more fetid than a suppurating wound — Bulldog dived in after him, grabbing the man's jacket with scant consideration for his injury.

"Are you hurt?" Lucas grabbed Kitty and opened her cloak.

Streaks of blood marred her dress, but it was drying — Harold's blood.

"Forgive me, my lady, I must examine you." Uncaring how inappropriate it was, Lucas checked Kitty as thoroughly as he was able without actually removing her clothes.

"Major Withers, fret not, I believe I am unharmed." Kitty gave a tremulous smile. "My cloak might be torn, and I do feel rather strange."

The world receded and for the first time in her life, Kitty fainted, folding onto the ground in a graceful heap.

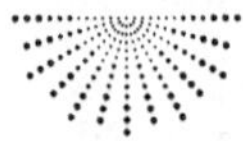

The sound of a carriage rattling along the street penetrated Adam's cogitation. Leaping to his feet, he was out of the library and crossing the hall to the front door before Louisa could stop him.

"Kitty." He wrenched open the heavy door. Grasping the handrail, he sprinted down the steps.

"Yes, she's here."

Adam heard the unruffled tones of Lucas Withers.

"She's a trifle battered and bruised, but otherwise unharmed, although I imagine she would appreciate a long soak in a hot bath." The humour in Lucas' voice settled Adam as little else would, knowing he would not be so genial if Kitty was badly hurt.

It was a trick advocated by senior officers in all branches of the military. When news was delivered with a sober demeanour, the recipient assumed it was grievous and gave up. Addressed in chirpy tones, they were assured they would survive.

. . .

Lucas assisted a bloodied and dishevelled figure out of the carriage.

Kitty stood on the path and breathed deeply. The chill air was lightly fragranced with woodsmoke coiling up from numerous chimneys, mixed with a hint of loam, courtesy of damp gardens.

Adam was there. Solid, handsome, beloved Adam. She had begun to think she would never see him, or their children, again.

"Thank you, Maj… Lucas." She smiled her gratitude. "I am in your debt."

He bowed. "Trust me, my lady. There is no debt. Live a long and happy life, that is repayment enough." His words echoed Harold's.

Kitty was still rather wobbly on her feet, and Lucas led her to where Adam waited. "Yours, I believe." He placed her hand on Adam's arm.

Indifferent to the fact they were in the middle of the street, in view of numerous spectators, Adam whisked Kitty against him to kiss her as though he would never let her go again. A sentiment he was seriously considering.

"Adam." Kitty giggled. "I am filthy and doubtless smelly. Your clothes will end up coated in grime."

"I do not care. Oh God, Kitty, I was so afraid…"

"Seems I have at least one guardian angel," Kitty murmured, for his ears only. She turned to Lucas. "Please do come in for some refreshments," she implored. "You must be exhausted and 'tis the least we can do after your sterling work."

Lucas shook his head. "Thank you, Kitty, I must decline your generous invitation. There is much left to do, including reports aplenty, and I would like to see my wife before day's end. She will be forgetting what I look like." He grinned. "I shall be in touch."

Tipping his hat, Lucas climbed back into the carriage, which trundled away.

Louisa expressed her delight at seeing Kitty, despite the circumstances. Affirming she would apprise David of the good news, and that they would pay a call after things had settled, the marchioness took her leave.

When Adam thanked his aunt for her kindness and support, she patted him on the cheek.

"It was nothing. I am glad to have been of some small help. Go." She flapped her hands at the two of them. "A bath then bed, that will work wonders."

With a smile and a wave, Louisa was gone.

Adam lifted Kitty and carried her up the steps into the house.

"Adam I can walk." She spluttered with laughter, the bell-like sound resounding around the cavernous space.

"I know." He pressed a kiss to her grubby face. "Indulge me. How is it I keep finding you coated in blood?" Heartened by the sound of her mirth, not to mention the feeling of her safely in his arms.

"Because you are my knight in shining armour." She kissed his jaw… the only part of his face she could reach.

As they ascended stairs, people appeared from every-where, exclaiming over her safe return.

"Thank you, so much." Kitty blushed, inordinately pleased by their rapturous welcome. "I am very glad to be home. Adam, please put me down." She wriggled.

Adam did as she asked, but entwined their fingers, his thumb rubbing over hers.

A barrage of questions rained down on her and she put up her hands in mock defence. "I am happy to tell you what happened, but it will be later. First, I must see the children, and then please may I beg you to fill my bath? I am unsure whether I shall ever feel clean again, but I ought to try." She gave them an impish grin and they fled to fulfil her request.

Hand in hand, Kitty and Adam walked along the corridor to the nursery.

Kitty pushed the door, and stood a moment, eyes fixed on her daughter. Lucas had confirmed Evie was unscathed, but Kitty would not be satisfied until she had seen for herself. The two children were absorbed in a game with Hettie, and Kitty had no mind to disturb them.

Pulling the door closed, she rested her head on Adam's chest. His arms slid around her, and a solicitous finger tilted her chin so he could study her face.

"Kitty?" Expecting her to burst into the room and hug the children, Adam was puzzled.

"I do not want either of them to see me like this, Adam. I am covered in blood and dirt. Not a sight for innocent babes. Another hour or so will make no difference."

Adam tightened his embrace. "Come then, let us get you out of these clothes."

Once the capacious bath was filled, Kitty shooed out the maid, assuring her she could manage. Adam unbuttoned her gown, then removed her underclothes piece by piece, kissing her tenderly as each garment fluttered to the floor.

He helped her into the bath, then knelt beside the tub, the subtle perfume from the salts enveloping them. Cupping his head, Kitty held his gaze for long moments, before pressing her lips to his cheeks, his scars, his eyes.

Dipping the soap into the steaming water, Adam began to bathe his betrothed, leisurely tracing her shape with the delicately scented ball.

Immersing herself, Kitty washed her hair, removing the last remnants of her night in captivity. A variety of bruises and abrasions, livid against her pale skin, were exposed as the blood and dirt dissolved.

The sight enraged Adam. *Oh, for five minutes with Silas Dryden.* With an effort, he set it aside and concentrated on Kitty.

Using a jug to rinse off the soap, he rang for a change of water.


The tub refilled, Kitty sank under the surface once again, to emerge, water cascading down her body and streaming from her hair.

Adam was watching her, one arm on the rim of the bath, his fingers dangling in the water.

"Join me?" Kitty invited.

Adam's eyes widened.

"Do you not think it would be heavenly?"

"I think it would more than heavenly, but perhaps not very sensible."

"I do not have any desire to be sensible. I want to be impulsive. I do not want to be restricted by the rules any more than is absolutely necessary. We are alone. We are affianced. Join me," she reiterated.

"But…"

Kitty stoked a slender finger along his cheek, then trailed it from the hollow at the base of her throat, to the valley between her breasts.

"Join me, Adam."

Near enough to see what she was doing, Adam's body reacted, to the point of acute discomfort. A fleeting internal debate ensued after which, he divested himself of his clothes with ungentlemanly haste.

"How am I supposed to fit?" he muttered.

Kitty shuffled forward and nodded over her shoulder. "Behind me."

Adam climbed in. It was cramped, but the feeling of Kitty settling between his legs, her body aligned with his, her head nestled on his shoulder and the hot water rippling around them was worth their slightly painful confines.

With a sigh of pure pleasure, Kitty relaxed against him, her fingers gliding up and down his calves.

Adam swallowed a groan.

"I love you, Adam." She clutched his fingers to kiss his knuckles.

"I love you too, Kitty." His free hand explored, as his lips found the soft skin behind her ear. He felt her quiver.

"Not the most suitable place or time to be making love." A statement belied as he continued his re-discovery.

"Perhaps, but don't stop," she entreated.

"We will flood the room, my sweet." He made a half-hearted attempt to divert her. "We have our whole lives ahead of us.

"I know, but I want this moment. 'Tis your turn to rescue me." Kitty squirmed around until she was on her knees facing him. Water sloshed over the rim of the tub.

Placing her palms on his chest, she bent forward, grazing her lips over the hardened planes of his torso. Her fingers skimmed his scars, before running through the smattering of dark hair on his chest.

Adam stilled.

"I am sorry I failed you." His tone hinted at the despair he had endured while she was missing.

"What nonsense. You did not fail me," Kitty refuted, strenuously.

"I have never felt so helpless."

"Oh, my darling, had your sight been unimpaired, you could not have found me. Yet in truth you still saved me."

He raised a sceptical brow. "How so?"

"You saved Evie. You trusted your instincts and you caught her. That is the greatest gift you could ever give me." She kissed him with fierce ardour, feeling his body tremble in response.

"Love me, Adam." She repeated her plea from the night they were first intimate.

While his lips teased and tormented, his fingers sought that most secret part of her, drawing her to the brink. Steam and heat coiled around them, heightening awareness.

Tracking ever lower, Kitty's inquisitive hands found and encircled his rigid manhood. Desire sizzled, and soft moans mingled with whispered endearments as their passion spiralled.


Not entirely certain how well they would be able to quench their thirst for each other in so constrained a space, Adam shifted Kitty until she was beneath him.

"Hold the edge," he rasped, his control evaporating.

Instead of clutching either side as Adam expected and never breaking eye contact, Kitty reached behind her head to grip the rim of the tub. Slanting his eyes, Adam saw her voluptuous body stretched out under him, glistening wet and ripe for the taking.

Using the side of the bath to balance his weight, he hovered above her, kissing her from her neck to her navel.

Kitty arched upwards, revelling in the glissade of sensations his lips were provoking. Her body craving his.

Their mouths met, tongues tangled, and the blaze kindled. Ignoring the odd twinge as knees and elbows encountered unyielding metal, they melded.

Though no less fervent than previously, the union of their bodies seemed gilded with a rare sweetness, a sensually seductive melody borne of trauma, loss, and grief.

A revival.

A reclaiming.

A rescue.

While Kitty and Adam began to obliterate the crushing horror of the previous two days, Lucas and his men were preoccupied with more mundane tasks.

Silas was transported to Newgate Prison where he was left to cool his heels. Harold's body was removed, and the quayside scrubbed clean.

By midday, anyone who happened by would be ignorant of the chaos which had unfolded scant hours previously.

In the carriage on her way home, Kitty had informed Lucas she wanted to pay for a proper burial for Harold. Despite his shady past, he *had* saved her life, and he had no one else.

To be tossed in a common grave felt disrespectful, given the circumstances of his death.

Lucas proposed he handle the arrangements, and would notify Kitty once finalised. An offer she gladly accepted.

Over the next few days, numerous interviews were conducted with the women found in Newell Street, and the sundry inhabitants of The Den as well as, those of Silas' cronies they could run to ground.

Silas' office was examined thoroughly, and anything relevant, collected, especially his nicely stacked sheaf of papers. Their search uncovered a network of businesses and schemes that would take weeks to unravel.

Lucas, Slater, and enough constables to prevent anyone absconding, met the ship when it docked at a lonely wharf, not far from where Kitty had been held. Captain and crew were escorted to Bow Street and interrogated, while their cargo was analysed.

Initially, the captain, averse to losing a thriving trade was tight-lipped — unlike his crew who readily gave up the whole operation. Lucas reminded the captain of the penalty for kidnap and smuggling. There was a speedy reversal of attitude, and the latter professed himself eager to shed light on Silas' affairs.

The investigation was exhaustive. Once Lucas was satisfied, they had collated every last piece of evidence, he went to Newgate to question Silas.

On a grey morning, three days after Silas was caught, Lucas was shown to a dismal room, which sported a table, and two chairs. One small window offered little light, and did nothing to soften the austerity. Moments later, Silas shuffled in, a guard on either side. He was chained, the irony of that not lost on Lucas.

Leading Silas to the spare chair, one guard stood behind the prisoner, while the other took up his position outside the door.

"We meet again, Mr Dryden," Lucas greeted the erstwhile mastermind, murderer, and malefactor.

Silas said nothing, his eyes fixed on the table.

In a voice devoid of inflection, Lucas outlined the case against him.

The murder of a viscount — attributed to Silas by his henchmen, although Lucas did not believe he had acted alone. Kidnap and smuggling of countless women. Owner and operator of at least half a dozen brothels masquerading as gaming hells. Abduction and attempted murder of Lady Asquith. Attempted abduction and endangerment of a child. Murder of Harold Simpkins. Assorted criminal activities. The list went on.

Lucas glanced at the accused several times during this litany, but Silas showed no visible reaction.

"Are you willing to divulge any more particulars in relation to your exploits?" Lucas concluded.

Silas lifted his head to glower mutinously at Lucas. "I am not guilty."

Lucas chuckled. "We have accumulated a formidable amount of proof to the contrary. I saw you shoot Mr Simpkins, Silas. I have witnesses to the abduction of Lady Asquith, not to mention you threatened to kill her in front of me."

Adopting a more accommodating stance, he leant forward, resting his elbows, on the table. "Come on, man, why? What does the viscountess have or know which possessed you to take such drastic action?"

Obstinately, Silas sat close-mouthed, and the silence lengthened. About to signal the guard, Lucas heard a resigned grunt.

"She saw me."

"Beg pardon?" Lucas was perplexed.

Silas shrugged and exhaled a philosophical sigh. "When I told her about 'er 'usband's involvement, she were genuinely shocked, but by then she'd seen me, could describe me. I couldn't risk 'er telling anyone. Mind, 'e were a rotter, worse'n me really," he mused.

Despite the gravity of the interview, Lucas hid a grin.

"'E had peculiar tastes and abused some of me girls terrible like. A few refused to service 'im, preferred to risk a belting, but 'is coin was good and reg'lar. 'E financed me operation and we split the profits. Then 'e got greedy and thought he could intimidate me. *Me.*" Silas jabbed at his chest confounded anyone could be idiotic enough to challenge him.

"I did fer 'im. Nobody double-crosses Silas Dryden." He paused, his lips moving as though arguing with himself. A slight shrug then. "I'll be 'onest wiv yer, 'e weren't the first person I'd killed, but 'is death was the one which gave me most satisfaction."

Lucas felt as though he ought to reprimand Silas. To remind him of the sanctity of life but, in his heart of hearts, he could not disagree. From all he had learned of Godfrey Lovell, the man lost his humanity long before he died and did not warrant a moment's pity.

# CHAPTER TWENTY-NINE

"So, Lady Asquith had seen you." Lucas guided the conversation back to the day in question.

"She'd seen both me and 'Arold. She knew no one had been arrested for her 'usband's murder and there's me bloody confessin' to it." Silas slapped his forehead.

"I tell yer, I made more mistakes that day than in the rest o' me life put togevver. Give 'Arold 'is due, 'e warned me, but there'd bin too many strange goin's on wiv me business, too many close calls." He frowned, still puzzled as to who was at the root of the issue.

Silas went on to explain why he suspected Kitty's involvement. "Like I said, when I saw 'er face," he shook his head. "Devil take me, she was innocent, but it were too late. I don't hold wiv killin' women but putting 'er on the next ship, now *that* were a good alternative. It'd get 'er out o' me 'air and no mess." He rocked back in his seat.

Heinous though Silas' deeds had been, Lucas acknowledged a grudging admiration for the man. Typical of most criminals working the sordid underbelly of London, he had found a niche and filled it, believing he was not *really* harming anyone else… or at least, anyone who mattered.

Godfrey Lovell had violated their unwritten code and paid for it. Those making their living on the wrong side of the law did not take prisoners and left no witnesses — hence Kitty's brush with death.

Now Silas had started talking, he was loath to stop, and the two men chatted for almost two hours, with Lucas jotting down copious notes. By the time Lucas was confident he had extracted everything he could, the sun had broken through the low cloud, giving the bleak room false cheer.


"I'm gonna hang for this, aren't I?" Silas asked when Lucas stood to leave.

Lucas did not believe in beating about the bush.

"I expect so." He held Silas' gaze. "For what it's worth, I understand your motives, but you committed murder twice that we know of, and were prepared to kill Lady Asquith, in front of a dozen men."

He paused and for no discernible reason, felt the need to give Silas a kernel of hope. "It depends on the judge. Perhaps given your rationale, life behind bars—"

"I'd rather 'ang," Silas interrupted, chewing his lip.

Aware of what constituted lifetime imprisonment, Lucas conceded it was probably the lesser punishment.

"Thank you, Silas, this has been an… enlightening morning."

"Major Wivvers, sir," Silas hesitated.

Lucas waited.

"If yer see 'er, will yer tell 'er I'm sorry." He had no need to elaborate.

"I will." Lucas banged on the door. The guard came in and Silas was led away. He turned once and gave a perfunctory nod. Lucas reciprocated, thinking how promptly men changed their tune when faced with their own mortality.

Back in his peaceful office on Bow Street, Lucas added his notes to the rapidly expanding file, and compiled his report for the court.

Then, needing a respite from the brutality of his job, went home for luncheon, where he was greeted with open arms and a heartfelt kiss by his wife.

Life at The Laurels reverted to its normal state of genteel bedlam.

Oscar was ecstatic when he woke from his nap to see Kitty sitting by his bed, Evie on her lap, and begged to hear all about her adventure.

He reminded Kitty of her twin brothers at the same age, who would only consent to read if it was a grisly tale. Avoiding the nightmare inducing elements of the previous two days, Kitty told her story.

Evie, too young to understand, clung to her mother chewing on a hunk of bread, her world set to rights.

As far as the children were concerned that was it. Mama was home, they were happy. Kitty's peace of mind was not so easily restored. Stalked by night terrors in the immediate aftermath, Kitty found sleep elusive, and Adam often woke to find her missing from their bed.

She was usually in library. Snuggled into one of the chairs, her feet tucked under her dressing gown, enjoying the warmth thrown out by the dying embers of the fire. A candle by her elbow, engrossed in some ancient tome.

Unable to settle without Kitty beside him, Adam joined her. It became a pleasant and unexpectedly cathartic habit for them to talk during the hours before dawn. Primarily, it helped Kitty come to terms with her experiences, but as the days went on, their conversations evolved into profound discussions about their lives.

Adam was persuaded into relating the events preceding, and subsequent to, the explosion, which had robbed him of his sight, his career and almost his sanity. In turn, Kitty answered his questions about her marriage, supplying Adam with a more detailed picture of her life with Godfrey.

Once recounted, the couple consigned their pasts to history, to be revisited only if necessary. Replacing them with far more congenial topics, such as their hopes and dreams, and their own future together.

Adam wanted to spend as many years as possible at Teasdale Mallow, a suggestion Kitty espoused eagerly. Plans began to take shape, were reviewed, amended, and revised. Their enthusiasm only increasing the more they talked.

One night while curled up together on the chaise not talking, simply cherishing the closeness, Adam disentangled himself, and walked across to the polished mahogany escritoire tucked under one of the windows.

Lifting the lid, he withdrew something, retraced his steps, and with studied nonchalance, handed Kitty a sheet of heavy vellum, rolled and tied with red ribbon.

"Pray tell what it this?" She smiled as he resumed his seat beside her.

"Open it and see."

Kitty untied the ribbon, and the paper unfurled. It was

covered in elegant copperplate script. She looked at Adam and back at the sheet, trying to hold it flat so she could read it in the glow of the candelabra perched on the table next to the chaise.

"Hold this please." She waved it under his nose.

Adam chuckled, and grasped the edge as requested, while Kitty did the same with the opposite side. It was a special marriage license. Expensive and not easy to obtain.

"When did you find the time to organise this?" she breathed, stunned.

"I went to the office in Doctors' Commons…" where such licenses were granted, "…on my way home after one of my hospital appointments."

"Over a fortnight ago?" Kitty, squeaked, flabbergasted. "Why this and not a traditional church ceremony?"

Adam reached for her hands. "I wish to pledge my life to you in our folly. I know it might sound fanciful, quixotic even. I want to declare my love to you before God and our families, but the folly has a special meaning, and I do not believe God is restricted to hallowed sanctuaries."

Kitty studied his face, spying a hint of apprehension in his expression. That he had come up with so romantic a setting for their nuptials, spoke volumes.

"Quixotic it may be, but it is also perfect." She twisted on the chaise to slide her hands around his neck. "I could not imagine anywhere more fitting. My Knight, your grand gesture demands a grand response. The rug looks so very comfortable, and the fire is warm." Gratified to see Adam's eyes darken.

"A moment." Kitty eased out of his arms to lock the door. "Yes, 'tis the middle of the night, but I would rather not be interrupted."

"Kitty Lovell, you are shameless." Adam chuckled.

"I know, is it not outrageous?" Kitty twinkled, and, taking

his hand, drew him down next to her, where she illustrated her delight with relish.

～

In due course, the case of Silas Dryden was brought to trial. In view of the charges — specifically those pertaining to the death of Lord Asquith and the abduction and attempted murder of his wife — it attracted widespread attention.

The courtroom was packed to bursting, with people loitering outside waiting avidly to hear the gory details.

Given the profusion of evidence against Silas, Kitty had been assured she need not testify either as a victim or a witness.

Her response, although couched much more politely, went along the lines of…

"…try to stop me."

Kitty had no doubt Silas would be convicted. Initially, she balked at the idea of reliving those awful hours, because it meant sharing her ordeal with the general public. That said, she also believed, to articulate what she had suffered, rather than allow it to fester was an essential part of the healing process.

By describing being snatched off the street, imprisoned without food or water, not knowing whether she would live or die and, if she *did* survive, what her future held, Kitty hoped the shackles of fear in which Silas had trapped her that day would disintegrate.

The court was quiet enough to hear a pin drop when Kitty gave her testimony. Her voice did not falter, and she held the gaze of whoever was asking the questions without wavering.

There were nods of approval when she detailed why she

had fired the gun... twice. Eyes became slits of disgust when she mentioned Silas throwing Evie. A collective hiss rippled around when she came to Harold's death.

Jubilant reporters scribbled pages of notes. This was a story to keep their readers spellbound for weeks.


When it was over, Kitty felt as though a lead weight had been lifted from her shoulders. A light-heartedness absent since her abduction — in fact, possibly since her marriage, suffused her being. By eliminating the last link in the chain binding her to Godfrey, the liberation Kitty craved was finally hers.


To the disappointment of the crowds, the trial only lasted two days. It could have been wrapped up in one, but this was a high-profile case. The presiding judge, basking in the publicity, liked playing to an audience, and stretched out proceedings.

The verdict was never in question. The plethora of evidence was sufficient to hang Silas multiple times, but the judge delayed his sentencing until the day after the trial concluded.

Everyone knew his declaration that he needed time to re-read the witness statements was nothing but a ploy to prolong the drama.

No one complained.

This was the highlight of the year.

Why rush it.

❧

Inevitably, Silas was condemned to hang. Kitty attended the hearing with Adam and tried to remain objective when the sentence was handed down. Despite everything, she experienced a stab of anguish for the man in the dock.

Lucas had passed on Silas' apology. Cynically, Kitty speculated whether Silas was genuinely sorry for his actions, or sorry he got caught, but was generous enough to give him the benefit of the doubt. To reject his attempt to make amends would be to her detriment, not his.

Silas' gesture, in conjunction with her own abhorrence of capital punishment, had prompted Kitty to petition the judge, in a private interview, to waive the death penalty.

She argued that hanging Silas was too easy a ruling, and surely to languish in prison, day in and day out, knowing the only release was death, would be far more fitting.

While sympathetic to her appeal, the judge refused to be swayed.


The sentence would be carried out immediately.


Alone, his life forfeit, Silas quailed, abruptly comprehending how his victims had felt.

He raised his head and looked straight at Kitty.

Deaf to the furore in the room, she held his gaze.

With a wry twitch of his lips, he bowed in tacit acknowledgement of his fate.

Expressionless, Kitty inclined her head, and watched the guards escort Silas from the courtroom.

The touch of a hand on her arm broke into her reverie and she turned to see Adam studying her, his forehead furrowed, solicitously.

"Do you wish to view the execution?" he asked, his tone indicating he hoped her answer would be in the negative.

"In this I am irresolute. In my heart, I have no desire to be a spectator, regardless of the man's crimes. That said, my fear is, if I am not witness to his demise, I may never be free of him." She squeezed Adam's arm. "It goes against my principles, but perhaps we might observe from a discreet distance. If only to put the whole sorry affair to rest."

He patted her gloved hand.

Lucas appeared at Kitty's elbow. "Come with me, Kitty, Adam. I know of a secluded vantage point." He led them through a maze of corridors and up several flights of stairs to an unoccupied room overlooking the gallows.

"Are you sure?" he pressed when the three were standing by the window. His question required no elucidation.

Adam, acutely conscious of the toll incurred when a life is taken, reiterated Lucas' remark.

Lifting her chin, Kitty nodded.


The crowds had increased, the noise ear-splitting. Unnoticed, at the back of the throng and half in shadow, stood a man with no distinguishing features. Dressed from head to toe in grey, hat pulled low over his face, he surveyed the scene in silence.

The moment came.
The sudden hush was as deafening as the cacophony.

At the last second, Kitty averted her eyes, unable to watch.

The trap was sprung.
The hooded figure dropped and jerked violently.

Loud cheers snapped Kitty's gaze back to the scene and she could not prevent a shocked gasp at the sight of the body, suspended in mid-air like a rag doll.

She gripped Adam's arm, determined not to weep. This was the second death she had experienced in less than a month and, however much she argued with herself that it had been justified, it was still the loss of a life.

"Take her home, Adam." Lucas' compassionate tone penetrated Kitty's distress.

"Thank you, Lucas." She offered a watery smile. "Perhaps now we can step out of the pall this man has cast across our lives." Her poetic words suited the sombre mood.

"I reiterate my thanks," Adam interposed. "I am endlessly glad we met. You are indeed a good man. Something Louisa Wells said," he clarified, in answer to Lucas' bemused expression.

They followed Lucas back the way they had come and walked out into the weak November sunshine.

Slowly, the crowds were dispersing, the spectacle over. The man in grey, long gone.

Turning once to wave, Adam and Kitty climbed into their coach and left the past behind. Their future beckoned.

# CHAPTER THIRTY

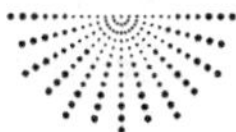

## NEW YEAR'S EVE ~ 1815

*E*asby Hall seethed with excitement. Today, Adam Reginald Marchmain, Marquis of Teasdale was to be joined in holy matrimony to Katherine Elizabeth Lovell née de Wilton, Viscountess Asquith.

Reverend Stainton, not in the least perturbed by the venue, would conduct the ceremony. As well as their families, staff, and friends, the guest list included Lucas and Jemima, along with as many of Lucas' team as could be spared.

Thick snow carpeted the ground and softened the stark branches of the leafless trees. The dazzling white was alleviated by swathes of dark green, courtesy of holly and juniper, cedar and pine.

Bright berries attracted those birds, hardy enough to tolerate winter in England, their dulcet chorus a cheerful backdrop to the celebrations.

. . .

In her bedchamber, Kitty was being assisted into her wedding raiment by Mabel. Wispy underclothes in the palest pink, underneath frothy layers of silk in a hue reminiscent of apple blossom. The gown, as Kitty had remarked to Mabel, was ridiculously frivolous, but when Madame Renaud had shown her the drawing, Kitty fell in love with the design.

The delicate shades complemented her alabaster complexion and blonde hair perfectly. She felt like the heroine from a fairy tale, and given Adam had always called her his princess, it seemed a felicitous choice.

The rose patterned satin of the fitted bodice — repeated in the frills, and the bows on the sleeves — was a colourful contrast to the plain pink silk, and ivory lace overlay of the skirts. Mabel twisted Kitty's shining locks into an ornate bun, interwoven with a matching ribbon.

Sliding her feet into pink silk slippers, Kitty stared at her reflection.

"Why, I look quite presentable." She turned this way and that. "Thank you, Mabel."

"You are most welcome, my lady, and you look exquisite. Do you need a few minutes? I've got your cloak."

"I would appreciate it." Kitty smiled her gratitude at the maid's perception. "I shall be there shortly."

Mabel left on the hunt for Oscar and Evie.

In the peace of her chambers, Kitty let her thoughts roam.

They had returned from London, perhaps a trifle subdued, but resolute. Without delay, Adam had discussed their remove to the Teasdale country estate, with his father who wholeheartedly approved.

"Kitty needs a place to recover from her tribulations and the pair of you need to begin married life in your own home.

I do not intend to forsake this earth for a goodly number of years, so go, be a family, without encumbrance." Reginald had decreed. A sentiment Prudence reiterated.

"We will miss you, all of you, but Teasdale Mallow is not too far away." With a loving kiss, she whispered, "I am so proud of you, my son. I *knew* you could overcome your limitations. You just needed the right incentive."

That had been a little over a month ago. All arrangements were in place, and everything was packed. Weather permitting, Kitty and Adam would leave on the morrow. Oscar and Evie were to stay with their grandparents for an extra fortnight, allowing the newlyweds quality time alone.

This took some persuasion. Neither Kitty nor Adam liked being apart from their children, but Prudence and Frederica took a stance against which even the most redoubtable would quake. Acknowledging the futility of their objections, the couple acquiesced.

They had chosen New Year's Eve deliberately. At the farewell of the old year, they could shut the door on what had gone before. The dawn of the new year symbolising the beginning of their life together as husband and wife.

Whimsical their reasoning may be, but Kitty and Adam, wearied of the rational and the predictable, championed the unorthodox.

Now, moments from the start of the rest of her life, Kitty summoned up the malignant elements from her past. In a curious gesture, she held out her hand, visualised each facet and rolled them into a ball, which she imagined to be suspended over her outstretched palm.

With a swift flick of her fingers, she relegated it to history.

Smiling, she smoothed out her skirts and stepped forward.

~

In Adam's old suite of rooms in the opposite wing of the house, Mr Wilderby was brushing non-existent fluff from the back of the groom's jacket. Adam was attired in a dark charcoal suit of the finest wool, and white shirt.

Recruiting the help of Mabel and Mrs Wilderby, and without them revealing any specifics, he arranged to have a waistcoat made in a rich cherry brocade, which bore hints of the same pink found in Kitty's gown.

Matching cravat and handkerchief completed the outfit. His feet encased in black leather shoes; Adam was ready.

"You look very handsome, my lord, if I may say so." Mr Wilderby folded his arms and studied Adam.

"Thank you, Wilderby." Adam faced the mirror, squinting at the indistinct figure within.

"I shall return shortly," the butler intoned and backed out, leaving Adam to his thoughts.

In the peace of his chambers, Adam reflected on the past year. Twelve months ago, he could not have anticipated meeting another who could cause his heart to trip or his breathing to stutter. He had resigned himself to a solitary life, reliant on others, the only light in his gloomy future, Oscar.

Then came Kitty, whose own plight had left her unrecognisable to him. A practically minded man, Adam was willing to concede it was more than happenstance, steered them along this intricate path. Somehow, their lives had converged at the precise moment each needed the other, however unconsciously.

A smile tweaked at his lips. His darling betrothed had finally reverted to the Kitty of his recall. Spirited, vivacious, and fiery; sweet, kind, and tender. The events in London, although tragic, ended the chapter of her life which had quashed her natural exuberance. Like a butterfly emerging from a cocoon, she had unfurled her wings and taken flight.

"You are becoming fanciful in your old age, Adan March-main," he muttered with a dry chuckle, as another notion nudged at him.

*Had the obstacles and crises which littered their journey to this point been a necessary evil, giving them the courage to remain steadfast and embrace their second chance at true happiness?*

He pondered this for a moment. It was feasible, and he was not about to question whichever celestial being had issued the decree.

A rap at the door heralded Mr Wilderby, and shortly thereafter Adam was crossing the stepping stones to the folly.

~

A warm, ivory-hued cloak slung around her shoulders, Kitty walked towards the lake on the arm of her proud father. The sight which met her eyes prompted a rush of tears. She blinked them back furiously and concentrated on not tripping over in the snow.

. . .

The staff, elated their young master and his betrothed were to marry at the Hall, had taken it upon themselves to decorate the folly. Tendrils of ivy festooned the white pillars, the bases of which were wreathed with boughs of laurel and fir, bedecked with silver and gold ribbon.

Not a breath of wind ruffled the silvery, glass-like surface of the lake. A flock of swans floated regally around the little island, for all the world as though they were watching proceedings.

A shimmering white landscape framed the water, muffling all sound. The sky was grey, more snow in the offing, although a weak winter sun was trying to break through.

At the edge of the lake, leaving a natural aisle leading to the stepping stones, the guests had foregathered, chattering in hushed tones.

Oscar and Evie, clothed in brand new outfits which matched those of their respective parents, were jumping up and down, trying to spot Kitty. Evie loved her new dress and kept twirling around. Oscar, on the other hand, tugging at his cravat was disgruntled. *How was he supposed to play in such fancy clothes? They were too stiff.* His pleas not to wear the dratted outfit fell on deaf ears.

"'Tis only for a short time," Adam had cajoled, "and it will make Mama very happy."

Since Oscar would do anything for Mama, he had, with bad grace, capitulated. Slightly mollified when Kitty assured him, he could change straight after the ceremony.

"There she is," Oscar yelled. Evie repeated his words like a ditty. Their antics, barely restrained by doting grandparents, drew a benevolent chuckle as the company watched a blushing Kitty approach.

. . .

When Kitty reached the cluster of people, she saw Reverend Stainton say something to Adam, who turned and, without equivocation, looked directly at her. She knew he could not see her but swore their eyes locked.

Lord Grafton led his daughter through the throng and ushered her onto the first stone.

"Thank you, Papa," she said. "I love you."

"I love you too, precious." He smiled and kissed her cheek. "Forgive me for approving Asquith's suit. Had I known…" His countenance, contrite.

Kitty stared at her father in astonishment. "It was not your fault, Papa. The boor hoodwinked us all but, had I not married him, I doubt we would be here today." She spread her hands, encompassing the entire scene. "So, perhaps it was a blessing in disguise. Albeit a particularly *devious* disguise."

She winked at her father. Beaming at the guests, and flouting dignity, Kitty lifted her skirts to skip across the damp stones. Laughter rippled over the group and, suddenly, everyone relaxed.

Sliding to a halt next to Adam, Kitty reached for his hand, feeling him entwine their fingers. They faced each other and the ceremony began.

The simplicity of the age-old liturgy resonated through those listening, as the bride and groom made their vows, pledging their lives to each other, responses ringing across the tranquil scene.

The ritual came to its conclusion.

Kitty and Adam were married.

Held in the grand ballroom, the wedding breakfast was a veritable feast. Mountains of food kept coming until Prudence was heard to remark they would not require another morsel for at least a week.

Adam and Kitty circulated among their guests, thanking them for coming especially those who had travelled a fair distance. Kitty introduced Adam to Lucas' men, all of whom peppered him with questions about his time at sea.

Their conversation soon evolved into a detailed discussion about the lunacy of war, drawing in the other menfolk who gravitated to one end of the ballroom.

The ladies gathered at the opposite end, while the children tore up and down between them, Oscar teaching Evie how to slide along the polished floor on her bottom. Kitty had not the heart to stop them, quietly mourning the likelihood their clothes would be naught but rags by the end of the afternoon.

The day disappeared in a whirl of merriment, chatter, an abundance of goodwill… and more food. When the clock struck midnight, welcoming in 1816, the stragglers began to wend their way to bed, tired and happy.

Alone at last, Adam and Kitty climbed the stairs, arms around each other. Kitty was not quite steady on her feet and confessed, with a smothered chortle, to feeling a mite tipsy. Suppressing his mirth, Adam ushered her into their bedchamber where Kitty came to a stunned standstill.

Atop every available surface stood a candelabra. The tiny flames flickered in the draft caused by the opening of the door and, along with the fire dancing in the hearth, created intricate shadow play across the walls. Miniature vases laden with hellebore and phlox, were tucked among the candelabra. The colour of the blooms, mimicking Kitty's gown.

"I am speechless," Kitty murmured. "This is nothing short of enchanting."

"Tell me." Adam could not make out anything except Kitty and her glossy hair and that extraordinary dress, of which he itched to divest her, as fast as humanely possible.

"They have decorated our chambers." She described the room.

"*You* are nothing short of enchanting," Adam countered, "but I concur, it sounds as though this comes close."

"Oh you, old romantic," she swatted him, lightly.

Catching Kitty's hand, he whisked her against his tall frame. "*Old?* You dare to call me *old?* The audacity. I shall show you." Sweeping his brand-new wife off her feet, Adam carried her to the chaise, sinking onto it with Kitty, who was gurgling with laughter, on his knee.

He unpinned her hair, which spilled over her shoulders in a waterfall of blonde silk. Probing fingers threading through the shining tresses found the line of tiny buttons on the back of her gown. As Adam began to unfasten them, the shoulders of the dress slithered off, the bodice gaping slightly to reveal the rise of her breast.

"Kitty Marchmain, you are perfection." Adam's lips scorched a line from the base of her throat to her décolletage, feeling her quiver.

"Kitty Marchmain. I love the sound of that." Fumbling a little, Kitty unbuttoned his waistcoat, pulled it off and flung it behind her, as Adam's fingers searched under the frothy layers of her dress.

"Do you still have legs under there?" he groused, at the same moment as his fingers came into contact with a stockinged foot. Kitty wriggled on his lap, making him groan. "Careful, wife, or this will be over far more quickly than I intended."

With a provocative grin, Kitty did it again.

"Kitty," he croaked, a hand gliding up each leg, to unhook her garters and roll down the silk.

Kitty gasped as his fingers tiptoed back up her inner thigh.

"Take me," she beseeched, fiddling with the fall of his trousers. "Take me now,"

"Tis our wedding night, Kitty," Adam admonished on a rasp. "Let me seduce you."

"You have all night to seduce me, my darling, but right now I want you so badly, I might burst with it." She cupped his face and their eyes met.

Adam's dark gaze smouldered with passion for her.

"Let us start our marriage as we mean to go on, with wanton disregard for convention."

She freed him, fingers teasing, making him shudder. "Take me, husband."

It was Kitty's first time claiming him as her spouse. Adam had neither the will nor the desire to argue. Pushing her skirts out of the way, he granted her request. Their coupling, frenzied and fast.


Panting hard, riding a wave of euphoria, Kitty's head dropped to Adam's shoulder, her chest heaving.

"What was that about old?" Adam quipped, with a lopsided grin.

"I… shall… never… call… you… old… again," Kitty puffed.

He kissed her, tenderly. "Better, wife."

"I adore hearing that," she husked.

"Kitty Marchmain, my marchioness, my princess, my

wife. Hmmm… I concur. I like the last best," Adam mused, his lips grazing the dip of her cleavage.

Savouring the intimacy, they remained wrapped together. Then Adam took his wife's hand and helped her upright.

"Now, 'tis time for seduction." Spinning her around, he undid her gown's remaining buttons, scattering kisses across her shoulders as the material pooled on the floor. One by one, Adam peeled away the layers, his ardour intensifying as he tossed another flimsy gossamer under-garment to the haphazard pile.

Equally stirred, Kitty returned the favour, with rather more urgency than care.

Naked, husband and wife tumbled onto the luxurious covers. As he had promised hours earlier, Adam loved, cherished, and adored Kitty until they fell into an exhausted slumber, limbs and bedding hopelessly entangled.


The knight had won his princess.
The princess had rescued her knight.
Their fairy tale was complete…
…almost.

# EPILOGUE

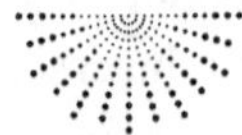

TEASDALE MALLOW ~ SUMMER 1820

On a colourful rug, in the shade of a huge weeping willow near the bank of a babbling brook, Kitty Marchmain was taking advantage of a few moments' uninterrupted peace.

Oscar, along with one of his school friends, was supposed to be unpacking his trunks. This probably meant the two boys were playing pirates or crusaders or soldiers along the many corridors.

Kitty loved hearing her son's voice resounding through the house, his bright chatter was sorely missed when he was at school.

Evie, a rambunctious seven, was helping make biscuits — although helping was probably the last word Anna, the Marchmain's long-suffering cook, would use. Kitty smiled, thinking about how many times Evie snuck into the kitchens, presuming her parents did not know.

Little did she realise, her mother who had been apprised the first time it happened, assured her staff that, as long as Evie wasn't causing them any problems, she had no objections.

"If she gets under your feet, mind you banish her forthwith," had been Kitty's only proviso. "Evie will harass you all day if you let her."

In truth, Kitty was pleased her daughter enjoyed spending time in the domestic sphere, it gave her an appreciation of how hard the staff worked. Kitty herself, continued to conduct Evie's lessons; the thrill in being able to impart knowledge had never waned.

Kitty's ear caught a plaintive whimper and she peered into a large basket, woven for the purpose. Within, a scrap of humanity — cheeks red, face scrunched, and fists clenched — was about to make her disgruntlement known.

"Hey there, poppet," Kitty cooed. "Are you hungry?" Lifting out the wriggling bundle, she adjusted her gown, allowing the babe to take her fill.

Born four months ago on a blustery day at the end of March, Elinor Prudence Marchmain — currently known as Nell — had the entire household wrapped around her tiny fingers.

Her Papa, who had missed the first months of Oscar's life, was entranced by this tiny creature. He spent hours with her tucked into his shoulder telling her stories or taking her for long walks around the well-trodden gardens, explaining how an estate was administered. For all the world as though she understood every word.

Evie shouldered the role of older sister with aplomb, her eager offers of assistance always accepted. The bond between

Kitty and her firstborn strengthening and deepening through these treasured moments.

Oscar, who had tried to pretend he was far too grown up to be interested in a baby, was often found peering over the crib chatting to Nell about school and the pranks he and his friends got up to.

Adam and Kitty had taken to loitering outside the nursery whenever Oscar vanished in that direction, specifically to overhear these conversations. Kitty had committed them to her journal, determined to capture golden memories.

Replete, Nell drowsed in her mother's arms. Kitty crooned a lullaby, stroking the child's downy hair, dark at the moment, of a shade similar to Adam's. Kitty hoped it stayed that way.

Seeing her daughter had fallen into the sleep of the well-fed, she placed the infant carefully in the basket, covering her with a soft muslin sheet.

~

Kitty had been stunned when she discovered she was increasing, four years after her marriage. Even though the couple were intimate with exquisitely gratifying frequency, they were without issue, leading Kitty to presume a new addition to their little family was improbable.

When the doctor confirmed her vague suspicions, Kitty had plonked down inelegantly in the chair. Her mouth agape, she spluttered that he was surely mistaken, it was naught but an upset stomach.

"How?" She had reached for Adam's hand, her expression one of wonder mingled with disbelief.

Dr Bertram did not bother to hide his amusement. "I

recall us having this exact same conversation six years ago, Kitty Marchmain. I repeat because your husband bedded you."

He chuckled and glanced over at Adam who had insisted on accompanying his wife to her appointment. "I am very pleased this news is cause for celebration not consternation. How is young Evie by the way?"

Kitty updated the affable physician on the scallywag ways of Evie and Oscar. This led to a brief conversation about other members of her family, after which husband and wife said their goodbyes.


In the balmy heat of that July morning on a quiet street in one the most fashionable districts of London, Adam kissed his wife into delightful delirium.

"Adam," she had chastised when he deigned to relinquish her lips. Her infectious smile belying her admonishment.

"Kitty," he had replied in the same tone, not in the slightest repentant.

She had batted him on the chest. "We are in the middle of the road, my love."

"Do I look as though I care?" He had rubbed her nose with his, making her giggle.

"A child, our child. I was beginning to think I was too old, that…" she had stopped speaking, unwilling to admit how many nights she had prayed for this moment.

"I know, my princess. You think because I cannot see, you can hide your anxieties. I sense them no less clearly. Although it is my greatest desire to have a child who is a part of you and a part of me, that we had yet to be blessed, meant we were afforded the chance to do things the presence of a babe would have curtailed.

"Think of what we have accomplished since our

marriage. Those glorious months travelling with Oscar and Evie." Referring to their regular jaunts around England; once they even crossed the channel to visit Paris.

"The complete refurbishment of Teasdale Mallow." The two years of dust and banging and clattering, during which they removed to the gatehouse for a period, would have been an extremely unhealthy environment for a baby.

"To go up to London on a whim, to entertain our friends, have house parties. While all those things can be modified to suit the care of a newborn, I confess, I am glad we have the opportunity to do so as a couple. To give each our... almost..." he had winked, "...undivided attention has been a precious gift."

Taking her hand, Adam had pressed his lips to her knuckles. "One I would not have missed for the world."

Kitty had moved into him, stretching up on tiptoe to loop her arms around his neck and kiss him, their surroundings fading into insignificance.

Lost in contemplation, Kitty gave a startled squeak when she felt a gentle hand cup the back of her neck.

"I thought I might find you here." An amused voice spoke from above her head.

"You scared me. I might have woken Nell," Kitty chided severely, pulling her husband down on the rug next to her.

"If that daughter of mine has just drunk her fill, she will sleep through a thunderstorm." Adam chuckled, squeezing the slender fingers enclosed in his.

Gathering Kitty into his arms, he kissed the sensitive skin behind her ear. "Good afternoon, wife. How was your day?"

"Hectic." She grinned. "Have you seen Oscar and Winston?"

"They are defeating the French as we speak." He nuzzled her hair. "Evie informed me her cakes will be divine," he mimicked Evie's artless tone.

"Poor Anna." Kitty shook her head, tolerantly.

"Anna adores that child, and you know it. She is endlessly tickled Evie wants to be at her elbow," Adam retorted.

Settling himself against the trunk of the willow, he shuffled Kitty until she was on his lap, her back to his chest. "Now, less about our madcap offspring and more about you."

His fingers teased from her nape to her throat.

He felt the tremor undulate through her and heard her hissed breath.

"Once upon a time." Adam kissed the exposed skin of her right shoulder.

"In a land faraway." He repeated the gesture on her left shoulder.

"There was a beautiful princess, whose name was Caterina. She had curly blonde hair, and green eyes."

Kitty swivelled around and knelt between his outstretched legs.

"One day, she was out riding her horse—"

"Whose name was..." Kitty interrupted, her eyes sparkling.

"Bluebell," Adam replied with a wink.

"I love bluebells." She beamed.

"I know. Do you want to hear the story or not?"

"Of course." She leant forward and brushed her lips to his.

"Well hush then." His mouth quirked. "The princess rode Bluebell through the woods and through the meadows, until they came to the river which marked the border of her father's lands.

"She had never travelled beyond the boundary and wanted to explore. The fast-flowing river was deep, and Bluebell faltered at the water's edge. Caterina, failing to recognise the danger, urged the mare into the torrent.

"Bluebell fought to keep her footing, causing Caterina to panic and cry for help. Bluebell joined in, neighing loudly, and between them, they created a tremendous racket.

"On the opposite bank, an *incredibly* handsome stranger riding a huge black stallion, appeared. Without hesitation, the rider guided his horse into the river, seized Bluebell's reins and led them to safety.

"Bowing his head, the stranger was about to ride away when the princess spoke—"

"Wait, you saved my life, or at the very least preserved me from a drenching. Your selfless act of courage deserves a reward," Kitty interjected, humour lacing her tones.

"Tsk, who is telling this story." Adam tweaked her nose "'No reward is necessary.' the stranger replied. 'It is my honour and my pleasure to rescue so charming a maiden.'

'Thank you, sir knight. I am in your debt.' The princess executed a flawless curtsy.

'Fair lady, if perchance you might bestow a kiss on a humble knight, there is no debt.' Her saviour dared request."

Making a show of being coy, Kitty stretched across the gap to kiss Adam's cheek.

"I will gladly grant your request," she replied, her lips tracking along his jawline, "but am uncertain I can stop at one kiss. You, my gallant knight, are so handsome, and tall, and strong, I find myself tempted to seduce you here on the riverbank."

"It would be most impolite of me to prevent your expression of gratitude." Adam's left hand began a delicious dance from her ankle, all the way up her bare leg. "No stockings? Kitty Marchmain, you wanton hussy."

"My lover encourages me to break the rules." Kitty gave a soft mewl as his remorseless fingers reached their goal.

"Is that so?" He began to unbutton her gown.

"He is *quite* the rake." She sniggered at Adam's mock appalled expression.


Adam stilled.

Close enough to see the mischief in his wife's radiant eyes, breathe in the intoxicating fragrance that was quintessentially Kitty, and sense the heat pulsing through her ravishing body.

"Adam…?" She canted her head and cupped his jaw, thumb rubbing over his bottom lip.

"From the day you tripped and cut your knee you have been my princess." He smiled in reminiscence, the hand under her skirts seeking and stroking said cut. "That has never changed, in spite of the different paths we took. Our journey has been an adventure worthy of any fairy tale."

Kitty stared, her mouth falling open slightly at her husband's whimsical turn of phrase.

"You know I can be quite the poet when I choose." He waggled his dark brows and contorted his face into a hideous grimace.

Kitty burst out laughing. "You are not the ogre of this tale, Adam Marchmain."

"No…?" he growled, the sound rumbling through his chest. "In truth, I was not much of a knight. You had to rescue me."

"We rescued each other, and you *are* my knight. You will

*always* be my knight." She tugged at his buckskins. "Whose princess has a request."

"And a knight never denies a princess," Adam groaned as she captured him, her fingers sublime torture.

"I've thought of an ending for your story," Kitty murmured dreamily, sometime later. They were lying on the rug, her head on Adam's shoulder, her fingers seeking under his shirt to stroke each of the scars on his chest.

"Hmmm?" One arm around his wife, Adam curled an errant lock of golden hair around his finger.

"The knight returned, battle-weary, wounded, and despondent. Caterina saw him, standing on the bank of the same river from which he had rescued her all those years ago. She stretched out her hand and drew him back from the brink.

"Something magical began to blossom, but the knight fought against it, believing he had nothing to offer a princess. Caterina knew the man beneath the scars — a noble warrior who would always love and protect her, and decided it was her turn..."

"...to rescue him," Adam finished.

"Of course," she replied, pertly, "and they lived happily ever after."

"I do not think I ever thanked you." Adam lifted Kitty so he could steal her lips.

"For what?" Kitty drew back, studying him in puzzlement
"Rescuing me."

"Rest assured, you did, but if you feel moved to reiterate your gratitude, I would not be averse." Kitty's languid reply was belied by the glint in her eye.

"Your every wish…" Adam needed no second invitation.

Veiled by the trailing stems of the willow, and to the peaceful burble of the stream, a tall, handsome — if somewhat scarred knight — gave his imp of a princess a *very* thorough demonstration of his appreciation.

# EXCERPT FROM LOVE KINDLED

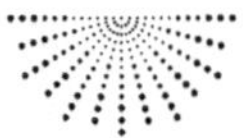

## LONDON ~ MAY 1816

*I*t was all Lady Amelia Gresham could do not to scream. Here was she, newly widowed, Hayward barely cold in his grave, and already they were talking about marrying her off to that boor, Ambrose.

She had been sitting quietly for the last hour or so while everyone talked around her. Her head was beginning to ache and her temper to bubble. Apparently, even as a widow she still had no voice, or so they thought.

Amelia stood, drew herself up to her considerable height, and coughed.

It took several moments before anyone acknowledged her presence, which only served to vex her further.

"Might I be permitted to speak?" she asked, her voice dangerously bland.

Lord Hungerford, her father-in-law, turned his flinty gaze on her, continuing to argue that marriage to Ambrose was the perfect solution.

Nobody had ever seen fit to ask her opinion, not once in her whole life, and Amelia was tired of being ignored. She wasn't stupid. She knew daughters of nobility were simply pawns in their father's schemes to bolster influence or wealth. The better the match, the higher the status.

Such frivolous emotions as love or tenderness or even respect were never considered essential to any discussion. Aware some unions muddled along quite nicely, as far as Amelia could tell, most lacked any affection whatsoever.

Her own marriage had been soulless. It was not that had they disliked each other. Dislike suggested some strength of feeling or concern in the other's well-being was involved, even if it were negative. Amelia and Hayward had been utterly indifferent to one another. So indifferent, they could not summon up enough interest to consummate their nuptials. A detail Amelia was determined to keep to herself.

Hayward Ingram, Earl of Gresham, had died a week previously, following a duel with one of his rivals in the racing fraternity.

Amelia hated horse racing with a passion and, despite being a competent horsewoman, wasn't overly enamoured of the creatures at all, except as a means to an end. Thus, she struggled to understand what prompted such a rash challenge.

The two involved were grievously injured, Hayward fatally so, although Amelia had heard it was likely her husband's opponent would survive.

Now here she was, a widow at three and twenty. Looking back over her life, Amelia realised she had never done anything impetuous or spontaneous. Her behaviour – always that expected by her somewhat overbearing parents – one of sedate refinement. It did not behove her to ruffle the surface.

Of late, an almost uncontrollable urge to defy all conventions and constraints had begun to stir within her. The tug of freedom – tantalising. Hayward's unfortunate demise seemed to open a door just wide enough for her to see beyond the confines of her limited world, and she would prefer it did not slam shut. Not just yet.

Straightening her shoulders, Amelia stepped forward.


Amelia dipped a deep curtsy in deference to her father-in-law, and spoke in tones rather more assertive than usual.

"My lord, am I not entitled to a period of mourning? Gresham is barely cold, and you are arranging his replacement. I do believe you owe him and me a little respect."

There were hushed gasps from the other three in the room. Amelia's mother-in-law, Lady Priscilla Hungerford. Ambrose, currently Viscount Hastings but in line to inherit his father's earldom. Mr Williams, the Hungerfords' solicitor, who was present to read Hayward's will.

Their brief and uneventful marriage notwithstanding, it transpired her husband had ensured – all things remaining equal – Amelia should be comfortable in the unfortunate event of him dying prior to inheriting the marquisate.

Lamentably, Hayward had not taken into consideration his own vices.

"It is imperative we keep the Hungerford money within the family." Abruptly, Lord Hungerford stopped speaking. Money was a delicate subject, and women were not usually privy to such conversations.

Amelia, however, knew to what he alluded.

"My lord, I am cognisant of my husband's debts."

Lord Hungerford narrowed his eyes, wary now.

.   .   .

Amelia noticed Mr Williams bite his lip to prevent a smile. She had spent many hours with the solicitor, prior to and since her husband's death, and knew everything about the financial straits of the family.

Hayward had been an inveterate gambler and a bad one. Money slipped through his fingers like water, leaving Amelia to control what she could in order to prevent the Gresham estates falling into rack and ruin. The solicitor was a font of knowledge, undaunted by Amelia's questions, his help invaluable.

Until her marriage, Amelia was shielded from any of the business aspects being a member of the *ton* entailed. Ladies should not bother their, obviously, empty heads with such matters.

Amelia had discovered, to her surprise, she possessed an uncanny knack for understanding how to manage an estate. Unbeknownst to the rest of her husband's family – with Mr Williams' assistance, she had kept Gresham Park afloat.

There was absolutely no chance of her giving that up. Not without a fight.

An idea had begun percolating during the morning, and for once, Amelia was determined to get her own way.


"I have long been aware of Gresham's gambling. How could I not know? He was going through his money as though it grows on trees. I was the one left to safeguard the estate and work out how to pay staff with the pitiful sum he left available to me each month," she paused. "I have a proposition to make."

Lord Hungerford regarded her steadily, his aristocratic features showing no expression. After long moments he inclined his head. "Speak, woman, but make it quick."

"I have been a dutiful daughter and, for the last two years, wife. I maintained Gresham Park, and despite your son's best intents, I expect it to turn a slight profit this coming year. I am frugal and recently employed a most reliable steward, in whose hands I can trust the management of the estate.

"This has come at some cost to me and, in light of recent events, I am resolved to give myself time to adjust. I have a hankering to travel. To see something of this England in which we live but are rarely afforded the chance to appreciate.

"I shall take six months after which, I may – I only say may – be prepared to engage in discussion regarding a possible marriage to Ambrose. However..." Amelia raised her hand as her father-in-law interrupted, stuttering and stammering at her audacity. "I am a widow and a countess in my own right. I am wearied of being dictated to, of allowing others to decide my fate. While I had no control, my hands were tied. That ends today. I have reached my majority. My life is my life, and you have no cause to instruct me. Hayward's will made that clear."

Amelia was trembling with anxiety at her recklessness but held her nerve. She refused to remain silent anymore. To speak thus was liberating, prompting another decision. Not only was she going to do this, but also it would be without the trappings of luxury. She fixed her gaze on Lord Hungerford.

They stared at each other for several seconds, and it was Hayward's father who dropped his eyes first.

A small victory but no less rewarding.


Mr Williams cleared his throat, the sound breaking through an atmosphere already strained.

"May I suggest we conclude our business here this morning? 'Tis not a comfortable subject, and I have no desire to prolong it."

Hungerford nodded, and the affable solicitor explained the last few particulars of the will. He was about to take his leave when Amelia requested a moment of his time.

Without waiting for permission, she tucked her arm through his, and led him through the open French doors, onto the terrace.

"Mr Williams, I would like to thank you for all your help and ask that you keep me apprised of any... err... untoward developments. If I find somewhere to stay for more than a week, I will inform you of my address. Mr Halifax, my steward, has your details should he require any advice, but he has proven to be efficient and trustworthy. I do not foresee any problems."

Mr Williams patted her hand. "I hope you have a pleasant sojourn, Lady Gresham. I wish Lord Hungerford knew of your tireless efforts to protect his good name. Alas, the nobility often cannot see past the end of their own noses." He dropped a sly wink, making Amelia chuckle.

She shrugged her shoulders. "'Tis of no matter. The most important thing is now I have said my piece, I can leave as soon as is practicable. For the next six months, I will no longer be Lady Gresham, rather I will be simply Mrs Amelia Danneville."

She grinned, a wholly unaffected gesture.

To the elderly solicitor, it was as though she was bathed in the glow of a hundred candles.

"I trust you find what it is you seek," he said quietly.

Pressing her hand one more time he bowed, walked back into the study, collected his papers, and said his goodbyes.

. . .

Amelia leant against the frame of the elegant door, admiring the pretty garden, ruminating over his words. *Was she seeking something?* It was conceivable, but what she had yet to discern.

Shaking her head, she turned her back on the profusion of blossoms and faced her father-in-law.

~

Two days and at least three acrimonious exchanges later, Amelia departed Hungerford House en route to Gresham Park. Hayward's father had tried every trick in the book to dissuade her from, what he referred to as, her lunatic scheme. Finally, he had accepted she was steadfast. To be fair he, albeit grudgingly, wished her well, pleading with her to consider marriage to Ambrose while away.

In spite of Lord Hungerford's rather cantankerous disposition, he had a soft spot for Amelia and, in truth, only wanted what he believed to be the best for her. He came from a world where women were little more than chattels to be married off to the wealthiest or most influential bidder.

To have his decisions thwarted was a shock. His own wife, while perfectly lovely, would not dream of questioning anything her husband did or said.

He would never admit it, but Lord Hungerford held a secret admiration for Amelia's fortitude and, following her departure was stunned to discover precisely how capable she had been in overseeing his son's property.

~

Amelia heaved a sigh of relief when her carriage rattled out of London and turned up the Great North Road. Her journey would take two or three days, depending on the weather and state of the roads. This time of the year, with spring rains, they could be treacherous.

Her faithful maid, Jenny, accompanied her, as did Trotter, her driver and stalwart defender. The hood was down, the day bright, and Amelia, breathing in the clean fresh country air, began to relax for the first time in as long as she could remember.

# ABOUT THE AUTHOR

Rosie Chapel lives in Perth, Australia with her hubby and three furkids. When not writing, she loves catching up with friends, burying herself in a book (or three), discovering the wonders of Western Australia, or — and the best — a quiet evening at home with her husband, enjoying a glass of wine and a movie.

Website: www.rosiechapel.com

OTHER BOOKS BY ROSIE CHAPEL

<u>Historical Fiction</u>
*The Hannah's Heirloom Sequence*
The Pomegranate Tree - Book One
Echoes of Stone and Fire - Book Two
Embers of Destiny - Book Three
Etched in Starlight - Prequel
Hannah's Heirloom Trilogy - Compilation – e-book only

Prelude to Fate

<u>Regency Romances</u>
*The Linen and Lace Series*
Once Upon An Earl - Book One
To Unlock Her Heart - Book Two
Love on a Winter's Tide - Book Three
A Love Unquenchable - Book Four
A Hidden Rose - Five

The Daffodil Garden
The Unconventional Duchess

His Fiery Hoyden
A Regency Duet
A Regency Christmas Double
Fate is Curious
A Christmas Prayer with Ashlee Shades

The Lady's Wager

Winning Emma

A Love Impossible

<u>Fairy Tale Romance</u>

Chasing Bluebells

<u>Contemporary Romances</u>

Of Ruins and Romance

All At Once It's You

Cobweb Dreams

Just One Step

His Heart's Second Sigh

### The Pomegranate Tree

*Hannah's Heirloom - Book One*

Hoping to trace the origins of an ancient ruby clasp, a gift from her long dead grandmother, Hannah Wilson travels to the fortress of Masada with her best friend, Max. Strange dreams concerning a rebel ambush begin to haunt Hannah and following a tragic accident, she slips into the world of Ancient Masada.

A woman out of time, Hannah must rely on her instincts and her knowledge of what will befall this citadel to survive. Will she escape, or is she doomed to die along with hundreds of others as Masada falls – and what does any of this have to do with an ancient ruby clasp?

### Echoes of Stone and Fire

*Hannah's Heirloom - Book Two*

Pompeii - a vibrant city lost in time following the AD79 eruption of Vesuvius. Now rediscovered, archaeologists yearn for an opportunity to uncover the town's past. Some things, however, are best left alone - revealing the secrets hidden beneath the stones could prove perilous. Hannah and Max are brought to Pompeii by a surprise invitation to join an excavation team who are trying to uncover the city's long history.

After entering an excavated house that bears a Hebrew inscription, Hannah's two worlds collide, and she falls back through time to ancient Pompeii. A place where her ancestor is a physician to gladiators engaged in mortal combat, where riotous mobs run amok and where a ghost from the past returns to haunt her.

Will Hannah and her loved ones manage to escape the devastation she knows is coming, before the town is engulfed in volcanic ash?

Will she ever find her way back to Max the love of her life, waiting not so patiently millennia away? Or will echoes be all that remain?

## Embers of Destiny

*Hannah's Heirloom - Book Three*

AD80 - Hannah and Maxentius must embark on a new journey to Northern Britannia. This harsh frontier is far from the comforts of Rome and danger lurks where least expected; a garrison of soldiers, some unhappy with their isolated posting; local tribes, outwardly accepting of their Roman occupier, but who may still resent the seizure of their lands.

Millennia away, Hannah Vallier finds a familiar item while working in a museum near Hadrian's Wall. It is the pomegranate; carved by Maxentius on Masada. Before Hannah can discuss it with Max, disaster strikes! Believing her husband has been killed, Hannah retreats into the past, her soul melding with that of her ancestor, but with little idea of what they could face. Is the risk from the conquered tribes, or much closer to home?

As rebellion threatens to shatter a fragile peace, Hannah's heart whispers that just maybe Max isn't dead and that he is calling her home. Can she trust her heart, or will she remain caught out of time, her destiny floating away like embers on a breeze?

## Etched in Starlight

*Hannah's Heirloom - Prequel*

Maxentius - a Roman soldier fresh from the battlefields of Armenia, arrives to take command of the military outpost of Masada, Herod's isolated citadel in the Judaean desert. A seemingly mundane posting after years of warfare, Maxentius finds it more challenging to maintain a focused garrison than to face the wrath of the Parthians across a disputed frontier.

Hannah - a young Hebrew physician spends her days dealing with injuries from street brawls, deprivation, disease and loss. As her beloved Jerusalem plunges into chaos; her brother — who belongs to a band of rebels determined to drive out their Roman occupiers — tells her of their plans to storm a desert fortress and steal the weapons stored there, persuading his reluctant sister to go with him.

Masada - following the ambush, Hannah finds and treats three badly wounded Roman soldiers. In the aftermath and against impossible odds, Hannah and Maxentius realise that they are more than healer and captive, their fate already etched in starlight.

**Prelude to Fate**

For Lucia, staring into the jaws of an horrific death, escape seems impossible.

Rufius Atellus, a veteran Roman soldier, is appalled when he recognises one of the victims about to be executed. Surely this is a ghastly mistake?

A ferocious she-wolf, anticipating a tasty meal, suddenly finds herself under a human's control.

In an unexpected twist, and as danger threatens, the lives of all three become inextricably entwined.

Was it chance brought them together in that theatre of bloodshed, or simply a prelude to fate?

**Love on a Winter's Tide**

*Linen and Lace - Book Three*


Every day, Helena disappears into a world few acknowledge, helping the poor, downtrodden, and abused. A husband is the last thing she can be bothered with.

Busy managing his shipping line, Hugh Drummond sees no need for a wife, whose only joy is dancing and frivolity. If — and it was a huge if — he ever married, it would be to a woman as capable as he, not some giddy society Miss.

Then, Hugh meets Helena and despite their resolve, fate, it seems, has other ideas. As their attraction deepens however, treachery threatens to tear them apart. Will they uncover the perpetrator in time, or will their love be swept away, lost forever on a winter's tide?


**A Love Unquenchable**

*Linen and Lace - Book Four*


Jessica Drummond, a bright and cheerful young woman, rarely gives romance, let alone love, a thought. Long hours working in her brother's shipping office affords little chance of her ever meeting an eligible bachelor.

Duncan Barrington, veteran of the Napoleonic Wars, believes himself wounded in both body and soul. He has no intention of inflicting his demons on anyone, certainly not a beautiful and, in his opinion, irresponsible city lady.

One cold and snowy morning, the plight of a bedraggled puppy throws Jessica and Duncan together and, as a spark of something indefinable yet wholly unquenchable begins to burn, it is unclear who rescued whom.


**A Hidden Rose**

*Linen and Lace - Book Five*

After witnessing his mother's grief at the loss of his father, Nick
Drummond resolved never to cause someone he loved such distress.
Even the happiness of his siblings would not sway him – until he
met Rose.

Rose Archer was almost content assisting her doctor father in a tiny
fishing village in the north of Yorkshire. To experience the world
beyond, a tantalising dream – until she met Nick.

Unexpectedly, the impossible becomes possible, and the renounced
– desired above all things, but the shipwreck that brought them
together, may yet tear them apart. Will Nick learn to trust his heart,
or will his love for Rose remain forever hidden

∾

**The Daffodil Garden**

Horrifically scarred during the war, William Harcourt - Marquis of
Blackthorne - prefers to spend his days in the quiet of his daffodil
garden; plants do not pity, turn away, or judge.

Lucy Truscott, whose life is far removed from that of the *ton*, has no
idea that by saving the life of a young woman, to whom she bears an
uncanny resemblance, her own will be placed in mortal danger.

A chance encounter leads to something more. William begins to
trust that Lucy sees the man beneath the scars, while Lucy is
persuaded that love might actually transcend status.

Unfortunately, before their courtship has really begun, someone has
every intention of ending it - permanently.

∾

**The Unconventional Duchess**

Refusing to suffer the humiliation of her husband flaunting his
mistress at Society events, the newly married Duchess of

Wallingstead, Ella Lennox, takes control of her life. She leaves London for the family's country seat in remote Yorkshire.

A woman alone, Ella spends the next four years turning a cold, grim house into a home, and transforming the fortunes of the estate. Not afraid of hard work, she soon earns the respect of those around her with her determination and unconventional attitude.

Out of the blue, the duke arrives. Resigned to another arduous visit, Ella is stunned when it seems he is attempting to court her.

Impossible!

Could her dream of a happy marriage be about to come true?

Everything hangs on a snowstorm, a herd of cows and an uninvited guest!

❧

### His Fiery Hoyden

*A Novella*

Livvy has no respect for the nobility; they let her down when she most needed them. Why should she accede to their demands now?

Philip, Lord Harrington, is stunned to discover the young heir to the dukedom lives a stone's throw away in a ramshackle cottage, and resolves to restore the child to his birthright.

They meet in a clash of wills, but just when it seems Livvy might surrender, the victory Philip desires, may not taste all that sweet.

❧

### A Regency Duet

*Luck be a Pirate*

Luck wasn't something retired pirate Kennet Alexson believed in – good or bad. However, even he had to concede that landing a job at Trentams shipyard, and meeting Lynette Collins, was more than coincidence.

Fortune it seemed, was smiling on him for once.

As Kennet adjusts to life on dry land, his friendship with Lynette deepens into something far more enduring, and what once seemed elusive now becomes possible.

Unfortunately, fate has other plans, and Kennet's good luck is about to run out.

The Highwayman's Kiss

*Surrendered Hearts – Book One*

Nothing exciting had ever happened to Juliette St Clair. Her days were spent assisting her father or calling on friends, wandering art galleries, taking constitutionals or, and more preferably, escaping into her books. Her evenings her evenings — an endless round of balls, where she preferred to remain invisible.

Until the day she was robbed by a highwayman.

**A Regency Christmas Double**

*Heart Rescued*

Four years since Jasper lost the woman he was hoping to marry. Four years since he closed his heart and withdrew from Society. He has no idea his reclusive existence is about to be shattered.

Enter his sister's best friend, Harriet, a flame haired beauty, who needs his help.

Reluctantly he agrees and as they spend time together, it is clear their feelings run deep. Although Harriet affects Jasper in a way no woman ever has, he believes her to be out of his league ~ but it's Christmas and she might just be the one to melt his frozen heart

*Catch a Snowflake*

Romance often blossoms in the most unlikely of places - but in a ward full of wounded soldiers - surely not?

When Lucas Withers comes face to face with Jemima Parsons - a young woman who blames him for her brother's injury - falling in love is the last thing on their minds. What neither of them anticipated, was the magic of snowflakes.

~

**Fate is Curious**

*A Novella*

Happily, ever after? No such thing! Bereft, following her beloved husband's sudden death, Lady Charlotte Sherbrooke has lost her belief in such romantic nonsense.

Successful shipping merchant, Zacharie Romain, is no stranger to loss; his business can be hazardous. Moreover, his wife died in childbirth and even though it happened a decade ago, he has no mind to expose himself to such sorrow again.

They meet in less than joyful circumstances but, as the year turns and grief diminishes, the woes of a small boy become the catalyst for something wholly unexpected. Can Charlotte and Zacharie trust what Fate has in store or will past heartbreak prevent them from taking a chance on love?

~

**A Christmas Prayer**

*with Ashlee Shades*

*A Short Story*

An entreaty from a frightened child.

Orphaned and only nine, Caroline Thorne has to grow up before her time. She is doing everything she can to keep what is left of her family together and out of the workhouse but is terrified her prayers are not being heard. Or maybe they are…

A petition from a woman desperate for a family.

A chance meeting with three orphaned siblings, tugs at Elizabeth Barrington's heart strings. Thus far, she and her husband have not been blessed with children and, as Christmas approaches, a plan begins to form - one which might just be the answer to her prayers.

Two Christmas prayers, as different as they are the same.

Will they hear and, more importantly, heed the answer?

**The Lady's Wager**

*Surrendered Hearts- Book Two*

*A Novelette*

Ged Mowbray will do anything to avoid being married off to the suitable prospects his parents insist on parading in front of him.

Melissa Bouchard is under no illusion her sizeable dowry is the attraction to suitors, not her.

An overheard conversation leads to an offer too good to refuse, but what happens when a lady's wager, becomes a gamble on the happily ever after, you did not even realise you wanted?

**Winning Emma**

*Surrendered Hearts - Book Three*

*A Novelette*

Randolph Craythorpe — earl, covert operative, and occasional highwayman — believed his dalliance with Lady Felicity Hartwich would lead to marriage. It did, but not to him! The arrival of an unwelcome guest, however, provides the perfect opportunity to indulge in a little retaliation.

Emma Newbury accompanies her cousin, Lady Charity Anscombe, to London for the Christmas season. Once there, she comes face to face with the three men who witnessed the humiliating aftermath of her father's disgrace — one of whom, to her irritation, has taken up residence in her dreams.

Their infrequent encounters only serve to confuse but, while winter tightens its grip on the city, what was inconceivable becomes the one thing for which they both yearn, yet bound by Society's rules, cannot admit.

As the snow falls, Randolph begins to understand that to win Emma, he will have to surrender.

### A Love Impossible

*A Regency M/M Novelette*

Tasked with investigating a heinous crime, Edward Lindsay travels from London to Dublin — a city which holds too many memories — in the guise of guardian to his sister. He knew it could be hazardous, and relished the challenge, but that wasn't what caused his stomach to tighten as they approached landfall.

Dublin held more than just a murderer.

There was also Aidan.

While attending a party, Aidan Griffen is astonished when he comes face to face with a man who fled Dublin two years previously. A man he has desperately tried to forget.

As Edward closes in on his quarry, a fire, deliberately extinguished, is rekindled. But what of it? Edward and Aidan share a love impossible, and to acknowledge their feelings — more dangerous than confronting a killer.

Is there any hope of a happily ever after?

## Chasing Bluebells

*A Novella*

Once upon a time, somewhere in France, there was a man whose reckless obsession led him down a dark path — one which, ultimately, cost him his life. That ought to have been the end of it. Regrettably, as is so often the case, those who least deserve it, suffer for the actions of others.

A decade after being sent away, Sebastien Daviau returns to the little village where everything began. Hoping to lay the ghosts of his childhood to rest, he studiously ignores the possibility, he might run into Charlotte de Montbeliard.

As luck would have it, Charlotte is the one who runs into him… well, his horse… and although the brief encounter leaves a lasting impression, neither recognises the other.

A name revealed causes a freak accident, catapulting Sebastien's past into his present, and bringing him face to face with a man whose reputation would intimidate the most ardent of suitors.

Can whatever is blossoming between Charlotte and Sebastien survive the challenge imposed, or is their happily ever after about to fade as quickly as the bluebells they loved to chase?

### Of Ruins and Romance

Kassandra Winters has intrigued Gabriel St Germain since he accidentally knocked her flying outside her university professor's office. Her face haunts his dreams, yet he never expected to see her again. So, he is surprised when she appears, as though destined to do so, in the middle of a ruin, and he concocts a plan to win her heart.

Gabriel's old-fashioned courtship touches something deep inside Kassie and, although struggling to believe someone as handsome as Gabriel could possibly be interested in her, she soon realises she has fallen irrevocably in love with him. However, just as Kassie shares everything of herself with Gabriel, her world comes crashing down.

Can their romance survive or will it fall in ruins, like the relics of antiquity that brought them together.

~

### All At Once It's You

When Alex arrives in the small village of Rosedale Abbey, to take up a position as a research assistant for a renowned archaeologist, the last thing she is looking for, or expects to find, is love.

Jake was perfectly happy with the status quo. When it came to relationships, he didn't do committed or long term. He called the shots, and if his current flame didn't like it, she knew what to do. A philosophy, which served him well - until he met Alex.

Romance blooms, but even as the untamed wilderness of the North Yorkshire moors weaves its spell, a long-buried secret might yet jeopardise their happily ever after.

~

**Cobweb Dreams**

*A Novella*

A holiday on the Scottish isle of Mull was just the break Chloe Shepherd needed, an escape from her boring office job and her complete lack of anything resembling a social life. Romance, it seems, isn't on the cards and, although Chloe dreams of finding her soulmate she is beginning to believe love is like cobwebs — spun overnight, only to vanish in the early morning breeze.

Under sufferance, Dominic Winters makes a flying visit to Mull to check on a rental property owned by his family. He hasn't got time for this — so indulging in a holiday fling is the last thing on his mind.

A lamb stuck in a bog proves a most unexpected matchmaker and, while Mull weaves its magic, Chloe wonders whether those fragile cobwebs might be far more stubborn than she thought.

**Just One Step**

*A Short Story*

In the aftermath of an horrific car accident, Daisy Forrester travels to Italy - hoping, so far from her memories, she might begin to heal.

Archaeologist, and single father, Adam Willoughby is too busy looking after his young daughter to give romance let alone love, a thought.

Neither expects a chance encounter in an ancient ruin to be anything more, but sometimes, that's all it takes.

**His Heart's Second Sigh**

*A Novella*

Reuben Faulkner and Paige Latimer are two happily single people, who have no desire to upset the status quo.

Unexpectedly, they are thrown together, only to discover both want far more than a casual friendship.

Just when things take an interesting turn, Reuben's past catches up with them, and threatens to derail their blossoming romance before it has chance to start.